Journey to New Salem

by

Mark Rosendorf

The Witches of Vegas Series

Journey to New Salem

Cover Art by *Jennifer Greeff*

The Wild Rose Press, Inc.
PO Box 708
Adams Basin, NY 14410-0708
Visit us at www.thewildrosepress.com

Publishing History
First Edition, 2021
Trade Paperback ISBN 978-1-5092-3534-6
Digital ISBN 978-1-5092-3535-3

The Witches of Vegas Series
Published in the United States of America

Isis ran back behind the wall. She then commanded the illusion of herself behind the far left wall to step through and stare out into the audience with a hand on its hip. It received a collective gasp. To them, it was as if Isis had stepped through one wall on one side of the stage, and then come out of another wall on the opposite side of the stage. She had practiced this many times, but this was the best she had ever pulled it off. It was now time to bring it home…

Whoa!

A pain ran through Isis' chest. It felt like a mallet slamming against her heart. She tried to take a deep breath, but it was a struggle, like sucking a watermelon down her throat. An image formed in her head. It was Valeria, the Wiccan vampire who turned their lives upside down. Isis hadn't thought about her, or the torture she endured at her hands, in a long while. Why now all of a sudden, and while her chest screamed in pain?

Isis leaned her back against the wall. Everything circled as if she were in the eye of a tornado. She had felt this sensation before, but never with such intensity. Her hands trembled. Something was happening, but she didn't know what. "Not again, not right now." She blinked her eyes rapidly. It's been over a year since Valeria was in their lives. She demanded of her brain to never think of her again. Time to refocus on the now.

Praise for *THE WITCHES OF VEGAS*

Shelf Unbound 2020 Best Indie Book - Notable Indie

~*~

Finalist in the Young Adult Category of the 2020 International Digital Awards

~*~

"What I loved most was how fresh this storyline was for the fantasy genre. I haven't read anything like it, which was a HUGE plus for me. The Witches of Vegas is one I'll be reading again!"

~ *HeyitsCarlyRae*

~*~

"The author lists this as a Young Adult novel, but this 43-year-old reader enjoyed it without any shame."

~ *Rob Stanley,*
Author of The Bite of Brenna Barlow

~*~

"The Witches of Vegas is a dandy Read, Happily Recommended especially for the young adult target audience, and all who enjoy a well written, 'who dunnit' yarn having overtones of magic, 5 stars."

~ *The Compulsive Reader*

~*~

"The story will tug at your heartstrings in so many ways. The author does a fantastic job of weaving a tale of heartbreak, first love, the thrill of accomplishment and self-sacrifice.

~*InD'tale, Five Star, Crowned Heart*

Isis ran back behind the wall. She then commanded the illusion of herself behind the far left wall to step through and stare out into the audience with a hand on its hip. It received a collective gasp. To them, it was as if Isis had stepped through one wall on one side of the stage, and then come out of another wall on the opposite side of the stage. She had practiced this many times, but this was the best she had ever pulled it off. It was now time to bring it home…

Whoa!

A pain ran through Isis' chest. It felt like a mallet slamming against her heart. She tried to take a deep breath, but it was a struggle, like sucking a watermelon down her throat. An image formed in her head. It was Valeria, the Wiccan vampire who turned their lives upside down. Isis hadn't thought about her, or the torture she endured at her hands, in a long while. Why now all of a sudden, and while her chest screamed in pain?

Isis leaned her back against the wall. Everything circled as if she were in the eye of a tornado. She had felt this sensation before, but never with such intensity. Her hands trembled. Something was happening, but she didn't know what. "Not again, not right now." She blinked her eyes rapidly. It's been over a year since Valeria was in their lives. She demanded of her brain to never think of her again. Time to refocus on the now.

Praise for *THE WITCHES OF VEGAS*

Shelf Unbound 2020 Best Indie Book - Notable Indie

~*~

Finalist in the Young Adult Category of the 2020 International Digital Awards

~*~

"What I loved most was how fresh this storyline was for the fantasy genre. I haven't read anything like it, which was a HUGE plus for me. The Witches of Vegas is one I'll be reading again!"

~ *HeyitsCarlyRae*

~*~

"The author lists this as a Young Adult novel, but this 43-year-old reader enjoyed it without any shame."

~ *Rob Stanley,*
Author of The Bite of Brenna Barlow

~*~

"The Witches of Vegas is a dandy Read, Happily Recommended especially for the young adult target audience, and all who enjoy a well written, 'who dunnit' yarn having overtones of magic, 5 stars."

~ *The Compulsive Reader*

~*~

"The story will tug at your heartstrings in so many ways. The author does a fantastic job of weaving a tale of heartbreak, first love, the thrill of accomplishment and self-sacrifice.

~InD'tale, Five Star, Crowned Heart

Dedication

To my wife, my family, my friends, and my readers.
This one is for you…

Prologue

One week ago…

Tia should have been fast asleep. She couldn't remember the last time she snoozed through an entire night. But that wasn't a surprise. No other nineteen-year-old anywhere on Earth had as much on their plate as she did. Lucky her home produced the strongest and tastiest coffee ever made.

Her bed shook as if there was an earthquake. Tia glanced over to the guy who had been sharing this California king bed with her for the last two years. He let out a moan. His six-foot frame rolled from stomach to back. His fist slammed the mattress over and over. There were so many reasons she cared deeply for him, only one of which was that they came from the same settlement in Northern Africa.

"Jas?" You okay, hon?" Tia shook him but Jas didn't wake up.

He threw his hands across his forehead. "No, no!" he shouted. His eyes were still shut tight.

Tia sat up. She reached to her nightstand and turned on the lamp. Jas, which was short for Jasper, let out a deep exhale from his mouth. Her love demanded she pull him from whatever deep, dark nightmare ran through his brain. But this was his Wiccan power. Those bad dreams had benefited their people time and

1

time again. She had to let him see it through, no matter the duress it caused.

Jasper shot into a sitting position. His eyes opened wide, as if he had just seen a ghost. "Jas, are you okay?" Tia asked again.

"Yes," he responded between heavy breaths. "I am okay." He sure didn't look okay. Jas stood from the bed. He walked to the window and looked up at the full moon illuminating the night sky. "No, we cannot let this happen," he mumbled.

Unlike Tia who slept in full-length pink pajamas with a purple bathrobe nearby, Jas only wore boxer shorts each night. He peered back at her with a rapid blink and a shaky jaw. It was a look she had come to recognize as a warning that required her full attention.

"Jas, sweetie, talk to me—"

"Give me a moment!" He threw up his hand, cutting Tia off. "I need to focus on every detail before it fades." He paced from one end of the room to the other, running a hand through his buzz-cut. Jas finally stopped at the foot of the bed, his wide eyes focusing on Tia. "There was a war on our land. It was a battle between witches," he said.

"Our witches?" Tia tossed aside the thin brown blanket and stood from the bed.

"No, they were strangers. Powerful ones." Jas tipped his head toward the ceiling. "They will come one week from this morning. Our witches will bear witness, but they will not engage even though the battle will affect our village forever."

"Affect us in what way?" Tia asked.

"I don't know." Jas shook his head. "But, in my dream, it did…which means it will, but it is unclear to me in what way."

Tia walked around the bed until she was face to chest with Jas. She reached up, throwing her hands around the back of his neck. "Do you know what they will be fighting about? Do you know why they come or why we allow it to happen?"

"I do not. As always, much of what went through my mind was unclear. But one statement still lingers."

She leaned in. "You remember what it said?"

"I do, but I am unsure what it means."

"Tell me." Tia placed a hand on his cheek.

"The statement…no one in particular said it, but it was known by all." After a moment's hesitation, he answered. "The immortal witch has won the day."

Tia wrapped her arms around Jas' pronounced chest. She squeezed so he would feel her embrace. Jas' dreams hadn't always been accurate, though many had proven to be useful premonitions. But sometimes they were just dreams. She made a point to investigate them all. Six weeks ago, when he dreamt of the dining hall being destroyed by fire, Tia personally checked out the place that night after it closed. A gas stove was left on in the kitchen. Tia turned it off and had the gas cleared out of the kitchen. Later that night, they had a major storm. A lightning bolt shot through the kitchen window. The damage was minimal, but if not for Jas' warning, the room would have been filled with gas. Had it ignited, it could have created the massive fire he saw in his dream.

Tia prided herself on always keeping an open mind, but the premonition in Jas's dream didn't make much sense. It did, however, spark her curiosity. Who were these witches that were coming to their home?

Where were they from and why were they at war? She certainly would like to meet them, but how accurate was the danger Jas foresaw? She had never seen him so spooked.

Tia's curiosity always got the better of her. Perhaps, this time, she would have to set that aside for the safety of her people.

Chapter One

Now...

Her birth name was Isis Flores Rivera, but she chose to go by Isis Quinn-Santell. It was a compliment to the family that saved her life, took her in, and gave her purpose. That purpose led to them saving the world thanks to their Wiccan abilities. But to their audience, it was all part of the show. To them, Isis was simply the sixteen-year-old member of The Witches of Vegas, the greatest, and last stage magic act in the city.

"Ladies and gentlemen, we hope you've enjoyed our show so far," Isis' adopted dad Sebastian Santell announced from the center of the stage. "But we are not done yet. Prepare yourselves to be once again amazed. We will now bring up three walls for our grand finale!"

Sebastian stretched out his arms. "Walls rise!" he shouted so the audience could hear him without the microphone near his mouth.

Isis stood offstage while three brick walls, each around one quarter the size of the stage, rose from the floor. The walls stood an equal amount of space from one another and faced the audience. She stood back for most of the show and watched her family perform. Now it was her turn to shine.

"Hey." An arm wrapped around Isis's stomach. "This is it, your big finale. Are you ready?"

"I am," she answered with a smile.

Isis turned to look into Zack Galloway's handsome green eyes. They complemented his golden-blond hair and blue collared shirt. Zack was just nine weeks older than Isis. Unlike the others, he was not a witch, but an actual magician. Well, he was a magician's assistant for his uncle, the late Herb Galloway, but he had so much knowledge on the subject. Now he was one of The Witches of Vegas, a member of their coven. They considered him part of the family. Isis didn't think of him that way, and nothing could make her happier.

"After the show," Isis said to him, "do you want to take me out dancing again?"

"You sure your folks won't mind?" he asked.

Isis rested a hand on Zack's elbow and grinned. "We can always ask."

Isis leaned in and kissed him. She loved feeling Zack's soft lips against her own. Her adopted mom Selena and Aunt Sacha returned to the backstage area. They pulled apart as the pair passed. It was no secret to her family that they were together. But Isis and Zack agreed it was better not to flaunt it in front of them.

"The audience is all warmed up," Sacha called out to Isis. "Go get 'em, kiddo."

"Let her focus, Sach," Selena said. "This is a whole new way for Isis to use the energy, she will need to concentrate."

"You hear that, Isis? Your mom's in worry mode again," Sacha responded with a blatant eyeroll. "You'd better come back in one piece."

"I know you don't need it," Zack whispered in Isis' ear. "But good luck, anyway."

"Thanks," Isis giggled.

"At this time, ladies and gentlemen, I welcome once again to the stage," Sebastian shouted with paternal pride in his voice, "my little princess and the future goddess of magic, *Isis!*"

A light melody—one chosen by Zack—played through the auditorium speakers. Isis' heart raced much as it did during her first performance one-year ago. The reason was that today she would be doing something new and exciting. After a month of practice with Dad, she couldn't wait for the moment she could do it in front of an audience. That moment was now.

Isis stepped out to a smattering of applause, stopping next to the wall closest to her. She closed her eyes and concentrated. Although this was part of the show, for Isis, it was a lesson. In fact, it was the equivalent of a mid-term exam.

In her mind, she pictured duplicate versions of herself standing behind the walls on the left and center of the stage. They had the same brown hair tied in a ponytail. They wore the same purple blouse and mini skirt. Earlier she stared at herself in the mirror, memorizing every detail including the cute watch with the pink band on her left wrist that Zack gave her for their one-year anniversary.

She opened her eyes. Sure enough, two mirror images of herself stood behind each of those walls. Isis held her watch-wearing hand out for the audience to see before sticking it back behind the wall. On command, the illusion of herself behind the center wall stuck out its hand and wiggled its fingers. Both Isis and the illusion pulled back their arms. Now, it was time to do the same with her head.

"Don't forget to look at the audience," Zack

whispered from offstage.

Isis nodded. The two illusions of herself did the same. She threw the audience a knowing grin, then hopped back behind her wall. The illusion on the far left stuck its head out from behind that wall. The image flashed to the audience the same grin. Isis willed the image to pull back behind the wall. At that point, Isis brought her head out behind her wall. To the audience, it looked like Isis was teleporting from behind one wall to the other. The effect received a smattering of applause. The preliminaries were over. It was now time to step it up.

Isis faced the concrete in front of her face. "Phase through," she mumbled to herself. Against the wall she saw what looked like static on a television screen. Isis leapt forward and stepped through, coming out on the other side. The wall was thin, but solid. The audience gave her a collective "Ooh." Now that she was through, she sensed the wall solidify behind her.

Isis ran back behind the wall. She then commanded the illusion of herself behind the far left wall to step through and stare out into the audience with a hand on its hip. The image received a collective gasp. To them, it was as if Isis had stepped through one wall on one side of the stage, and then come out of another wall on the opposite side of the stage. She had practiced this many times, but this was the best she had ever pulled it off. It was now time to bring it home…

Whoa!

A pain ran through Isis' chest. It felt like a mallet slamming against her heart. She tried to take a deep breath, but it was a struggle, like sucking a watermelon down her throat. An image formed in her head. It was

Valeria, the Wiccan vampire who turned their lives upside down. Isis hadn't thought about her, or the torture she endured at her hands, in a long while. Why now all of a sudden, and while her chest screamed in pain?

Isis leaned her back against the wall. Everything circled as if she were in the eye of a tornado. She had felt this sensation before, but never with such intensity. Her hands trembled. Something was happening, but she didn't know what. "Not again, not right now." She blinked her eyes rapidly. It's been over a year since Valeria was in their lives. She demanded of her brain to never think of her again. Time to refocus on the now.

At the sound of audience members gasping, she picked up her head. Different voices all yelled the same thing, "Where did she go?" Isis glanced over. Her illusions, including the one on the far left had vanished before ducking behind her wall. She had to bring at least one of those illusions back to finish the act. Stay focused on the spell.

A few deep breaths pushed away the dizziness. Same with the pain in her chest. Her hands no longer shook. Talk about a close call. Isis focused on the back of the center wall. The image of herself returned. "Rise, rise," Isis whispered. On command, her illusion slowly levitated above the wall, looking out at the audience, its head turning from right to left. High up, the image hovered in place.

Isis took in a mouthful of air and allowed her body to levitate. As she went up, the image simultaneously drifted down. Once behind its wall, the illusion disappeared completely. Isis called this routine "Elevator." The audience cheered as the walls dropped forward, leaving only Isis hovering several feet above the stage floor.

Sebastian ran out, microphone in hand. "Ladies and gentlemen, let's hear it for our youngest witch, *Isis*!"

The crowd roared. Isis floated down to the stage floor with a huge smile across her face. Dad had worked with her on creating and controlling more than one illusion at the same time. It wasn't easy but if they believed in her ability to pull off such a complicated spell, how could she not believe in herself as well? She had to demonstrate to her family, and herself, that she was old enough and ready to handle such focus. In the end, they were right. She did it.

Isis took a bow and skipped offstage, her symptoms a fleeing memory.

"We hope you enjoyed our show," Sebastian continued. Selena joined him on the stage, taking his hand. "Come back anytime to see *THE WITCHES OF VEGAS*!"

The audience exploded in cheer. The lights in the auditorium came on.

Isis stopped in front of Zack, who was waiting near the dressing room's open door for her. "So, how did it look?" she asked, her lips stretching into a huge grin. "I think it looked good. Did it look good?" God, they'd been together for a year and her heart still fluttered around him. They'd been through so much together she couldn't imagine life without him.

She expected Zack to return her smile with one of his own, then embrace her with a big hug. That was what usually happened. In fact, it was the main reason Isis was so quick to run off the stage. But that wasn't what happened this time. This time, Zack's eyes were tight with worry. "Isis, what the hell happened out there?" he asked.

"What was wrong?" The words flew out of Isis' mouth before she even thought to ask them. "I thought I nailed it."

"I saw your eyes blinking and your hands shaking. You were about to pass out."

Isis's mouth popped open. "You saw that? Did they see it, too?"

"Sacha's in the dressing room and your folks didn't have the angle. They were near the front of the stage. The wall blocked their view of you. But I saw it. I saw your face when the illusion fluttered and disappeared. They thought your concentration broke, but I know that's not what happened. Something was wrong."

"I'm okay, Zack," Isis insisted. "Can we talk about this later?"

"Later? Why?" His head tipped left. "Has this happened before?"

"Yeah, it's happened a few times." Isis shrugged. "But never during a performance. Not until this time."

"A performance?" Zack shouted. "That's not what I'm worried about! Were you ever going to tell me?"

Isis shushed him. She clenched her fists. "Zack, can we please talk about this later?"

She tried to step away, but he grabbed her wrist and pulled her back. It was an aggression she'd never seen from him. The way his mouth dropped, his actions must have surprised himself as well. He took a deep breath. "I'm sorry, just…at least tell me if I should be worried."

Isis clenched her jaw. This boy just couldn't take a hint. "No, Zack, I'm—"

"Worried about what?" Sebastian asked.

Isis swirled around. She gasped at the sight of her folks standing behind her. She hadn't sensed their approach. Damn, she thought she was getting better at that sixth sense thing. This was not a family conversation she wanted to have at this moment, not while she was covered in sweat from the stage's hot lights.

"Is everything okay with you two?" Selena asked.

Zack's mouth opened. She forced his jaw to close. His eyes shifted her way. She had never used her power against him. She didn't want to this time. It was an instinctive reaction. Guess they were both having those. They'd have to make that up to each other later.

"Everything's fine with us." Isis stepped away from Zack and in front of Selena. "Mom, are you sure *you're* okay?"

Selena took Isis's hands and squeezed. "Oh, sweetie, I told you, I'm fine. You don't have to worry so much about me. It's our job to worry about you, remember?"

"I know, you and Dad tell me that all the time. But I do."

"I know you do." Selena released Isis's hands. "I know I was in a bad way for a while, but I'm fine. I'm performing again, aren't I?"

"Yeah, and you were great out there," Isis answered. The shows were always better when the whole family took the stage. "Hey, Zack and I were going to head out tonight, spend some time on the strip. Is that okay?"

"On a Sunday night?" Sebastian folded his arms across his chest. "Zack has school tomorrow, and you have some lessons of your own, as well."

"We won't stay out too late," she replied. "I promise."

Isis opened her deep brown eyes wide and pointed them up at Sebastian. It was her "Daddy, please?" face, and it made him a lot more agreeable. She could already see the word "no" melting off his tongue. He threw a glance at Selena and that was a good thing. She was a bit more easygoing than him when it came to parenting.

"It was her first time closing the show," Selena answered. "I can understand them wanting to celebrate." She glanced back and forth from Zack to Isis. "Just make sure you're back no later than eleven o'clock, okay?"

"Make it ten-thirty," Sebastian added.

"Eleven o'clock would be great." Isis threw a smile at Zack. "I'll be ready in a half hour?"

Once again, Zack did not return the smile. His head was down as if he were deep in thought. The grimace on his face gave away exactly what he was thinking. "Yeah, sure," he snapped. "Let's pretend nothing's going on and just have fun. Maybe that's all I'm good for?" Zack stormed off in a huff.

"What was that all about?" Selena asked. "Are you two fighting?"

"I don't think we are," Isis answered with eyes on Zack heading down the hallway. "I don't know. Maybe. We've never really had one before."

"Do you want me to talk to him?" Sebastian asked. "I noticed he's been a lot less jumpy around me. Maybe he'll open up if we speak man to man."

"No, I'm sure we're fine." Isis strolled toward the

dressing room. "I should go get ready."

"Remember, no later than eleven o'clock," Selena reminded her.

"Ten-thirty," Sebastian added.

The door to the dressing room was wide open. Isis stepped through the doorway. Sacha occupied the chair in front of the vanity mirror. Isis caught her cool aunt's smirk in the mirror directed her way.

"Men! Right, kiddo?" Sacha quipped.

"You heard?" Isis asked even though the answer was obvious.

"These aren't exactly thick walls, and the door's wide open. What happened that he's so upset?"

"I don't know why he's upset at me," Isis said. "I didn't do anything wrong."

The comment made Sacha snicker. "At least he didn't cancel on you for tonight. That means he wants a reason to let whatever it is go. Just stroke his ego a bit and whatever's bothering him, he'll forget all about it."

"Stroke his ego?"

"Throw him a few compliments and reassurances. Use that precious little smile of yours." Sacha gave Isis a wink. "The boy is crazy about you. I'm sure you'll have him eating out of your palm in no time."

Isis nodded as Sacha returned her attention to makeup removal. Sacha was the right one to get advice on men. She'd certainly been with plenty of them.

What Sacha said did make sense, at least Zack was still willing to go out. But Isis was worried. She'd never seen him this upset. She thought things were good between them despite that little setback a few months ago when she teleported into his hotel room across the hall after her folks went to bed. They were intimate, then fell asleep in each other's arms. It was a great night, until Isis' scary dream set the blanket on fire. The fire alarms turned it into an embarrassing situation that they couldn't hide from her folks. Since then, Isis still visited him at night, but Zack had been reluctant to let her sleep over. Apparently, causing a fire in bed was a great deterrent to intimacy.

Isis still enjoyed their dates, but not if they were having issues. She especially wanted her relationship with Zack to be on good terms tonight. Last week was the first time she agreed to go dancing with him. He took her to a nearby nightclub and it turned out to be a lot more fun than she expected. Isis really wanted to do that again.

Chapter Two

Zack sat across from Isis at the middle of five tables in the yogurt shop. It was one of their go-to location after evening performances. He was happiest when they'd arrive and the center table was available. It wasn't too close to the door and it wasn't near the crowded yogurt machines. Normally, Zack spent the time staring at Isis. He loved the innocent grin she always sported while digging into her yogurt. Isis was extremely skinny, which came from years of abuse before her adoption by The Witches of Vegas, but she was still so adorable, especially with those dimples. Zack saw himself as the luckiest guy in the world in that he had her whole family's unconditional love and trust.

Or so he thought.

"You are part of my coven now, Zack Galloway," Sebastian said to him a year ago. "That also makes you part of my family and part of our lives. I promise you will be treated accordingly." Those words now rang hollow. Isis said whatever happened to her on that stage had happened before. Zack saw that as a legitimate family crisis. The others had to know; Isis was like an open book with her family. Apparently, Zack was the last to find out. He was left out of the loop.

"Earth to Zack?" Isis tapped the table with her knuckles. "What's up with you?"

"Huh?" Zack lifted his head. "What do you mean?"

"You've barely touched your yogurt. It's turning all liquidy."

Zack took a scoop of yogurt with his spoon. He held it above the bowl for several seconds while staring across the table at Isis. He then dropped it back into the bowl. Isis' face scrunched. Perhaps she really didn't get why he was upset.

"Your opening act was great tonight, Zack," Isis said. "Was that a new card trick you did at the end?" Isis blinked her eyes rapidly. Okay, so maybe flirting wasn't her greatest strength.

"Can we get into what happened to you on stage?" Zack asked.

"Is that what you're upset about?" Isis shrugged. "I got a dizzy spell and had trouble catching my breath, but it went away."

"And it's happened before."

"It wasn't the first time." Isis leaned in across the table. "Are you upset because I didn't tell you about it? If that's it, I'm sorry. I didn't think it was a big deal."

Because no one told him, that's why he was upset. He didn't know if that was because he was an afterthought, or if there was another reason. Like maybe it was a witch issue, or a family issue, and maybe he wasn't really either. But she was sharing now. At least now he could catch up. "I'm concerned about why this is happening. When did this start? How many times?"

"I told you, just a few times and they never last long." Isis took a gulp of what was left of her candy-covered chocolate yogurt. "The first was a few months ago. It happened twice since. I shook them off. Today was the first bad one, but even then, it passed kinda quickly. I don't know why it's happening, maybe I'm just stressed."

"What's stressing you?" Zack stuck a spoonful of yogurt in his mouth. Isis was right, it was melting. It tasted like milk with cookie crumbs mixed in.

"I don't know." She twirled her spoon in what was left of her yogurt. "I've been having some weird dreams. Mostly about, well…her. I think when the dreams stop and I'm sleeping through the night, the dizzy spells will stop, too."

"I've seen you have bad dreams. Like when you set my bed on fire."

"Well, yeah." Isis bit her bottom lip. "God, that is so much worse than wetting the bed. I thought that habit was long behind me." Zack wished it were long behind her too.

"What do your folks think?" Zack leaned in and whispered. "Do they know if it's a…witch thing?"

Isis stayed quiet. The smile disappeared. Her eyes went wide with guilt, like an adolescent caught with a hand in the cookie jar.

"Wait—they don't know, either?" Zack gasped. "You really haven't told them?"

Isis shook her head back and forth. Zack expected his jaw to fall off and smack the table. Isis shared everything with her family. She even told them about the time the two of them…she shared everything. "I don't get it," Zack said. "You don't keep secrets from them. Why are you hiding this?"

"I'm not hiding it."

"You didn't tell me. You didn't even tell them. It seems like you're hiding this, and I don't understand why you would—"

"*It's too soon!*" she shouted.

Isis threw a hand across her face, no doubt trying to hide tears. A couple at a nearby table focused their way. The woman had a look of concern aimed at Isis. She then glared at Zack. Great, now he felt like a total jerk. The last thing he wanted to do was make Isis cry.

Isis brought her hand down and sniffled. "You know how excited we all were," she sobbed. "They'd been trying, like, forever but we all kind of accepted that they couldn't. Finally, they beat the odds."

"Isis, you don't have to—"

She continued. "Mom had a connection with the baby after just six weeks. She already knew it was a boy. What happened after that, well, it's been almost a month, but I know she's not over it. I can see it all over her face. I'm sure Dad isn't either although he tries to act like he's all good."

Zack wanted to say something encouraging, but just like the day Selena lost the baby, he had no magical words to offer. He witnessed firsthand how this ordinarily jovial family went through a period of sorrow and depression. Hell, he even caught Sacha crying, and he never thought she let that nonchalant armor crack. Unfortunately, the time to grieve was limited as the show had to go on. They were all back on the stage in two weeks, Selena in three.

"Is that why you were mad, Zack?" Isis reached over and cupped her hand over his. "You thought I told them but not you?"

"Well, yeah." Thoughts of diving under the table crossed his mind. "You're all super close and sometimes I feel like an outsider…"

"You're not an outsider, Zack, especially not to

me." Isis squeezed his hand tight. "Your uncle gave his life last year so we, and Luther, could stop Valeria. After that, my family took you in and my dad made you part of our coven. That means you're one of us now. I respect that. Plus, I trust you as much as I trust them. I'd never treat you like an outsider."

"I appreciate you saying that, Isis." It was Zack's biggest lingering concern. Uncle Herb was the only family he had until that day. There was no one else to turn to for a home. He appreciated their oath to treat him like their own, even though he wasn't a witch. Deep down, he questioned how much they really meant it.

Isis' brown eyes connected with Zack's. "You're my soulmate, Zack Galloway. I want to be with you until the end of time. I've known that since the day we met."

Zack's lips stretched into a slight grin. "The day we met we were under a love spell created by a legit wicked witch."

Isis giggled. "Yeah, we were. But that spell wore off a while ago and my feelings for you haven't changed." Isis stretched out her arms as if she was on the stage and her act was a roaring success. "Here I am, at your table, nobody else's, just yours," she sang, then flashed him a cheese face.

In that moment, Zack found himself lost in her wide eyes and smile. It was like a wave of euphoria splashing through his body. No one had ever made him feel this way, no one except for Isis. At times, he questioned if she was using her power on him. But after being under an actual spell, Zack was sure he knew the difference. The happiness that came over him whenever they hung out together—or every time she appeared in his room at night—it had to be real.

Isis stood, walked around the table, and sat in Zack's lap. Her eyes widened to the size of silver dollars. "So, are we good?"

"Yeah, we're good," Zack said with a nod and a grin. "You really should let them in on this, Isis."

"I know. I just don't want to give them something else to worry about," Isis said. "At least, not about me."

"You're the most important thing in their lives," Zack responded. "If you're having a problem, they'd want to know about it. Especially if they can help."

Isis's blank stare pointed towards Zack for several seconds. Finally, she broke the awkward silence. "You're right. I'll tell them in the morning."

"You sure you want to wait?"

"Yes." Isis wrapped her arms around Zack's neck and squeezed him tight. She whispered in his ear. "Right now, I'm on a date with my boyfriend and I'm hoping he wants to take me dancing again."

Zack let his cheek touch hers. "Are you sure you're okay to go dancing?"

"I'm fine," Isis assured him. "In fact, I've never felt better. Not in a while."

Zack had more to say and questions to ask. He decided instead not to ruin the moment. The rest of this conversation could wait until later, and it should involve the whole family. "Well, I did read about a place called Club 90's. It's in the basement of a resort not too far down the strip from here. They play all the great music from that decade. Want to check it out?"

Her head tipped back. "How'd you get into the 90's? That's long before we were born."

"I had to research the decade for a project in school. I really got into it." Pride resonated through Zack. "I got an A on the project."

"And that's why you wear that blue fanny pack now?" Isis stood from Zack's lap and pointed down at his waist. "To feel more '90's'?"

Zack gave the pack a firm tug. It had the words Sapphire Resort written across the front in Roman lettering. "I saw it in a store at the hotel's mall. I like the fanny pack. It gives me a place to keep some of my magic supplies wherever I go."

"Because people are stopping you all the time to perform magic," Isis giggled.

"Hey, you never know. Someone may recognize me as one of The Witches of Vegas. It has happened." Zack stood from his chair and took a bow. "So, what do you say, should we check the place out?"

"Yeah, sure, let's do it!"

Isis reached for Zack's arm, which he gave freely. She grabbed her small black pocketbook from the table with her free hand. Zack dropped what remained of their yogurt in the trash and the two headed out. Next stop: Club 90's.

Chapter Three

Isis had lived in the middle of Las Vegas Boulevard since she was nine years old. She loved the way the huge neon signs lit up the sky and how droves of people were always on the move. Most of those sights she saw from the window of her bedroom in the hotel's penthouse suite.

Isis never really got out much in all that time; she was a bit scared to venture too far from the hotel she knew as home. That was until she met Zack. He knew the area and all the fun stuff to do for people their age. That's why she always let him pick the places they went to for their dates.

Every place he chose was either exciting or romantic. Sometimes they checked off both boxes. Of course, this was Las Vegas, a place that was all about odds, and odds were they'd eventually hit a dud. Club 90's qualified as a dud.

The place wasn't overly crowded—maybe around thirty people filled the club—but it was small, so it felt packed. Many were shoulder-to-shoulder on the tiny dance floor under one huge strobe light. Others crowded the pool table and the arcade machines in the back. The walls were covered in framed pictures of items such as old video game systems, see-through phones, and cartoon characters. There were also old pictures of real people. Isis only recognized a few of them like Will Smith and Britney Spears. The others, not so much.

Isis sat with Zack on stools in front of the bar with her pocketbook resting on her lap. They waited for the abnormally tall female bartender with tattoos all over her exposed arms and a short, pixie cut hairstyle to notice them. At the moment, she stood at the other end of the bar chatting it up with an older couple.

There was a huge portrait on the wall above the wine rack. It was just a multi-colored pattern, but the sign below the picture said that an image would form by staring at it without blinking. So far it didn't work for Isis.

A new song blared through the speakers. It had a loud and somewhat violent opening beat. Then, the vocals began.

"Load up on guns, bring your friends," Isis said, repeating the opening line. She tried to listen some more but couldn't follow anything the singer said after that. She nudged Zack with her elbow. "You really like this stuff?"

"This is where alternative rock music began." Zack pointed up at the speakers along the walls. "Grunge started with this band. In the mid-nineties, it was truly teen spirit. You can feel it in your bones."

"Um, okay." Her bones yearned for last night's club.

A tap on Isis' shoulder swung her around on the stool. A tall boy with shoulder-length hair even blonder than Zack's peered down. His gray T-shirt said UNLV in red lettering. By his side was a much smaller girl around the guy's age with curly black hair that hung to her waistline. Along with a pink T-shirt that had Greek letters across the chest, she wore thick black glasses and the tightest jeans Isis had ever seen.

"Hey, lemme ask you something," the guy said, looking Isis over with a cocked head. "By chance, are you The Witches of Vegas?"

"Yes, that's us," Isis said with a shy grin.

"Oh my God, Marv, you were right," the girl shouted over the music. "We've seen your show, like three times this year. Each show you all do different stuff, and we can't figure out how you do any of it. You guys are so amazing."

"I'm Marvin," the guy said. "This is my girlfriend, Diane."

"Hi, I'm—"

"You're Isis. We were there a few weeks ago. You flew over our heads." Marvin glanced at Zack. "And you're the card guy from the beginning of the show, right?"

"That's me, I am the card guy," Zack said with a smile. "Cards are my specialty." His left hand reached for the fanny pack where he kept his card decks. Isis took the hand, pulled it to her lap, and cupped it between her palms. The last thing she wanted was to lose him for an hour as he did tricks for a new audience. It happened twice before. The second time was at a restaurant for the family at the next table who didn't even recognize Isis or Zack. They were just being friendly.

"Wow, you two are, like, an item?" Diane asked as if she had just learned an amazing piece of gossip.

"Yeah, we are," Isis said with pride. "We've been together for about a year."

"Are you guys hanging here?" Zack asked.

"Nah, we're heading out," Marvin answered. "This place is kind of lame. We're going to hit another club a block down from the boulevard. They have way better music there."

"But it was so cool meeting you," Diane added. "We'll totally be at your show again."

"Thank you." Isis gave them a genuine smile.

Marvin shook Zack's hand. He and Diane walked across the dance floor and out the door. As much as she hated to admit it, Isis liked being recognized. It filled her with a sense of pride. It never happened when her family was around, although that could have been any of their doing. They did prefer privacy when outside the Sapphire.

"Hey, why did you stop me from pulling out my cards?" Zack asked in that tone that said he was slightly annoyed.

Isis widened her eyes as she leaned in and gazed at him with the "please forgive me, boyfriend" look. It was the same as her "please forgive me, Daddy" look. It worked on both men in her life. "I'm sorry, Zack, but tonight I want to keep you all to myself."

"I guess that's fair." Zack nodded, a sign he was accepting her explanation. His eyebrows rose as he looked across the club. "I wonder why they think this place is lame."

Isis turned her head away and smirked. "I have no idea."

Finally, the bartender made her way in front of them. "What can I get you two?" she asked through what had to be the phoniest smile Isis ever laid eyes on.

"Two club sodas, please," Zack answered.

"I'd like a mimosa." Isis glanced over at Zack's

tilted head. "I've always wanted to try one."

The bartender snorted. "I'm going to need to see I.D. for that."

Isis had learned a lot about her connection to the planet's energy and how to manipulate it. Her mom and Sacha trained her on moving objects while her dad taught her how to create illusions. Dad also knew how to use his connection to force hypnotic suggestions into people's minds. Although he hadn't yet taught that skill to Isis, she had seen him do it more than a few times. It basically ran on the same principle as all the other reality-manipulating powers of a witch. Time to put it to the test.

Isis reached into her pocketbook and pulled out her hotel room keycard. She looked the bartender directly in the eyes. "I am showing you my I.D. and it says I am old enough to drink an alcoholic beverage." She focused her thoughts on the bartender's mind. "You see my picture and my age at twenty-one. Now that you have seen my age, you can place a mimosa on the counter for me to try."

The bartender laughed. "That was cute. Two club sodas coming up." She reached under the counter and placed two bottles in front of Isis and Zack. "That'll be eight bucks. You can leave it on the counter." She then moved onto another group of customers.

"Well, damn." Isis shook her head. "That didn't work out at all. I guess hypnosis just isn't my thing."

Isis held out her open palm, pointed at the club sodas. One bottle glided across the countertop to her hand like a piece of metal being pulled to a magnet. At least that ability was still working.

"Or maybe your heart just wasn't into committing

a crime." Zack reached for his bottle and picked it up off the counter.

"I'm sure you're right." Isis took a swig of the soda while staring off at the dance floor. "Still, I wonder why her blood tastes like syrup."

"I'm sorry, what?" Zack's face whipped her way. His eyes squinted.

"What?"

"Did you just say something about tasting the bartender's blood?"

"Did I say that?" Isis honestly couldn't remember those words coming out of her mouth, yet they sounded so familiar.

Zack stood from his bar stool and clenched her wrist. "Isis, are you all right?"

Isis stared at the strobe light above the dance floor. Somehow, it seemed brighter, or darker. Or... something. She could hear Zack shouting her name. It echoed as if they were on opposite ends of a tunnel. A striking pain crossed her chest. Everything around her blurred, just like when she'd teleport herself to a new location. But she was sure that wasn't what was happening. She inhaled but couldn't catch her breath. "Zack, I think I'm not...okay..." Did she say that out loud or did she think it? Isis couldn't be sure.

Her attention turned back to the bar from the sound of one or both bottles exploding. Her forearm stung from a piece of glass piercing her skin. Zack called out her name.

Then everything went dark.

****

"Isis, what's happening to you?" Zack heard the justifiable panic in his voice.

He hooked an arm across Isis' back and led her body down to the floor as if she were a rag doll. Her head and hands shook at rapid speed. The bar's countertop ignited in flames. Zack glanced around with no idea what to do as patrons and club staff ran for the doors. The only one not panicking was the bartender who grabbed a fire extinguisher from behind the bar and sprayed the fire. Her calm demeanor turned to fright at the realization that the foam from the extinguisher wasn't doing a bit of good.

"Isis, you have to snap out of this!" Zack held a hand against her chest. "We have to get out of here, now!" But Isis' body kept shaking. Her eyes were stretched wide, and blank.

A man with jet-black hair and a horseshoe mustache leaned next to Isis facing Zack. He had to be in his late twenties. "My name is Thomas. I'm an RN at North General. I can help."

"I don't know what's happening to her." Zack's jaw shook even harder than Isis' body.

"It looks like a seizure, maybe a reaction to the fire?" Thomas said. "Right now, we have to get her out of here. If you can take her upper body, I'll grab the legs."

Zack nodded. He hooked his arms under Isis' shoulders and lifted. Her body had stopped shaking. Her eyes closed. Thomas lifted Isis by the ankles. Lucky she was barely a hundred pounds which made it easy to get her across the empty dance floor and out of the building. Outside, they eased her onto the cement sidewalk. A crowd had formed around the sidewalk and street. All eyes were on the club's entrance.

Thomas wrapped his thumb and forefinger around

Isis' wrist. "I'm getting a pulse, but it's low," he said. "She needs to get to the hospital right now." Thomas reached for his shirt pocket and flinched. "Dammit, I think I lost my phone in there. Do you have one on you?"

Zack pulled his phone out of the fanny pack. "Well, yeah, I do, but I really need to call her family. They can help."

Thomas snatched it from Zack's hand. "They can meet us there," he said while dialing. "Right now, you need to turn her on her side. If she has another seizure, she's in danger of swallowing her tongue."

"Ah, crap!" Zack did as Thomas instructed. He rolled Isis onto her side and held her in position. Her eyes had shut tight. Zack could barely tell if she was breathing. "I need to get her family here." He reached for the phone.

Thomas stood up before he could grab it. "I need an ambulance in the front of Club 90's," Thomas shouted over the sounds of people scattering and a fire truck's siren blaring. "There's a teenage girl down, possibly critical, barely breathing! It looks like she just suffered a seizure."

"Thomas, listen to me!" Zack shouted. "I need to call her folks!" But it was clear Thomas couldn't hear him.

"Sebastian, Selena, can you hear me?" Zack whispered to himself. He had seen the family use their Wiccan power to heal. Hell, Sebastian was shot in the stomach with a pistol at point blank range. Sacha healed him within minutes. No doubt they could do the same for Isis far quicker than anything they'd do for her in the hospital. Unfortunately, not being a witch, Zack had no idea how to send his thoughts all the way across the boulevard. Hell, with all the noise around him, he could barely hear those thoughts in his own head. Plus, there was no way he'd leave Isis' side, even for the moment it would take to snatch his phone back from Thomas.

Another siren blared past the firetrucks. It came from an ambulance that sped around the other vehicles and stopped short in front of them. Thomas waved his hand and pointed down at Isis. The doors swung open. Thomas ran to the passenger's door and spoke to the people inside.

Within seconds, two EMT's exited the ambulance and placed an oxygen mask onto Isis' face. A third exited through the back and laid a stretcher next to Isis. They lifted her body onto the stretcher and off the ground.

In a flash, Zack found himself sitting in the back of the ambulance looking on as one of the EMT's was taking Isis' vitals. She was still unconscious.

That's when Zack realized he never got his phone back from Thomas.

Chapter Four

Isis' eyes opened to black and white tiles staring down at her from the ceiling. She had no idea where she was, but between the tiles and the hard bed under her body, she knew it wasn't her bedroom in the Sapphire suite. Her head felt like someone had used it as a basketball. A stinging sensation in Isis' right arm grabbed her attention. There was a needle attached to a long tube protruding from her skin. It was inches from a bandage stuck to her forearm.

"What the hell happened?" she asked.

"I'm glad to see you're awake." A woman's voice made Isis' heart jump. It wasn't her mom's. It wasn't Sacha's voice either.

The woman's heels tapped the floor as she walked to the bed. She was a middle-aged lady with glasses against the tip of her nose that made her eyes expand. The short grayish-brown hair and black pantsuit made her look like a librarian. So did the abnormally thin lips. The woman held a clipboard with a blue pen harnessed to it with a string.

Isis lifted her head. It gave her the sensation of a bright light shining in her eyes. She let her head drop back onto the pillow. "Where…where am I?" Isis asked.

"You are in Vegas North General hospital," came the response.

"Are you a doctor?" She already knew the answer, this woman was not a doctor.

"No. My name is Ms. Clarke. I am a social worker with Children's Protective Services." The woman peered down at Isis. "What is your name?"

"Isis. Isis Santell."

"Santell." The woman took the pen between her fingers and scribbled on paper attached to the clipboard. "I see."

"What am I doing here?" Isis shut her eyes tight, then reopened them. It helped clear her vision, but not by much.

"According to reports, you had a seizure at a nightclub in town," Ms. Clarke explained. "You've been in a coma for the last hour, Isis."

"A coma?"

"Yes." Ms. Clarke walked up to the bed and hunched over Isis. "Have you had these seizures before?"

"My family. Are they here?"

"We will contact them soon enough," Ms. Clarke replied. "First, I would like to learn all about you."

"What about Zack? Where is he?"

"Zack is the boy you came in with?" Once again, Ms. Clarke scribbled in her notebook. "He is in another room speaking with an LVPD detective."

"Why? What did we do?"

Isis peeked past Ms. Clarke at the door which was wide open. A man in a police uniform stood in the hallway with his arms folded over his chest. His massive frame blocked the doorway.

The social worker's eyes narrowed until her eyebrows touched. "Tell me, Isis, what is your current living situation?"

"I live with my family."

"You live with a family. Where?"

"Here in Las Vegas."

Ms. Clarke's pen moved along the page. Isis was sure she was writing down each answer. "How long have you been living with this family in Las Vegas?" Ms. Clarke asked.

"I don't understand, what's going on?" Isis made another attempt to lift her head. The result was the same. "Am I in some kind of trouble?"

"I was hoping you could answer that question for me," the social worker answered. "The young man you came in with refused to divulge your name, which meant the hospital had to admit you as a Jane Doe. In the case of a minor admitted without identity and with signs of abuse, policy dictates that, in conjunction with the LVPD, DNA is taken and run through the national database. That's how we found out who you are."

"Abuse? Me?" Isis' mouth opened wide. "I'm in the database?"

"Yes, you are. I have notes from your file right here." Ms. Clarke flipped the top page of her clipboard and studied it for a moment before responding. "You're Isis Rivera. You were in the New York City foster care system until you went missing over seven years ago. They still have an open case on you."

Uh-oh. Isis tried to come up with something clever, an explanation that would satisfy this woman so she would go away. Nothing came to mind. She could try the truth, but that didn't strike her as a good idea. "I'm a witch my 'new' family saved from getting roasted alive from the foster family that hated me even before they decided I was the devil. Now, I use my Wiccan powers to perform on stage. We even saved the world last year."

Good chance none of that would fly. This woman seemed way too tight to think outside her box. Still, Isis had to say something.

"Have you ever seen The Witches of Vegas show?" Isis asked. She didn't get a response, just a blank stare. "Um, who did you say you were again?"

"Ms. Clarke with the Las Vegas Children's Protective Services."

"That's for abused kids, right?"

"Among other things, yes."

Isis rubbed her eyes and shook her head. "Why are you here? You think I'm abused?"

"I was hoping you can tell me." Her response was dismissive, as if she had already made the determination. "You were in a coma when you were brought here, Isis. Your blood pressure is abnormally low, and you have a dangerously low body temperature. Meanwhile, the doctors can't figure out why this is happening to you. Despite the symptoms, they found no drugs in your system, at least ones they can detect."

"You think I'm on drugs?" Isis mumbled.

"Understand, my job is to help keep you safe," Ms. Clarke answered in an almost robotic tone which Isis found creepy. "I'm here to help you however I can, which includes getting you out of a situation where you may feel uncomfortable or even scared."

"You mean like this one?" Isis' reply was followed by dead silence. Not even a slight chuckle.

The social worker was only doing her job, but Isis wanted nothing more than to get rid of her. So far, the conversation only made her headache worse. Normally, Isis had the power to make her go away in over a dozen different ways. Right now, though, her thoughts were so cloudy she couldn't focus on a single idea let alone the concentration to make anything happen.

God, she needed the family by her side. They'd know how to get rid of the social worker and heal Isis from whatever was happening to her. Did they even know she was in the hospital? It had to be long past eleven o'clock by now. Isis and Zack had missed curfew before, and they always found her folks waiting up in order to give them "the talk." But they'd never been this late.

By now, Mom and Dad had to be worried, especially if they used their powers to sense her and Zack's location—which they have done in the past— and found they were in the Las Vegas hospital. But if they did that, where were they? Why weren't they here? Was that officer outside the door waiting to arrest them?

"I don't feel we are getting anywhere," Miss Clarke said. "So, let's start from the beginning. What is your living situation?"

Chapter Five

Zack sat in the metal folding chair at the end of the desk with his arms folded. An angry looking man sat across from him in the big suede chair with his back to the door. He clearly did not work for the hospital. That was obvious even before he introduced himself as Detective Chen with the Las Vegas police department's special victims' unit. Zack always thought police wore yellow uniforms, but this one was in a white collared shirt and a red tie. He was sure the detective spun the desk around prior to their meeting so Zack's back would end up against the wall.

Detective Chen had Zack's fanny pack on the desk in front of him, unzipped. He wiped his stringy hair from his eyes and removed items from the fanny pack one at a time, an action that made Zack feel violated. It was like going through a strip search.

"Another deck of cards." Detective Chen dropped the box on top of the first two he'd removed. "Are you a card player or something?"

"I'm a magician," Zack answered. "Card tricks are my specialty."

"I see." Chen removed Zack's hotel keycard and examined it. "The Sapphire." He then eyed the hotel's logo on the fanny pack. "Nice place. Is that where you're staying?"

"It's where I perform," Zack said. "Why am I here

and why are you going through my stuff?"

"Searching you is protocol," Chen replied. "You are here because I have some questions I need answered. Most of them are about the girl that you brought to this hospital."

"Is she okay?"

"She's being treated as we speak." Chen pulled out a pair of handcuffs. He threw a raised eyebrow at Zack.

"They're a prop in my act," Zack explained. "I can escape them without a key."

"Uh-huh." Chen reached back in and pulled out small sheets of red tissue paper. The detective held them under his nose and sniffed. "These are flammable?"

"It's flash paper. It's used for—"

"I'm familiar with flash paper and how it works. I'm guessing that's what the lighter in here is for as well?"

Zack nodded. "You said you had questions about the girl I brought in?"

"Indeed. I do." Chen folded his hands across the desk. "What can you tell me about Isis Rivera?"

"You know her name?" Zack now understood how his audience felt when he stunned them by pulling out a selected card they were sure he couldn't know. It left them completely thrown off, much the way he felt when the detective referred to Isis by name, a name Zack refused to give up.

"Isis Rivera," he repeated. "What is your relationship with her?"

"She's a fellow magician. She is also a good friend."

"Just a good friend, or something more?"

Zack did a doubletake. "What do you mean by that?"

"So, you are in a romantic relationship with her. Interesting."

Wow, it was like the detective could see right through Zack's brain and catch lies or omissions. He was good, like the magicians who convince their audiences they read minds through careful listening and keen observations.

Detective Chen leaned in. "Tell me, Zack, according to your school records, you are the adopted ward of your uncle, Herbert Galloway. Is that correct?"

"You have access to my school records." Zack had never told the detective his last name. He'd be wildly impressed by this man if he wasn't making Zack nervous to the point it was a struggle to contain his bladder.

"My office does, yes," came the answer. "The problem is that we tried to get in touch with Herbert Galloway. We've had no luck. It seems Mister Galloway is unaccounted for. In fact, he has been for a while. Am I right, Zack?"

No point in lying, the guy obviously knew. "He has been, yes."

"Do you want to catch me up on that? Perhaps you can tell me where you're living and who is there with you?" He pointed a thumb behind him. "I'm betting Isis Rivera for one?"

Zack let out a deep sigh. "Listen, there's nothing crazy going on here. I'm a magician, I perform on stage. The show is pretty well known around here. We're The Witches of Vegas!"

Chen did not respond. He simply stared across the

desk with what Zack took to be an adult's stink eye.

"You must have heard of us," Zack said. "Our logo is on a huge neon sign in front of The Sapphire—

"I'm familiar with The Witches of Vegas," Chen interrupted. "I've even seen the show. I am from around here, after all. So, you're claiming the two young performers are you and her?"

"Exactly! That's us." Zack raised his arms out. "I'm the opening act and she's the finale. We're pretty much minor celebrities here in Las Vegas. People go crazy when they see us." Zack decided to leave out the fact that, except on a few occasions, both he and Isis could walk down any street in Las Vegas and not get recognized by anyone.

"I'll try my best to contain myself." Chen folded his hands on the desk and smirked. "Here's the thing, Zack, even if what you're telling me is the truth, it still doesn't tell me what I need to know."

"What do you need to know?"

Chen slammed his right fist against the desk inches from Zack's body which shot back. Zack's heartbeat sped up.

"Right now, Zack, I have a very sick girl in this hospital, who may be dying, and who disappeared from the other end of the country years ago." To Zack's surprise, Chen's voice stayed monotone as he spoke. His eyes never left Zack's. "I also have you, whose guardian, as far as I can tell, has been missing for at least several months. Now, the two of you are together. This is one hell of a mystery, Zack, and I get the feeling you're giving me the runaround."

Detective Chen raised his hand from the desk and pointed a finger into Zack's face. "Right now, that girl's life, celebrity or not, is in serious danger. So, I need you to be forthcoming and tell me everything, from the beginning. If not, I'm going to have to introduce you to *my* handcuffs, and they *do* require a key to escape. At that point, we can finish this discussion at the precinct. Do you understand me?"

Zack leaned as far back as the chair would allow. Even with Chen across the table, Zack felt as if the detective had a virtual hand wrapped around his throat.

"I...I understand." Zack's voice had suddenly become hoarse. The last thing he wanted was to take a trip to the police station. Not while Isis was somewhere in this hospital.

"Good," Chen snapped. "Then start talking. Tell me everything you know, from the beginning."

Oh boy. Zack felt his lower jaw shake. He had to come up with something to tell this annoying but intimidating detective. He could claim he and Isis were both emancipated. Chen would need to call his office to verify. Of course, it wouldn't pass but at least it would buy some time. But then what? At least it was something.

Zack straightened his back, folded his hands, and smiled. "So, here's the story, Detective—"

"I can tell you are about to lie to me," Chen said in a stern tone that drowned Zack out. "Let me give you a piece of advice. Don't! It won't work out well for you."

A slight wind passed behind Detective Chen, blowing his slick black hair. A transparent vision of Sacha flashed. She was here, but invisible. Zack jerked his head up. He only peeked up for a moment, but it was enough for the detective to notice. Chen swiveled around in his chair and scanned the empty room.

A hand clenched Zack's left shoulder. Selena materialized next to him. Chen turned back and, in one motion, leaped out of his chair. "What the hell?" he shrieked as Sacha materialized behind him. Chen's hand reached to the holster attached to his belt. Sacha held a palm near the back of the detective's head.

"Sleep," the sisters said in unison. "Close your eyes and fall asleep."

Chen's eyes closed. His body fell back and slumped into the suede chair. Zack let out a sigh of relief. "About time you guys got here," he muttered.

"Zack Galloway," Sacha said in a teasing manner. "You gots some 'splainin' to do."

"Later," Selena snapped. "Right now, we need to get the two of you, and us, out of this hospital as soon as possible. There's a number of police officers here, especially on this floor."

"Where's Sebastian?" Zack asked.

"He went to get Isis," Sacha responded. "We came here to spring you."

Zack gathered his belongings and shoved them into the pack. He knew what was coming next. Time to take a deep breath and prepare for teleportation.

Chapter Six

Isis exchanged stares with Ms. Clarke for what felt like an eternity. At least her head was feeling better. Her thoughts were clearer and the social worker's tapping the clipboard with her pen no longer sounded like a jackhammer digging a hole into her skull. She hoped to outlast the lady, but it was clear she wasn't leaving without the answers she sought.

"I'm in a good home," Isis explained. "With a loving and caring family. That's the truth. You don't have to worry about me."

"I'll need more than that, Isis," Ms. Clarke replied. "For starters, I need to know who you live with and how you came to be under their care."

"If I tell you, will I get to see them?"

"That's not my call. However, the more forthcoming you are with me, the more information I can bring to my supervisors. Any contact will be determined by…"

A voice raced through Isis' head, one she recognized. It said her name. "Dad," she whispered.

"Dad?" Ms. Clarke repeated. "Okay, so there's a father figure in the home. Can you tell me his name?"

"I'm here," Sebastian's voice said to her. "Can you connect with the energy to use it?"

"I'm…not sure."

"You're not sure of his name?" The social worker

wrote on her notepad as she spoke. "I have to say, that is a sign for concern, Isis. Can you tell me who else is in the home with you? Are there any other children in the home?"

"I need you to concentrate on your connection to the energy, Isis," Sebastian said. "Focus on invisibility. Remember back to the games we played when you were first getting comfortable with your power."

Isis remembered those days with glee. She had been with them for around six months when her training had moved past the basics. It was now under the guise of playing games with her new family. One of those games was "hide and seek." In their version, Isis had to hide in plain sight by turning herself invisible. They always knew where she was—Isis realized that looking back—but if she pulled off the effect, they would act like they couldn't find her until she would reveal herself.

"Try to be quick about this, Isis," Sebastian said in her head. "I had to get rid of the officer before I could enter the room, but he will be back soon."

"How?"

"How what?" Ms. Clarke responded to the question she assumed was directed to her.

Sebastian answered, "I made him think he had to pee and couldn't hold it. He's in the bathroom now as we speak."

Isis giggled. This made the social worker's face squish. "What is so funny?" she asked. "Isis, are you feeling okay? Do you need the doctor to come and see you?"

Isis pointed toward the doorway. "The guard just left."

Clarke turned to the door. The sudden flinch meant a police officer leaving their post wasn't a common occurrence. At least it provided the distraction she needed.

Isis took a deep breath. "Hide in plain sight," she said under her breath and focused the Earth's energy around her body. It was that control which classified her as a witch. Isis focused down at her hands. They faded, then disappeared.

Clarke turned back to the bed and shrieked. She looked around the room in a frantic manner. The social worker then ran to the bed and placed a hand on the mattress just inches from Isis' face.

"Where? How?" Clarke gasped. Her right hand covered her wide-open mouth. Clarke dropped to one knee, leaned down, and peeked underneath the bed. Clarke jumped to her feet and spun back to the open doorway. Her head darted around the room with clear confusion radiating across her face.

"This is a problem, a huge problem," she moaned. She ran through the doorway like a cat with its tail on fire. With the social worker gone, the door slid shut. The lock in the knob turned. Sebastian appeared in front of the bed.

"Dad," Isis said with a deep exhale. "Where's Mom? Where's Sacha?"

"Rescuing Zack. They should all be here shortly." Sebastian sat at the edge of the bed and touched her forehead with the back of his hand. "What the hell happened to you, Isis?"

Isis shrugged. "I…got dizzy, then must have fainted. I woke up here."

"Just like that?" Sebastian felt her cheek, then the

side of her throat. "No warning signs?"

Isis hated to admit it, but Zack was right. She should have told her family about the dizzy spells long ago. She had convinced herself that they'd pass, that they weren't anything to worry about. For all the family had done for her, Isis didn't want to add to their stress, not so soon after losing the baby. Now she may have just brought even more trouble to their lives.

"Isis?" Sebastian said.

No choice anymore. It was time to confess. "I…I got dizzy a few times for, like, the last bunch of weeks." Ugh, this was not how she wanted them to find out. "It was nothing like this. I never passed out before like I did at the club. I just didn't think it was a big deal." She looked up into his blue eyes. They had signs of both worry and anger. "I know I should have told you about it."

"Yes, Isis, you really should have."

Isis wrapped her arms around Sebastian's waist and buried her head in his abdomen. As always, when she needed her family, they were there for her. And they were her family, no matter what that social worker implied.

"We will talk about this later." Sebastian stood and held a hand over Isis' body. "For now, let's heal whatever's going on inside of you."

"I like that idea."

Sebastian chanted the words, "Heal her illness." Within moments, Isis' entire body tingled, as if every single bone had fallen asleep. It had been over a year since Isis needed such an intense healing. She remembered feeling better almost immediately. But not this time.

"I don't understand," Sebastian said to himself.

The center of the room blurred like the place was inside a kaleidoscope. The distortion faded revealing Zack, Selena, and Sacha standing together in its place.

"Hey, kiddo, you're looking great," Sacha called out. Selena and Zack rushed to the bed.

"Thanks," Isis said through a slight grin. "I feel great, too."

Selena put a hand on Sebastian's shoulder. He threw her a nervous glance. "What is it?" she asked.

"I don't know what's happening here." Sebastian pulled his hand back. The tingling stopped. The headache did not. "She's not healing."

"What do you mean?" Selena asked with concern. "How can that be?"

"I don't know. I used a spell but nothing happened—"

The doorknob shook. It was followed by a loud bang, like a shoulder ramming the door from the other side. "Open this door now!" a voice shouted through the wood.

"Oh damn, that's Detective Chen," Zack gasped.

"I think this is a good time for us to leave," Sebastian said.

Sacha took Selena's hand. Both sisters shut their eyes. Isis forced herself to sit up. The room around them faded away. The last thing she saw was the door flying open and the same police officer, done with his pee break, charging in. He was followed by Ms. Clarke and a well-dressed man who had to be Detective Chen.

47

Chapter Seven

The witches' penthouse suite at the Sapphire materialized around them. It felt safe, but only for now. Zack wanted to kick himself. Letting them take Isis to the hospital was a mistake. But how could he have prevented it? In the moment and with no control of the situation, not a single option came to mind. Now their lives were ruined. The witches were on the run for a crime from over seven years ago that wasn't an actual crime, but they couldn't explain it away. At least not without revealing themselves as witches. This was a threat far different than what they faced against Valeria.

Isis was laid out on the living room couch while Zack and the others surrounded her. Selena took a seat at the end, cupping a hand under Isis' head. Zack's eyes stayed on the suite's front door.

"You all realize that eventually they're going to come here looking for us, right?" Zack heard the tremble in his voice as he spoke. "They think you kidnapped Isis."

"Well, technically, we did," Sacha said. "But for all the right reasons."

"We need to regroup," Sebastian said. "We have to figure out our next step."

"Our next step is healing Isis," Selena stated. "Sacha, let's see what we can do."

Without one of her usual snide remarks, Sacha

stood across from Selena in front of Isis' feet. She raised her hands over Isis. Selena stood from the couch and did the same. "Try to relax, kiddo," Sacha said to her niece who, from her scrunched face, was anything but relaxed. "We'll have you up and running in no time."

Zack's confidence bolstered. Individually, Selena and Sacha had amazing control of the planet's Wiccan energy. Combined, their power more than doubled. He had seen this in action firsthand. According to Sacha, it was due to their sibling connection. The planet somehow knew and rewarded them for acting as one. That was fortunate for Isis. The sisters chanted in unison, "Heal the body, heal the mind. Heal the body, heal the mind."

"How exactly does the healing effect work?" Zack whispered to Sebastian. It was one of the few questions about their power that he hadn't asked over the last year.

"The power speeds up the body's natural healing process at an exponential rate," he whispered back. One thing Zack really liked about the witches was their patience with him. In the past year, he must have asked at least a million questions. No matter which of them he asked, they always offered him a clear and concise answer. Even Isis answered his questions, although she was a bit more open about letting Zack know when he bordered on annoying.

The sisters put down their arms and stared at each other from across the couch. Sacha shook her head back and forth. "That's never happened before."

"We'll keep trying," Selena said to her.

Isis sat up. "I think I'm f-feeling better." Her words

slurred and her eyes still had a glaze to them.

Selena sat behind Isis and wrapped her arms around her waist. Isis rested her head on Selena's shoulder. "Have faith in us and the energy, Isis. We're going to beat this," Selena whispered.

"I know you will, Mom," Isis replied. "You're the strongest Wiccan of the world. You can figure me right on up through the sky."

Zack did a double take. Her sentence sounded more like random words thrown together. From the look on her face, Selena noticed, too. "I don't understand. What are you trying to say, sweetie?" she asked.

"I'm…I don't want to taste."

"Hey, guys." Zack took a step back. "This is what happened at the nightclub before her seizure."

Isis' eyelids fluttered. Her body tensed. She inhaled a deep breath as her hands and feet convulsed. Isis' seizure and the damage it caused crept back into Zack's brain. He was inches away from the fire. He dropped to his knees, bracing himself in case it happened again.

This time, the entire room shook like it was the epicenter of an earthquake. Sebastian and Sacha lost their footing and dropped to the floor. Pictures and paintings flew off the wall. Selena gripped the armrest of the couch, keeping her free hand pressed against Isis' chest. From the looks on the witches' faces, this was something they'd never dealt with before.

"Isis, can you hear me?" Selena shouted in her ear. Zack was sure Isis was oblivious to what was happening, just as was the case back at Club 90's.

"Zack, look out!" Sebastian shouted.

He pointed his palm at Zack. A wind formed. It engulfed him and rolled him across the floor. The chandelier plunged from the ceiling and crashed in the spot Zack originally occupied. The crash nearly made Zack's heart shoot out through his chest.

"You just saved my life," he screeched.

"Later," Sebastian shouted over the rumbling. "We have to contain this before she brings the whole building down!"

"Zack!" Sacha called out to him from the other side of the room. She pointed to the door directly behind him. It led into her bedroom. "My crystals! They're in a pocketbook at the top of my closet!"

"You keep enchanted crystals in a pocketbook?"

"Not time for questions, Zack!" she screeched at him. "Go!"

Zack was the closest to Sacha's room so he had the best shot at getting to the crystals. It was just a matter of not falling on his face with the floor vibrating at a heavy pace. He grabbed the doorknob to pull himself to his feet and maneuvered through the doorway. He was careful to stay balanced with each step. His magician training never prepared him for navigating an actual earthquake.

Sacha's room was a mess with all her dresser drawers open and her clothes—including ones Zack was sure he wasn't supposed to see—all over the floor. He yanked open the closet door. Sacha had as many purses as she did boxes of shoes, all of which had fallen across the closet floor. One bright red pocketbook still sat on the shelf above where the clothes hung. Despite the room shaking enough to make her hanging clothes sway, the purse didn't move at all. That had to be it.

Zack grabbed the purse and made his way back into the living room. He passed it to Sacha who unzipped the front pocket, reached in, and pulled out five diamond-shaped crystals. Sacha and Sebastian each took two stones and placed them on the floor around the couch. Sacha tossed the last one to Selena who laid it at the head of the couch. The crystals were equally apart, forming a pentagon shape around the couch.

Electricity rose from the crystals, connecting in the center high above Isis. Sacha stared into the pentagon. The rumbling stopped. Isis was out cold. Selena leaned down by Isis' head.

"Sacha, what did you do?" Zack asked.

Sacha let out a deep exhale. "I cut off her connection enough to stop her from making this super tall building quake."

"Not just the building."

All eyes went to Sebastian who was staring out the picture glass window.

Zack made his way next to Sebastian. Below, Vegas Boulevard traffic had come to a standstill. This was due to a line of cars directly in front of the Sapphire Resort, all of which had collided into each other. A fire hydrant lay on its side. Water shot up from an underground pipe.

"Holy…" Zack's opened his mouth wide.

"Real talk, folks." Sacha squeezed a handful of her shoulder-length red hair. "We have no idea what's happening to Isis, or how to cure her. We need help with this."

"Whatever is happening to her, it's Wiccan in nature." Sebastian groaned. "Where are we supposed to go to get help?"

The room went silent. It was a good question as none of them knew any other witches except each other.

In fact, the only expert they did know, their immortal mentor, Luther, was now trapped on a world in a whole other dimension babysitting Valeria, a psychopath vampire with impressive Wiccan powers. Not like they could call or reach him on social media.

Zack thought back to every fact he had learned or heard about witches and supernatural beings. It was a lot. But, unfortunately, all his teachers on this subject were in the room and they were clueless on how they could handle this. Still, there had to be an answer.

He thought back to every fact he was told and every story he had heard. That's when it hit him.

"Sacha," he said, unable to withhold his anxiety. "You told me about another family of witches from when you were young. You said they went to a village, a sanctuary for witches."

"Yes, I told you what I remembered of them, which wasn't much. I was only four." She turned to Selena. "Do you remember them, Sis?"

Selena stood from Isis' side. "Yes, it was a boy and a girl. They were twins, around eleven years old. I remember that because I asked Mom how they were the same age and still be sister and brother. Like us, they hadn't discovered their connection yet. But their parents, both witches like Mom, were sure it would happen soon enough." Selena paced, staring up at the ceiling like she was trying to pull memories from a vault that had long been sealed. "They wanted us to go with them. Mom didn't want that. I only remember because I was hoping we'd go. I had a little crush on the boy."

"You never mentioned *him* before," Sebastian said.

"Please, Sebastian, I was eight," she snapped. "It

was years before Mom took you in. Anyway, I remember their father saying it was a village. I think it was in Europe."

"It was in Europe. I do remember hearing that," Sacha said.

"Yes, it was on the outskirts of a country in Europe, but which one?" Selena's pacing stopped. She rubbed her temples. "I'm sure it started with an S. Scotland? Switzerland?"

"Could it be Spain or Scandinavia?" Sacha asked.

"No…maybe. I don't know…I'm sorry." Selena shook her head. "I'm trying, but I just don't remember."

"You don't even know if the village actually exists, or if it was a folktale," Sebastian pointed out. "Did you ever hear from this family after they left?"

"No, we never did," Selena answered.

"So, all we have is that it's somewhere in Europe, in a country that maybe starts with an S?" Zack asked. "And we're not sure if it's even real."

"Not helpful, I know," Selena responded. "It's just been so long, and I was a child at the time."

"I wonder," Sacha said, "if we could use the energy to get into your memories—"

Sebastian interrupted, "If not, we need to come up with something. Meanwhile, we can freeze time within the crystals. Put Isis in suspended animation just like we did with Luther when he was dying."

"You want to put my niece in suspended animation, Sebastian?" Sacha asked. "Especially while she's in this condition?"

"We have to." Sebastian took Selena by the hands. Their sad eyes met. "Selena, if she wakes up and has another attack, the entire building could come down, killing everyone in it. This is no longer just about her or us."

"I know, you're right," Selena sobbed. "At least until we can find a way to help her."

"The outskirts of a country that starts with an S," Zack muttered. "That's not enough. We need more than that."

"We're all concerned here, Zack," Sebastian said to him. "Frankly, even if Selena could remember, that still doesn't tell us exactly where the village is located."

"We can't just give up so easily," Zack snapped. "Are there really no other options that could help Isis?"

"It's not like we can thumb through a phonebook and find experts on the Wiccan world," Sacha said.

"We're not giving up," Selena said. "We just have to find a way—"

Zack wasn't completely sure what a phonebook was. However, it did give him an idea. It was a long shot, but he couldn't just stand around waiting for the witches to come up with something, especially when so far they were shooting blanks. Zack ran out the front door and left the suite. He had nothing to offer, at least not at this moment. But if he was going to find something, it would be in his own hotel room.

Chapter Eight

Zack sat on a rolling chair in front of the desk in his hotel room. The room was directly across from the witches' suite, which offered just enough privacy while still close enough that they could check on him at any time. They were good about it, rarely knocking on his door without a legitimate reason. Isis, on the other hand, entered his room constantly. But in her case, he looked forward to her visits.

This time, no one barged in, which allowed Zack time to search. He stared intently at his laptop screen, reexamining what he found. It was exactly what he came in and booted up the machine hoping to find. He allowed himself a well-deserved smile. If the situation weren't so dire, Zack would reach around and pat himself on the back. Hopefully, it wasn't too little, too late. He had already spent two hours typing and reading, two hours he wasn't sure they even had.

The laptop was connected to a color inkjet printer, both Christmas gifts from the witches to help him with his schooling. He didn't expect such lavish gifts. All he got them were pajamas and slippers from a store in the hotel mall where they received an employee discount. The laptop did help him with several research projects. If all went well, the same search skills he picked up researching those projects just saved Isis.

A knock on the door grabbed Zack's attention.

"Come in," he shouted. He knew they'd come looking for him eventually. No need to stand up and open the door for any of them to enter his room. They could all phase through solid objects.

Sacha did exactly that—she phased through the door. He didn't need Wiccan power to sense her annoyance. "Isis is awake. She's asking for you." Yup, her voice confirmed it. "We decided not to freeze time around her, but in case there's another seizure we're keeping her within the crystals so her power stays weak."

"That's probably a good idea."

"We're working on ideas that may help her. Your innovative thinking would be useful. Zack. Your presence would be helpful. I know you're upset, but we're all upset. It doesn't mean you can leave us and hide over here in your room—"

"I'm not hiding," Zack shot back. "I've been researching, and I think I found it!"

"Found what?"

Zack turned around in his chair. "It's Sweden. The country you and Selena were trying to remember is Sweden."

"What are you talking about?" Sacha's head tipped forward. "You sound sure of this."

"I am sure." Zack poked a thumb over his shoulder. "I was searching maps and locations for villages in Europe. Of course, thousands came up. That didn't help. So, I searched for rumored claims of supernatural sightings. I hit a lot of dead ends, but eventually, I stumbled onto a chat forum called 'Seeking the Supernatural.' I focused on posts about Europe."

"And you actually found the village on there?"

Sacha asked.

"Well, not at first," Zack replied. "Much of the posts were sightings of Sasquatch and people claiming they met vampires in Transylvania. Most of their descriptions were clearly phony based on old-time movie vampires."

"Get to the point, Zack."

"Right. I narrowed the search to witches. Again, most of it I could tell was a bunch of fiction with people talking about witches putting curses on their towns or claiming that Goth girls used magic potions to make them fall in love." Zack jumped out of his chair. "But there was one post from around seven months ago. It was a college girl from Cambridge University. She claimed to be raised in a small village that's a hidden sanctuary for witches."

Sacha rolled her hand in the air. Taking the hint, Zack continued, "According to this girl, she's not a witch but her brother is. The family immigrated there when she was fifteen. She even talked about Wiccan power coming from the Earth's energy. The village does exist, it's called New Salem and it's hidden in the Boreal Swamp Forests on the outskirts of the country."

"She actually posted all this on a public forum?" Sacha asked.

"I was surprised too, but yeah. She said the village was created in the 1600's by witches as an escape from the trials happening around the world. Her family was found and invited to live there when her brother's connection was discovered. As with most of the postings on this forum, the responses were full of mockery, dismissing her claims as fiction. She argued with them, insisting she was telling the truth.

Eventually, she stopped posting altogether. Before that, however, she posted the longitude and latitude coordinates of the village's location. I popped them into a search."

"And?"

"Nothing came up, just swamp. But what if the village is hidden from satellites and such?" Zack's excitement jumped three levels. "Witches can do that, right?"

"Well, yes, I'm sure we can."

"I'm guessing it's there, right where she said." Zack took a step forward. "They've been a community of witches for four hundred years. You can teleport us directly there and they can help Isis."

Zack expected to see elation from Sacha which matched his own. Instead, he received a deep sigh. "Zack," she said, "our power doesn't work like a GPS. You know this. We need to be able to visualize where we are going in order to send ourselves there."

Zack's lips stretched into a huge grin. He knew Sacha was going to say that, and he was prepared. "Would an actual photo do the job?"

"You have one?"

"She posted a picture of what she called The Village Quad." Zack ripped the paper from his printer and held it out for Sacha. Sure, he could have led with it, but being raised on a stage, Zack had a flair for the dramatic. "It's a huge farming area surrounded by four large buildings, one on each side. As you can see, she took that photo from one of those building's rooftop. It's an open area in the middle of their village."

"New Salem, huh?" Sacha stared at the photo for several seconds. She rewarded Zack's effort with a proud grin and a ruffle of his hair. "Let's show this to the others."

****

Once back in the witches' suite, Sacha took the liberty of sharing everything Zack had found on the internet. She included every detail, including New Salem's history dating back to the sixteen hundreds. As she spoke, Zack's eyes shifted to Isis. She was awake, but barely. Eyes that were usually wide open and vibrant now were slits he could have blindfolded with dental floss. Her matted brown hair and forehead were soaked. Static originating from the crystals shot randomly around her. Each spark sizzled like bacon on a frying pan.

Sebastian took the picture from Sacha. He and Selena stared inquisitively at it. "This is from how long ago?" Sebastian asked.

"Seven months, give or take," Zack answered. "I'd bet not too much has changed since this picture was taken."

"We'd have to hope you're right," Sebastian said. "Otherwise, we could be teleporting ourselves right into a mountain, a wall, or anything solid. If that happens, we'd be dead in seconds."

"So, we are going there?" Zack asked.

"I don't see any other way," Selena responded. "You know we haven't sensed another witch since Isis, even here in Vegas."

As they spoke, Isis said Zack's name. He rushed to the couch and sat at her side, looking down into her face. Damn, he hoped being inside the pentagon didn't disrupt the hocus pocus the witches were using to keep Isis alive. So far, her condition didn't seem any worse.

"I'm right here, Isis," he said in a low voice.

"Hey, Zack." Isis smiled. "Sorry I ruined date night."

"Are you joking right now?" Even after a year, he still couldn't always tell.

Isis' eyes opened wide. "Thank you for coming into my life, Zack." Her voice was clear, as if he were hearing it in his head. "You brought joy to my heart."

"Isis, we're going to save you. We have a plan and everything." Zack put a hand on her stomach, hoping his touch would make her feel better. But he felt nothing. Instead, his hand passed through her body, hitting the couch pillow. "What in the... How?" She faded away. "It's an illusion." He gasped.

Zack jumped up from the couch once he saw Isis wobbling toward the living room's picture window. "*HEY*!" he shouted, which pulled the witches from their deep conversation over the picture.

"Isis, why are you up?" Selena asked, concern radiating from her tone.

Isis pointed a fist at the picture window and mumbled something under her breath. The glass shattered, leaving shards all over the floor. Isis kept her slow pace forward until Sebastian leaped in her way and grabbed her by the arms.

"What in the hell do you think you're doing?" he shouted.

"You're right, it's a waste to jump." Isis' eyes shut. Her words slurred. "Set me on fire. One of you can take my connection. Valeria told me that's how it's done."

"Isis, stop!" Selena shouted. "We're not going to set you on fire. We're certainly not going to let you kill yourself. Giving up is *not* an option."

Sebastian put a hand under her chin. "You are our daughter. We will find a way to help you."

"You don't even know what's wrong with me!" Isis' breathing became heavy and loud. "I can sense the people outside. One man is dead, three people are hurt. One's a little girl." She sniffled as tears rolled down her cheek. "I love you guys. You gave me a great life. But you have to let me go now. I don't want to keep hurting people."

"No! That's not how we're going to solve this, Isis," Sebastian said. "Not a chance."

"That's right." Selena pulled Isis from Sebastian and hugged her tight. Isis leaned her forehead into Selena's shoulder and wept. "Zack found it. We have a plan," Selena said into her ear. "We're going to this village. If they have a Wiccan society that has lasted for generations then I'm sure there are witches in this place that will understand what's happening to you."

"Great," Sacha said through a slight smirk. "Now all we have to do is figure out how to get to a place none of us have ever been to, or even known about, before. Not to mention, we've never teleported that far of a distance. Sweden's not exactly along the Vegas strip."

"The distance doesn't matter." Sebastian turned his attention to Selena. "At least, it shouldn't. Right?"

"We'll use the crystals," Selena led Isis back to the couch. "Our power is strong when it's focused within the crystals. Plus, Sacha's power and mine are strongest when combined. We can use the picture as a beacon to will ourselves to the location."

Isis dropped onto the couch. Her body slumped against the back pillow. Sebastian took a seat next to her. "Let's hope it works," he said with a hand against her forehead. "Because she's feeling a lot colder than before."

"Okay, then." Sacha rolled up the sleeves of her red blouse. "Let's do this."

"Zack," Sebastian said. "There is an element of danger if this doesn't work. You don't have to come and take that risk."

"You said I'm part of your coven, isn't that right, Sebastian?"

"I did, and you are."

"Then I'm coming with you."

"Understand," Selena said to him, "if the picture is wrong in any way—"

"The picture is not wrong." Zack sat at the edge of the couch. "And I believe in your abilities as witches."

"Very well," Sebastian said. "He comes. But let's not dawdle. We need to get there and hope they're willing to help us."

"They'll help us," Sacha added. "If not, they'll have a war on their hands."

"We're not going there for a war, Sach," Selena said. "But we will take whatever steps are necessary to convince them to help one of their own."

"All right, then. Let's do this," Sebastian said.

Selena and Sacha knelt at each end of the couch. They raised their hands in the air, gazing down at the picture which lay across Sebastian's lap. Zack took Isis' hand and squeezed tight. Next stop: the Boreal Swamp Forests of Sweden.

Chapter Nine

Zack's fingers wrapped around Isis' hand. She squeezed them in return. She wanted to open her eyes and watch her mom and Sacha at work. Despite being constantly spoken to about her "potential," Isis believed that, together, they were far more powerful than she could ever hope to be. The moment Isis tried to lift her eyelids, the light in the room made her head pound.

Her stomach hurt as well but that may have been hunger. The last time she remembered eating was the yogurt with Zack. Not eating left her weak, but that may have been a good thing. The weaker Isis felt, the less chance she'd put people in danger, or so she hoped. She didn't have any actual memory of her power spiraling out of control, only what she overheard.

God, she actually killed someone. A man died because Isis' powers went crazy from her seizure. The guilt ate at her heart like a worm digging through an apple. For all she knew, this man was heading home from work to see his family. He may have had a wife and kids, all of whom just learned they'd never see him again. Tears squeezed through her closed eyes.

For one long moment, Isis thought ending her life was the best option. She tried to act on it before the next seizure hurt anyone else. She didn't want the deaths of more innocent people falling on her conscience. Isis was never one to simply give up, but she had no idea what else to do. Her family, however, had another idea. They believed this village of witches could have the answer. It sounded like a long shot at best, but Isis decided long ago to trust them with her life. Since taking her in at nine years old, they'd never let her down. But now, it was no longer just about her life. Others were in danger because of her condition.

"To the village," Selena and Sacha said. They said it again, and then a third time.

The sisters had tapped into the Earth's energy. She could feel it all around them. It was like whenever meat hit the grill and the sizzle emitted through all her senses. The sensation radiated all around her no matter who was manipulating the Earth's energy. Her sensitivity to the power only started for her a few months ago, a sign that her connection had grown even stronger. Isis wondered if Mom, Dad, and Sacha felt it as well.

The suite around her fell out of focus. Amazing— they actually connected with a place they'd never been to. Was this a first in Wiccan history? Isis was sure it had to be a first just based on the constant warnings while learning teleportation. The number one warning was never try to connect with a place she'd never visited.

This would have been a cause for celebration any other time, if it weren't so necessary that they get to this mystery village. Wow, they were about to travel across the entire world. Isis wondered what it would look like. Did the people even speak English over there?

Everything gradually came back into focus. They were once again surrounded by broken glass and the big mess produced by Isis' unexpected earthquake.

"What happened?" Sebastian asked. "Did it not work?"

"Oh, it worked," Sacha said. "I felt us moving through space."

"As did I." Selena's hazel-colored irises peered around. "What happened?"

Sacha answered, "Somehow, we're back here."

"Is that even possible?" Zack asked.

Sacha responded by shaking her head.

Selena raised her arms back over the group. "Let's try this again!"

They chanted a second time. Isis felt the energy moving around them. This time, she kept her eyes open, watching the hotel suite's walls along with the TV and furniture turn into a distorted haze. Soon, the blur faded. This time she was sure they teleported yet they were still on the couch in the middle of their living room.

"This is bizarre." Selena's arms dropped to her sides. "I was sure the energy was transporting us, yet we keep bouncing back."

"There are witches on that side," Zack said. "Could they be blocking us from going there?"

Sebastian's head spun to Zack. "You may be right. Their village is hidden. They may also have created some type of Wiccan defense around their borders to keep strangers from popping in unexpectedly."

"A defense?" Sacha's eyebrows rose. "How would they be able to do that, unless..." She glanced down at one of the enchanted crystals on the carpet in front of the couch. "Could this entire place be surrounded by enchanted crystals? They could be using those to keep us from getting in."

"Like a magical firewall," Zack said with his head down.

"A what?" Sebastian asked.

"Um, never mind."

"I don't care how or why we are being held back," Selena announced. "We're going to push through. Let's knock on that door a bit louder."

"Ready when you are, Sis," Sacha said.

"To the village," they chanted once again. Their faces cringed as their closed eyes tightened. Isis was sure it wouldn't work this time either...unless she helped.

Growing up, the family kept talking about how Isis could conceivably be the most connected witch alive. It was time to find out if they were right. Isis closed her eyes and focused on her mom and Sacha. She'd utilize her control of the power to enhance theirs. It was an idea that lingered in Isis' mind for a while. Was that something that could be done with the energy? They had nothing to lose if she tried...

Several seconds passed. A heavy wind blew against Isis' face. It smelled of horse manure. Isis opened her eyes and tipped up her head. They no longer had a ceiling above their heads. Isis' elbow flew back against the leather pillow. Apparently, they took the couch with them.

"We did it!" Sacha screeched. "I don't believe it, we actually pulled it off."

"Hey, guys," Zack's voice stammered. "Take a look around."

Isis turned her head from right to left. She expected to see four buildings, one on each side, just as the picture Zack printed out showed. Instead, they were surrounded by debris. The buildings had been destroyed, leaving only their foundations. All around them was wreckage covered in walls of flames several feet high. Fire coated the branches of trees in the far distance. Even the sky was obliterated by a sheet of smoke.

"This can't be." Zack gasped. "It just can't."

A sense of defeat rushed through Isis. Well, at least if she had another seizure, she couldn't do any more damage than what surrounded them.

The sofa sat in the middle of a huge circle of dirt, much of which was deep puddles of mud. Zack had said something about farms, but signs of agriculture no longer existed, if it ever did in the first place. Isis still smelled the manure but there were no signs of horses, or a village, anywhere. Their trip, the longest trip ever taken by witches under their own power and enchanted crystals, was for nothing.

The three adults stood from the couch. Only Isis and Zack stayed. Zack leaned down near her face. "I'm sorry," he whispered in her ear.

"N-not your fault," she muttered.

"What the hell happened here?" Sacha shouted. "The place looks like it was hit by a bomb."

A quiet giggle forced its way out of Isis' throat. Not that it was funny, but at this point, her only choices were laugh or cry. And she was all out of tears.

Chapter Ten

Isis' head leaned against Zack's knee as if it were a pillow. Her body shook but did not spasm, which was probably thanks to the enchanted crystals that surrounded the couch. The witches, meanwhile, stepped away with expressions Zack could only describe as shock and disappointment. He felt the same way.

"I don't understand," Selena asked. "What could have happened in the span of seven months that wiped out an entire village?"

"It had to happen recently for everything to still be burning, right?" Sacha put a hand toward the flaming wreckage but jerked it back. "Like, real recent."

"What are we going to do?" Zack asked. "Are we going back?"

"Can't go back," Isis whispered. "I'm too dangerous."

"Oh no!" Sacha shrieked.

"Sach?" Selena touched her arm.

"Sis, the crystals!" Sacha dropped to a knee. "I'm not feeling the connection to them."

Selena's eyes widened. She stared down at one of the five crystals. They were no longer bright with the sun reflecting off their shiny surfaces. The crystals lost their color and energy, just like everything around them.

"You're right." Selena's eyes went wide. "I think

we fried them."

"I didn't know that was even possible," Zack said, thinking back on all he had learned from Sacha about enchanted crystals.

"They can lose their connection, but not after just one teleportation spell. That's not possible!" Sacha stood, looking back and forth. Her cheeks were bright red. "At least it shouldn't be. And now we're stuck across the world in the middle of a burnt down wasteland!"

Sebastian's head then darted toward the fire-stricken branches. "Maybe not," he said.

"What do you mean, Sebastian?" Selena asked.

"Look at the fire." His body swung 180 degrees toward the others. "It's not spreading. Neither is the smoke. It should be sucking all the oxygen from the air leaving us barely able to breathe. There should also be a sulfuric smell but there's not. We should also hear the fire burning, but all I hear is the wind."

"What are you saying?" Selena asked. "That none of this is real?"

"The horse poop smell." Isis picked her head up from Zack's knee. He could tell it was a struggle for her. "Dad's right. I...I see buildings," she mumbled under her breath. "And people." Now was she becoming delusional? Or was Isis somehow able to see what the rest of them couldn't?

"This is all an illusion, isn't it?" Zack asked.

"Yes, that's exactly what it is," Sebastian said to the entire group. "Illusions are my specialty. I can't believe I didn't pick up on it right away, but all of this around us is an image like what we've created on the stage."

Selena ran up to him. "Are you sure?"

Sebastian flashed a broad grin. "Absolutely. None of what we are seeing is real." He shouted at the top of his lungs, "*All of this is a Wiccan illusion!*"

The fire and wreckage faded, as did the burn-stricken trees. In their place stood the four buildings they'd seen in the photo, one on each side forming a square. One was five stories high. The building directly across the field was three stories high. One with double glass doors was circular in shape and only had two floors. The fourth building, across from the circular one, was long and rectangular in shape. Houses and garden-like pathways circled these buildings.

The destroyed trees were replaced with tall, vibrant ones filled with bright green leaves. The field between the buildings was mostly grass with several long strips of dirt surrounded by wood fences. Zack also saw a fenced-in barn near the cottages. Animals, such as chickens, pigs, and cows, wandered around the barn. Everything around them matched the photograph.

"I love that brain of yours," Selena whispered to Sebastian.

"Guys, heads up," Sacha exclaimed. "We're not alone."

One man and two women approached them. Zack's eyes went directly to the man's rifle which was pointed their way. Sebastian took a step forward, raising his hands in the air. The sisters did the same. Zack glanced around. The windows of the buildings were filled with many faces. A glistening light shone from the rooftop of the highest building.

The tall man, with long dirty-blond hair tied behind his head in a ponytail, pointed his weapon at

Sebastian's face. "Not another step forward," he said in a deep accent that said Scotland native. "You may be witches, but I can squeeze this trigger faster than you can twitch your nose."

So much for a warm welcome. Zack presumed by his words that he was not a witch. From the badge on his black button-down shirt, he had some sort of authority in this village. The lady behind him on his left, however, was definitely a witch. It wasn't because of her curly black hair that hung down to her waist, or the black boots she wore with a white low-cut dress. It was the fact that she hovered an inch off the ground. Unlike the other two, she didn't carry a weapon. She probably didn't need one.

The woman to the right with a buzzcut pointed a pistol their way. Her eyes shared the same intensity as the man's. She appeared far younger than the man but was still an adult. She had to be at least in her mid-twenties. Zack wasn't sure if she was a witch or not, but with that scowl across her face, she was one of the most intense people he had ever seen. The woman had a pale skin tone similar to Selena and Sacha's. Unlike the Quinn sisters, her arms and legs were the size of tree trunks. No wonder she wore nothing but black shorts and a green tank top. Who wouldn't want to show off that physique?

"I'm so glad you speak English," Sebastian said, displaying his pearly whites. "First, let me make it clear, we are not a threat to you; we are here as friends. We come seeking assistance for one of our own. I am sure you can offer this—"

The man lunged forward and rammed the end of his rifle into Sebastian's gut. The blow hunched him

72

over and knocked him to his knees.

"HEY!" Selena rushed to Sebastian's side. A yellow glow formed around her hands. "What the hell do you think you're doing?"

The witch with the long hair hovered closer. "Power down, now," she said in a tone Zack was sure had a Russian inflection.

Sacha moved next to Selena. "Say the word, Sis," she whispered with determination written across her face. "We'll turn pigtail guy inside out!"

"No, this is not what we came here for." Selena held her hands out for all to see. The glow dissipated. "I am backing down! Please, just hear us out. We are in desperate need of your help." Selena slowly dropped to her husband's side.

"What sort of help are you seeking?" a young woman's voice asked.

All heads looked the woman's way. She strolled to the guards' side with hands on her hips and confidence in her step. Zack's eyebrows rose to his forehead. He took her to be of African descent, although her eyes were the brightest blue he'd ever seen. Figure-wise, she came off like one of those super-fit cheerleaders from Zack's school that had no idea he existed. With each step, the walkie-talkie attached to the right side of her belt dangled.

The man with the rifle returned his focus on Selena. "Madam President, I strongly suggest you stay back," he growled.

"Madam President?" Zack mumbled to himself. She couldn't have been more than a few years older than Isis and himself.

"My curiosity got the better of me, Paul," she

answered, stopping her stride at his side. "Natasha, what do your senses say?"

The woman with the long hair hovered close to the president. "I sense a very strong connection with the Earth in each of them except for the boy." Her accent was thick. "They may be the most powerful witches here save for perhaps Doctor Mac. If it turns into a battle, I do not believe we would fare well against them."

"That's exactly why your being out here puts you in danger," Paul shouted toward the president.

"We already told you," Sacha snapped. "We are not a threat or looking for a battle! We're here for my niece!" Sacha waved to the couch where Isis lay on her back. Zack pointed down to emphasize Sacha's reference.

"I recommend caution," Paul said. "We've been duped before."

"We have," the president responded. "But it doesn't mean we are today. If appearances are true, then these strangers are not a danger. They're simply a like-minded family in need."

"Regardless," Paul responded. "Allow us to handle the interrogation and determine their motives before—"

A high-pitched male voice shouted, "Everybody, wait!"

A man was perched on the roof of the circular building. In one hand, he held a silvery cane. He leaped off the two-story structure. Zack clutched his forehead and cringed, expecting this man to break every bone in his body upon impact. Somehow, that wasn't the case. His salt and pepper hair blew from the wind caused by his descent. So did his red cape. Somehow, he landed

74

on his feet and the tip of the cane between Paul and the witches.

No one could have successfully made a jump from that height, especially one with this guy's slightly obese physique. Still, Zack was sure this man wasn't a witch—they used the energy to float as opposed to outright jumping and landing from great distances. His pale skin, however, meant he wasn't completely human, either. Well, at least not anymore. Although he wasn't nearly as albino as the two undead vampires Zack had met in the past, he was well on his way.

"Simon, what are you doing?" Paul growled.

"Hold on one moment, please." He waved his hands at Paul and the others as a gesture to back off. "I know these people. In fact, I know them well."

The vampire limped, leaning on his cane. He stopped in front of Selena who wrapped her arm around Sebastian's waist and helped him to his feet. The glance they exchanged confirmed what Zack expected, that they had no idea who this man was despite his claim of knowing them well.

"You are Sebastian Santell and Selena Quinn," the vampire said with a huge grin.

"Yes," Sebastian answered with clear confusion.

Simon waddled to Sacha. He moved well for a man, or vampire, with either an injury or a disability. "You are Sacha, Selena's younger sister." His eyes shifted to Zack. "I don't know who you are." His head tilted. "Are you a witch?"

"I'm Zack Galloway, and no, I'm a magician."

"Magician." Simon's eyes lit up. "Like Merlin?"

"Um, no, more like Houdini."

"Houdini?"

"Um, Copperfield? Angel? Penn? Teller?"

"Ah, that kind of magician. I see." He turned back to the others. "So, the boy with the fanny pack is Zack. And the girl at Zack's side, lying on the couch, that has to be Isis." He spread his arms. "Everyone, I introduce to you, The Witches of Vegas!"

"You know us," Sacha said. "You've seen the show?"

"Oh, no, I've never had the pleasure," Simon replied. "I've never even been to Las Vegas." He placed a hand on Sacha's shoulder. "My goodness, I haven't seen any of you in years."

"Yeah, it *has* been a long time." Sacha offered a nervous giggle then threw a wide-eyed glance at her sister.

"Excuse me for asking," Selena said. "But how *do* you know us?"

"Oh, wow." Simon gently slapped himself against the side of his head. "Forgive me, you must be so confused right now. Your mentor, Luther, stumbled upon me many years ago when I was first turned and left on my own to figure out what was done to me."

Simon threw his arm over Sebastian's shoulders as he went on. "I had no idea what I had become. Luther took me under his wing and taught me how to exist in this form. Before Luther, I thought I was simply reeling from the experience of getting attacked while on a hiking expedition and nearly killed. It hadn't occurred to me that I really was killed, then resurrected. What did I know from vampires, right?"

God, this vampire loved to hear himself talk. The thought made Zack smirk.

Simon motioned his cane from Sacha to Selena. "I

remember when Luther met your mother." He tapped Sebastian on the chest with the head of his cane. "And also, your Wiccan mentor. Luther used to send me photographs of all of you growing up. We lost touch once I came here to New Salem."

Simon removed his arm from Sebastian, turned to the couch, and stared down at Isis. "The last time I heard from Luther, you had just brought this young lady into your family. She was, what, ten years old at the time?"

"Nine," Sebastian said.

"I saw clips of your battle with that witch on my computer. Although it had been years since I last heard about you, I recognized each of you." Simon's smile disappeared. His head dipped. "They called it an improvisational performance, but I didn't think so, especially once I saw Luther disappear with her through that portal."

"Wait," Zack said. "You have internet here?"

"Of course, we do," Simon answered. "Why wouldn't we?"

"Simon," Paul interrupted, his threatening stance never wavering. "Bottom line, are you saying you can vouch for these people?"

Simon clapped his hands together. "Yes, I absolutely can and will vouch for them."

Paul placed his rifle in a holster across his back. The muscle lady followed his lead, lowering her pistol. "In that case, welcome to New Salem," Paul said with a smile. He offered Sebastian his hand to shake as Selena returned to the couch to check on Isis.

"Thanks." Sebastian obliged the handshake, his other hand still pressed against his gut. "I was trying to explain ourselves. What the hell was with that potshot?"

"I've been around witches for a long time, that includes my wife and teenage daughter," Paul replied. "Did you think I wouldn't recognize a persuasion effect being cast on myself?"

"It...it was instinct," Sebastian said between coughs.

The muscle lady walked up to Sacha. She offered her hand. "Carolyn," she said in a low and deep voice. Her narrow eyes and clenched jaw never wavered.

"Um, nice to meet you." Sacha shook her hand, then glanced down at the grip. "Sacha Quinn. My friends call me Sach."

Carolyn nodded, released Sacha's hand, then marched away. Sacha's head cocked.

"Witches of Vegas," Simon exclaimed. "Allow me to further the introductions and present to you our leader." He made a hand gesture her way. "This is New Salem's president, Tia."

"Let's table the introductions for now." Tia joined Selena in front of the couch. "You said you were here for help. For her, I presume?"

"Yes. This is Isis, and she is sick," Selena answered. "We've tried to heal her, but it hasn't worked. We don't believe it's a medical issue."

"Natasha," Tia said with a friendly but commanding tone. "Please transport Isis to the infirmary and catch Mac up on the situation." She refocused her attention on Selena and Sebastian. "Mac is our doctor. If anyone can help, medical or supernatural, it's him. Meanwhile, if the rest of you will join me in the dining hall, we can speak over lunch. I'll see to it that Isis receives something to eat as well, provided Mac sees no reason otherwise."

"With all due respect," Sebastian replied, "it may be best that we go to the medical center as well. Isis is also suffering from random seizures. During her last seizure, the energy around Isis spiraled out of control."

"I understand, but Mac prefers to work without an audience." She offered a smile. "He also utilizes empowered crystals, just as I see you do. He dampens all Wiccan connections in the infirmary except for his own. It makes it easier for him to diagnose and heal."

"Empowered?" Zack whispered to Sacha, who answered with a simple shrug.

"Seizures," Simon wheezed. "Madam President, allow me to assist Mac in the infirmary. I have a theory which I'm hoping we can rule out."

Sacha leaned in and whispered in Zack's ear, "That was cryptic."

"Go ahead, Simon, make sure to keep me up to date." Tia pointed to her walkie-talkie. "The rest of you, please join me. And will someone get rid of that couch in the middle of our field? It stands out like a sore thumb."

Chapter Eleven

When Zack heard "dining hall" he expected it to look like a school cafeteria. To his surprise, the hall had an ambiance that was more like the huge restaurants in the Vegas resorts. The tables, which were many in this large space, had fancy gold tablecloths. Antique-looking chandeliers hung throughout the dining hall. There was even elevator music playing low in the background. Waiters and waitresses traveled throughout serving food as busboys cleared tables once they were no longer in use.

While most tables were either circular or square, one at the end of the room was rectangular in shape. The president and Paul sat in the chairs facing the hall with their backs against the wall. Zack and the witches sat on the other end. A man dressed in a suit fancier than all the waiters and waitresses' dark blue uniforms placed a tray of small cooked chickens in the center of the table. The chickens were surrounded by bowls of mashed potatoes and mixed vegetables.

"The chicken smells good," Zack said to the server.

"It's Cornish hen," the man responded in a French accent. His eyes rolled. "Madam President, if there's nothing else?"

"That'll be fine, Maurice, thank you," Tia answered. She said to the table, "Maurice runs our dining hall. He's also one of our two head chefs. He's a

80

good man, but easily insulted when it comes to his food. So, please, eat up."

"We appreciate it," Selena said. "But right now, our concern is Isis."

"Understandable." Tia reached with her fork and removed a large hen, which she placed on her plate. "Rest assured, our doctor is excellent at what he does. I promise you, he or one of his people will call me the moment there is an update on her condition."

Tia motioned for them to take from the tray. Zack was the first to reach with his fork. He wanted to stand united with the witches, but hunger took over. Soon, the three helped themselves as well. Paul was the last to pluck the final piece of Cornish hen with his fork.

Zack peeked behind him. People were scattered throughout the dining hall at various tables. Based on the composition of adults and children eating together, it was clear New Salem had a lot of families. At a nearby table, Carolyn ate by herself with an eye on him and the group. Her focus never left them even as she bit into her meat, holding it in both her hands. The pistol sat on the table next to her plate.

Sacha leaned in. "Zack, stop staring," she whispered in his ear.

"Please forgive our paranoia when it comes to visitors to our land," Tia explained. "Neighbors have tried to infiltrate our borders. Norway once actually sent a witch here requesting asylum. We discovered quickly that she was a spy sending information back to her country."

"Such a small village compared to those large countries around you," Sebastian said. "Why are they so interested in a property that sits in the middle of a swamp?"

"Our crops grow faster and stronger than anywhere else in this region." Tia waved her fork with a piece of hen attached in the air as she spoke. "We export fruits and vegetables all over Europe for trade of goods. That is how we maintain our way of life. Most leaders respect our arrangement. Others have seen us as an independent land ripe for the taking."

"Your crops grow this way naturally?" Sacha bit into a carrot at the end of her fork.

Tia smirked. "It's natural in the sense that the witches of our village have a relationship with Mother Earth."

"But not you," Selena said. "I don't sense Wiccan power in you."

"As you know, the planet picks and chooses who it connects with," Tia replied. "And it's not necessarily through bloodlines. My grandparents were both witches, as was my mother. When I turned eighteen, it was finally accepted that I was not a late bloomer. I just did not have the connection."

Paul swallowed. "She may not have the gift, but she's extremely intelligent. She inherited that quality from her grandfather."

One topic for conversation tugged at Zack's tongue. It screamed to jump out of his mouth from the moment Tia first introduced herself as the president of the village. He couldn't hold it back any longer. "How old are you?" he asked.

"I'm nineteen," she answered with a confident nod and smile. "And you want to know how I came to be president?" Actually, that was exactly what Zack wanted to know.

"Well, since it's out there, I think we're all a bit curious," Sacha replied.

"My grandfather was the president of New Salem for fifteen years. My mother lived in Morocco back when she was pregnant with me. Unfortunately, she died during my delivery. My grandfather arranged for me to be brought here where he and my grandmother raised me to be a prominent member of our village."

"Tia was quite tiny when she first came here," Paul added. "She was born eight weeks premature. She also had many health issues, but she endured. Even at that age, Tia was strong-willed."

"I'm sorry you went through all that," Selena said.

Tia swatted her hand, waving off the apology. "It's been a good life. My grandfather made me his vice-president when I was sixteen. I presumed it was meant to be symbolic, but a sudden brain aneurism took his life two years ago. He died in his sleep. By village law, his position went to me."

"And the people are okay with you being in charge?" Zack asked

"We hold elections every five years if someone wishes to challenge the current leader," Tia explained. "That window opened up six months ago. Since no one chose to run, I'm taking it as a sign that my people are happy with the job I've done so far."

"There were a few who approached me about challenging for the position," Paul said. "They thought I'd stand a good chance. But I'm happy with my role as both the head of law enforcement and Tia's appointed vice president. I also detest having to speak in public."

"He really does," Tia laughed.

Zack leaned forward. "So, you're the president of a

village of witches, but you're not a witch."

"Currently, there are sixty-eight residents of New Salem Village," Tia answered. "At last count, thirty would be classified as witches."

"Thirty," Zack repeated. "That's less than half."

"The rest of our village is made up of the family members of witches," Paul added. "And descendants of Wiccan families. Many of our families have been here for hundreds of years. Some even longer than that."

"It's quite intimate here," Tia expressed with a proud grin.

"I notice that you all address one another by first names," Sebastian said. "Is that the reason, for intimacy?"

"Every resident of New Salem must give up their surnames," Tia explained. "Whether through birth or invitation, we are all part of the New Salem community. We are like one huge extended family and each individual member on our land matters. Although we have disagreements, we are without division. Formality is based on position and rank only."

Paul added, "Some of our families have been here so long and through so many generations, they don't even know their surnames."

"That is really weird," Zack said.

Someone kicked his leg under the table. Although Zack liked the idea of a huge family environment, he was rather fond of the name Galloway. That was enough of a reason he wouldn't want to live in New Salem. Although he had to admit, the way Tia spoke, she made it sound like a happy lifestyle. She'd have made a great real estate agent.

"You have a unique infrastructure here," Sebastian

said. "Four buildings facing one another and all your homes encircling them. It's certainly different."

"Thanks, I think," Tia said with a giggle. "There are actually three miles of homes surrounding the Quad."

"We're not really sure who designed New Salem," Paul explained. "Needless to say, that was long before any of us were born. But each of those buildings serves a purpose. The largest is our school. We offer an education from first grade to high school. The building opposite the school is our medical center. The circular building across from us is our auditorium."

Paul waved a hand from Tia to himself. "Our offices and others are on the floor above the auditorium. The building we are in right now has two double glass doors as a message that it is always open for all residents. Downstairs on our first floor is our marketplace. From there we distribute food, clothes, and other necessary home products. This dining hall offers service from early morning to late evening.

"Interesting. But what about income?" Sacha asked. "Don't you have an exchange of goods and services in this village?"

"With other nations, yes," Tia answered. "Within New Salem, everyone contributes as best they can, and their needs are provided. The more essential their contributions, the greater their entitlement to luxuries."

"And people accept this system without question?" Sebastian asked.

"With sixty-eight residents, the system works for us."

"It is a system that we have followed for hundreds of years." There was a clear defensiveness in Paul's tone. "The people of New Salem have and continue to thrive."

"I'm sure it helps that almost half of your people can defy the laws of science and keep your crops growing, no matter what," Sebastian said.

"Well, that certainly doesn't hurt." Tia folded her hands across the table. Her back straightened. "As you see, we are willing to answer all of your questions. However, we do have questions of our own. Starting with how you know about us and our location."

Sacha slapped Zack's shoulder. "Why don't you take this? You are the one who found them, after all."

"Found us?" Paul asked.

All eyes around the table fell on Zack. He swallowed what was in his mouth. "A college girl online said she came from here although she wasn't a witch. She posted a lot of details about the village, including the location and a photograph of your quad." Zack wiped his mouth with a napkin, then motioned toward the witches. "They were able to use the photograph to take us here."

An awkward silence surrounded the table. Paul and Tia exchanged a sideways glance. "Britney," Paul said. "It has to be."

"Who's Britney?" Sacha asked.

"We found her family in London and granted them asylum when her brother's connection manifested at the age of thirteen," Paul answered. "He created a fire with his mind and used it to fend off a group of bullies. Unfortunately, it happened in front of several witnesses. Their parents were appreciative for the opportunity to relocate and escape their son's persecution. Britney, however, was not happy about the move at all. That was clear from the moment they arrived. She did not like leaving her life behind."

"Britney and I were fifteen at the time," Tia said. "I tried to befriend the girl. I thought it would help. But she was a city girl and she just wouldn't accept her new life here. She was intelligent, though troubled. Our school graduates who wish to further their education do so abroad. When Britney reached eighteen and wanted to return to England for college, we arranged it through our connections in Parliament. Of course, we will welcome her back if she chooses, but we expect that was the last we will hear from her. She doesn't even reach out to see her family on holidays."

"It sounds like she's still causing us trouble," Paul said with an eye roll.

"Hold on." Selena raised a finger with curiosity written all over her face. "The boy and his family were in London, yet you were able to sense his manifestation from here? And you mentioned having connections in Parliament. People in the British government know about this village?"

"We have an understanding with a few government leaders throughout Europe, at least with the ones we believe can be trusted," Tia responded. "We also have scouts in various locations throughout the world who monitor spikes in the Earth's energy fields. They look to persuade the families to immigrate here before they are discovered and persecuted out there."

Wow, her answer came so quickly and full of confidence. Zack had to admit, he was impressed by Tia. Not in a romantic sort of way, those feelings were set aside for Isis. But the way she handled herself in such a presidential manner amazed him. She was only three years older, yet he felt like a child around her.

"I presume that's how you discovered Isis, am I right?" Tia asked. "I'm sure at your power levels, you can sense energy spikes."

"Normally, yes," Sebastian answered. "But we don't come across a lot of witches back in the states."

"Speaking of Isis," Selena said. "May we check on her?"

"I promise, Selena, we will be contacted as soon as there is something to report." Tia removed the walkie-talkie from her belt buckle and placed it on the table. "Right now, I'm interested in learning more about you. According to Natasha, the three of you hold a connection to the power far beyond anything we've seen in most witches."

"Is it the same with Isis?" Paul asked. "You mentioned her last seizure caused her power to spiral out of control. I'd like to hear more about that."

Zack eyed Sebastian and Selena. Were they about to tell these two protective leaders about the earthquake Isis inadvertently created? He had a hunch if they did Tia and especially Paul would ask them to leave immediately. They wouldn't be wrong to do so.

Before anyone could answer, Tia's walkie-talkie buzzed. "*Madam President,*" Simon's voice said through the speaker.

Tia snatched the transceiver and spoke into it. "Go ahead," she said.

"*Isis is awake. Doctor Mac is examining her as we speak. He asked me to contact you on his behalf.*"

"Copy that," Tia replied.

Selena and Sebastian dropped their silverware. Tia acknowledged their unspoken request with a nod. "Let him know we are on our way," the president said into her walkie-talkie. She reattached it to her belt. "I take it you are finished with lunch?"

"We are ready to go," Sebastian stated.

"Very well." Tia placed her fork across the plate and stood. "Let's go check on our patient."

Chapter Twelve

Isis lay across a metallic medical table atop a paper-thin mattress. The doctor, Mac, held an electronic thermometer over her forehead. As he waited on the thermometer, Isis stared up at his deep brown eyes and jet-black curly hair that may have been a dye job. She couldn't stop a grin from crossing her face. He was kind of cute for a guy somewhere around her dad's age.

After a few moments, the thermometer beeped. Max examined it. "Ninety-two point three," he said. "That's lower than before I attempted the healing process."

"That certainly is evidence toward my theory." The other man in the room, Simon, clutched Isis's chin and turned her head. "This scar on the left side of her neck does as well."

"But you're not sure."

Simon shook his head. "I may be among the undead, Doctor, but that doesn't make me a scientific expert on the subject. However, it does make sense."

The conversation confused the hell out of Isis. She must have slept through the first part. She wanted to sit up but the throbbing in her brain had returned. "What's going on with me?"

"Tell me, Isis." Simon placed a hand on her stomach. "That witch you battled alongside your family, was she a vampire like me?"

Isis nodded. "Luther knew her."

"And did she break skin?"

"I'm not sure." Isis took a moment to think on it. God, she couldn't believe it had been a whole year since Valeria abducted her. She remembered trying to escape her abduction when they were in New York. Valeria grabbed her by the throat, cutting off her air. She also recalled the vampire's fingernails digging into her neck. It may have pierced her. "Yeah, I think she did."

"I see." Simon threw a knowing glance at Mac. "What do you think, Doc?"

"You may be onto something here, Simon. It's worth looking into." The doctor turned from the bed to the countertop. "Let me take some blood and run a few tests. I should be able to either confirm your hypothesis or rule it out."

Isis gasped at the sight of the long, sharp needle in Mac's hand. The syringe had a rubber tube attached from the side. "Wait, you're…you're going to stick me with that?"

Doctor Mac patted the top of her hand. "Relax, I'm really quite gentle. You will feel a slight sting, but it will only last a moment."

Isis didn't like that idea at all. Her heart raced. "Is it…necessary?" She hated needles ever since she was five years old when a doctor dug into her arm with one to find a vein. Her arm hurt for days after that. Now she was sixteen and that anxiety never went away.

Simon leaned in, grabbing Isis's attention. "I'm quite surprised to hear this," he said with a look of feigned shock across his face. "Luther's letters described you as amazingly brave and with potential to be a true warrior."

"Luther wrote that about me?" Isis threw Simon a slanted glance. "He called me brave and a warrior? For real?"

"Oh, yes. He was quite fond of all of you. Luther spoke about his witches with pride." Her flinch made Simon chuckle. "I know Luther tries to come off as an uncaring, ancient vampire. Deep down, though, he is quite the immortal sweetheart."

"I...I guess he hid that well—*OW!*"

Isis shut her eyes tight. Her arm was held in place by a set of fingers wrapped around her wrist. That was definitely more than a slight sting.

"Just another moment," Mac said. "And...done."

The needle slid out of Isis's arm. She opened her eyes and saw a long test tube filled to the top with blood. Mac placed the needle on a tray next to the examining table. He raised his free hand over Isis's arm. After a slight tingle in her elbow, he stopped. "There we go," he said in a soothing tone. "Not even a hole left behind."

Isis held her arm in front of her face. A few drops of blood on her skin was all that remained.

"Mac." Simon grabbed Isis by the wrist and examined her arm. His skin was like ice, much like she remembered Luther's. "You poked a hole in her skin and then closed it."

"As I have done often with my patients," Mac replied. "Why are you now surprised by this?"

"Because of your patient's condition." Simon tapped her arm as if it were on display. "This means her body can be healed, but her illness cannot. Interesting, no?"

Mac's eyes darted to the ceiling. "That is interesting, indeed," he answered. "How familiar are you, exactly, with the process?"

"What process?" Isis was sure Doctor Mac wasn't referring to the Wiccan healing spell.

"Not much at all," Simon answered. "I was unconscious when it happened to me."

Mac picked up the test tube and examined the red contents. "If it is the case, there should be clues in this sample. We will know soon enough."

Isis pulled her arm out of Simon's grip. She didn't particularly like the fact they were talking about her as if she wasn't lying on a table directly under their noses.

"So, you're a doctor and a witch?" she asked for the sake of joining the conversation.

"Yes, I resemble both descriptions." Mac placed the test tube in a holder on the counter near the sink. "The kids here call me 'The Witchdoctor.' I take it as a compliment."

"Doctor Mac was a pediatrician back in the states," Simon explained. "I believe this was in San Francisco, am I correct?"

"I lived in Sacramento," Mac replied. "I was a year into my practice when I vacationed in Stockholm. The witches sensed my presence and brought me to the village. Well, actually, they abducted me."

"What?" Isis blinked her eyes rapidly. "They kidnapped you?"

"They were desperate," Mac answered. "An unusual strand of flu had spread throughout the village and their witches couldn't eradicate it. They suspected it was sent with intent by a neighboring nation that wanted to claim the land."

"It started with a young witch who claimed she found us after imprisonment and was requesting asylum," Simon added. "She disappeared immediately after the spread."

"Wow, that's terrible." Isis now understood why they didn't trust strangers.

Mac went on. "The president at the time was at a loss on what do and thought I would be able to provide assistance."

"Which he did," Simon added. "He cured all the infected and helped rid New Salem of the epidemic."

Mac's lips stretched into a prideful grin. "Once my work was done, I received a tour of New Salem and an offer to stay. They didn't have a doctor with my connection or qualifications, and they wanted me to fill the role."

"And you stayed?" Isis asked.

"Initially, I declined their offer and resumed my practice," Mac answered. "But after giving it much thought, I returned and made New Salem my home."

"And now, he's a married man with a child on the way," Simon said with glee.

Isis smiled wide. "Wow." Her eyes shut and her head tipped back. "That's so lighter than air."

"It's what?" Simon asked.

"Lighter than air." Exhilaration ran through her body like a river. "Lighter than air."

It was Isis's first time on the stage in front of an actual audience. This was something she'd been looking forward to for years. The pride resonated from her dad's introduction. She sensed the nervousness from her mom while walking out onto the stage. But there was no need for Mom or Dad to be nervous, Isis was ready. Every instinct told her it would all go well.

"*Isis!*" a voice filled with panic screamed. It belonged to Doctor Mac. Isis couldn't respond to him, not now when the show was about to begin. This is what she had been waiting for since her first time practicing in the empty theater. Now it was a sold-out audience.

Isis waved to the crowd. Excited smiles filled all their faces. "Lighter than air," she said again, just as she had practiced over and over. The crowd cheered as her body rose from the ground.

Behind the applause, Isis heard the chaotic screaming. "We have to make this stop," Simon shouted. God, they sounded scared. But they didn't need to be. Isis was over the crowd, ready to impress.

It was time to fly.

****

Tia led the group out of the dining hall and toward the village infirmary. The food was delicious. Zack could have eaten much more, but once they heard from the vampire on Tia's walkie-talkie, it was time to go. Zack's primary concern, like everybody else's, was Isis. He wanted more than anything to be at her side, holding her hand while she was examined. If he felt that way, imagine the distress the whole family was feeling. All things considered, they handled it well, at least on the outside.

A bunch of "what ifs" ran through Zack's head. What if Isis couldn't recover? What if this mysterious illness killed her? Every so often he saw the same concerns written on all three witches' faces. Their hopes and faith were left on the shoulders of a doctor they didn't know, in a place they knew almost nothing about. Still, from what he could see of New Salem, the place was impressive.

On the way to the infirmary, Zack looked back and forth at his surroundings. A group of eight children, all around ten years old and younger, sat Indian style on a patch of grass. In front of them, an older woman perched on a wooden bench reading them a story. At one point, she picked her head up from the book and addressed the children. All their hands raised to answer whatever her question may have been. The woman's old-fashioned brown dress reminded Zack of the style on that prairie show that ran during late night reruns.

Three men strolled through the long fields of crops. One of the men waved his hand over certain smaller crops. Zack was sure one of those long green leaf blades reacted to the gestures. Of course, the couch from the witches' suite was gone. So were the five crystals they burnt out on the trip.

Along with the four large buildings around what was known as The Quad, cottages stood as far as his eye could see. In the distance, the village was surrounded by the tallest trees Zack had ever seen. The place was truly secluded from civilization. No bright lights, no big city. Zack couldn't help but wonder if any of the cottages even had televisions. Simon did mention having a computer with an internet connection, but did they all have that or was he among the privileged? How did they even set up a connection? There wasn't a single wire running anywhere, at least above the ground. It could have been wireless, but connected to where?

Zack had to admit, everyone seemed jovial and genuinely satisfied. Maybe village life wasn't the worst thing in the world. Still, their entire population was sixty-eight people. After a lifetime in Las Vegas, Zack couldn't even fathom that concept. Sixty-eight—he had ten times that number in his high school. Of course, almost half of his high school population wasn't made up of witches.

With each person he passed, Zack found himself trying to guess if they were a witch or not. So far, the only one he knew for sure was Natasha. Tia wasn't a witch, and neither was Paul. Zack was pretty sure Carolyn didn't have Wiccan power either...or much of a personality. What about the two guards dressed in black that Zack caught following them from a distance? They were clearly around for President Tia's safety, but were either, or both, of them witches?

When they arrived in New Salem, they were met with an amazing illusion. It was better than anything Zack had ever seen Sebastian or Isis create. It had to have been conjured by a large group of witches. There was no way Natasha was powerful enough to make it on her own. Then again, maybe she was. Zack really had no idea—

Zack's feet picked up off the ground while in mid-step. His body rolled in the air and hovered like a child's balloon that untied from its string. His hands instinctively reached for the grass, but it was just out of reach. "What the hell?" Zack screeched, hoping to get someone's attention.

He looked toward the witches, but they, along with Tia, Paul, and the two guards behind them were in the same predicament. They all hovered inches from the ground.

"It's Isis," Sebastian shouted. "She's having

another seizure!"

"And this is what happens?" Paul exclaimed.

"It's her lighter than air spell." Sebastian stretched out his arms in an attempt to regain his balance. "Except it's happening to the entire village!"

"Sach!" Selena yelled to her younger sister. "We need to stop this, now!"

Zack twisted his body mid-air into an upright position. It was a technique magicians used to keep control of their bodies when performing a levitation act. This time, however, he wasn't wearing a harness or attached to a wire. This time, it was actual zero gravity floating.

Right now, they were only inches from the ground, but he already felt himself moving higher up. What if they ended up high in the sky? The fall from such a height could be deadly.

As he darted his head around, Zack realized this wasn't just happening to their group. The children, the teacher, and her bench were off the ground as well. To Zack's surprise, the children were handling it far better than he was. Only a few were shouting their heads off. The youngest screamed with joy like it was the best amusement park ride they'd ever experienced.

The three farmers were in the air, as were some of the crops. The farmers flailed their arms and legs as if they were plunging from an airplane without parachutes. Near the barn, cows and pigs floated in the air as well. From the murmuring all around, this had to be affecting the entire village. The buildings and trees rumbled. Only their size, weight, and foundations kept them from floating along with everything else. Their hope lay in Selena and Sacha, who swam through the air toward one another. Their plan was clear: bring their power together to offset the side effects of Isis' seizure. Sacha's wide eyes and grinding teeth meant that she wasn't sure they would succeed.

The sisters reached for one another. Before they could lock hands, they, and Zack, hit the ground. So did everyone and everything else. Zack's body bounced upon impact. Lucky they dropped from only about two feet in the air. Paul was the first to stand. He ran to Tia's side and helped her up. "Is everyone okay?" he called out. "Is anyone hurt?"

"Wow," Sacha said, pushing her upper body off the grass. "The seizure must have passed."

"We were lucky," Sebastian whispered to Selena while helping her stand. "This could have been a lot worse."

Tia brushed herself off. "Okay, folks, on we go." She marched in the direction of the medical center as if nothing happened.

Zack pulled himself up. He took a quick look in case anyone needed a hand but everyone around them were okay. He let out a deep sigh of relief. Sebastian was right; considering the earthquake Isis created in Las Vegas, they got off light this time.

But what about the next time?

Chapter Thirteen

Sebastian and Selena charged past Tia and into the medical room. Zack stopped in front of the open door and looked around in horror. The room was a complete mess. Broken glass covered the floor and countertops. Papers were scattered in every direction. Tables and medical equipment were knocked over. Simon sat on the floor rubbing the top of his head. His cane had flown across the room. Isis was laid out on a medical table with her eyes shut tight. Her body lay stiff, almost lifeless.

"Mac, fill us in," Tia said to the doctor who leaned against the wall, taking a deep breath.

"I think what happened was obvious," the doctor responded. "Isis had a dialeptic seizure. The electrical activity in her brain triggered a massive energy flux like I've never seen. I gave her a benzodiazepine to knock her out."

"You did what?" Zack asked.

"It's a tranquilizer." Mac waved an empty syringe in the air.

"When treating a witch, you always have your crystals in place to cut off their connection." Paul helped Simon off the floor. "Why not this time with her?"

"The crystals are in place, or at least they were." Mac stepped away from the wall. There was a slight stagger in his step. "Somehow, her power flux knocked one out of place. I can't imagine how that happened. She shouldn't have known they were here, let alone where in the room they're positioned."

Selena sat at the edge of the medical table and took hold of Isis' hand. Sebastian stood in front with his palm pressed against their daughter's forehead.

Zack sprinted across the room to get Simon's cane. He made his way back and handed it to him. "Thank you, young man," the vampire said.

Mac cleared his throat in order to get everyone's attention. It worked on Sebastian, at least, who did look up from Isis.

"I could use some perspective here," Mac said. "Exactly how connected to the planet's energy is Isis?"

"Real connected," Sacha said from behind the doctor.

"I need specifics. 'Real connected' means what, exactly?"

Sebastian answered, "It manifested in Isis just after her ninth birthday."

"She was *nine*?" Mac rubbed his thick eyebrows. "I've never heard of any of our kind manifesting at such a young age. The potential in her, it's on levels beyond anything we've seen here—"

"Do you know what is happening to her?" Sebastian snapped.

"I believe we have some idea," Mac answered. "Simon, if you would share your findings, please?"

Simon leaned on his cane near the table. He tapped a long fingernail against the side of Isis' neck. "First, do any of you know how she received this scar?"

Zack moved closer to the medical table. He had

seen the scratch many times, particularly when they were fooling around in his bed. He loved kissing Isis' neck, especially when it tickled her. This time, however, the mark was a darker red and more pronounced. He'd think the scratch infected, but based on Mac and Simon's concerns, it had to be more than that.

"The vampire scratched her," Sebastian answered. "That's who you saw us battling in Vegas."

Simon shook his head. "That does explain a lot. This is how it begins."

"How what begins?" Selena asked.

"The turn," Simon immediately replied. "Mythology claims resurrection is through the exchange of blood. That is only partially true; it is the plasma in the bloodstream that contains the vampire virus and keeps our bodies animated long after death. The first step in the turn is a vampire puncturing the chosen's skin. We then just need to let a few drops of our blood enter the chosen's bloodstream. I believe that is exactly what is circulating through Isis.

"Wait, a vampire doesn't have to kill their victim to turn them?" Zack asked.

Simon let out a sigh. "That is the second step. Once the vampire's plasma is flowing through the chosen's body, the next phase involves death, then resuscitation. The vampire breathes renewed life into the chosen. It is always through the mouth, at least as far as I've ever known."

"Mouth to mouth resuscitation," Sacha said.

"Yes, but with the vampire's breath connecting with the reanimated body fluids circulating through the bloodstream, it will genetically change the chosen's blood, allowing an awakening but in an undead state." Simon motioned towards Isis. "Without completing the turn, a living human body cannot handle a vampire's genetic materials coursing through their system."

"She was scratched a year ago," Sebastian said. "And there have been no symptoms of this until now."

"Well..." It was time for Zack to confess. "That's not entirely true." All heads went Zack's way.

"What does that mean?" Selena asked through grinding teeth.

Zack took a huge gulp. He was suddenly under a rather dangerous spotlight. "Isis was experiencing dizzy spells and difficulty breathing. She didn't mention them because they didn't last long, but I caught it during her last act."

"And you didn't think it was important to tell us?" Sebastian growled.

"That was the first time I noticed it happening. I confronted her about it when we went out after the show. She promised to tell you about it in the morning, but then at the club..."

"I don't understand. Why would she keep it from us in the first place?" Selena asked.

Zack didn't want to answer. He simply stared at Selena in silence. He hadn't realized that his eyes had dropped to her stomach. Not until she turned away and said, "Oh."

"How long had she been experiencing these episodes?" Mac asked.

"She said there were three over the last few months, but they weren't severe." Zack threw a glance at Selena and Sebastian. "Isis thought it was just stress from everything that was happening."

"Clearly, it wasn't just stress," Simon responded. "Isis has vampire DNA running through her body. Without completing the turn, it is like a virus tearing her apart from the inside."

"With all due respect, Simon," Sebastian said. "Could you please not sound so damned gallant when discussing our daughter's impending death?"

Simon stretched his arms out and bowed his head. His eccentric way of offering an apology, perhaps?

"Doctor Mac, can you confirm any of this?" Tia asked.

"Not at all. Vampire is way outside of my expertise," Mac answered. "But I don't have a medical or a Wiccan explanation for Isis' condition. I can confirm she is showing far lower than normal oxygen levels in her bloodstream. I have no choice but to go with Simon's assessment. It's the only possible conclusion."

"How long does she have?" Selena sobbed, never looking up from Isis.

Simon shrugged. "I can't say. Most of what I know, I learned from Luther, but he did educate me on this process. Seeing as how the turn was not completed, it is an absolute miracle she survived even the first seizure."

"Maybe not a miracle." Mac leaned against the counter with his arms folded across his chest. "If Isis truly manifested at nine years old, then her connection is strong, perhaps stronger than any witch we've ever seen in this village. She may be instinctively using the planet's energy to fight off the virus. That would explain the coma she falls into after the seizure causes a spike of electrical activity in her brain. She's shutting down after absorbing an overwhelming amount of the energy to flush her system. Unfortunately, as the virus grows stronger, it is a fight she will inevitably lose."

A chill filled the air. Tears tried to push their way through Zack's ducts. He fought back the sensation. In the faces of Sebastian and Selena, there was only shock. Finally, Sacha broke the silence. "There has to be a cure, right?"

"I'm afraid there is no cure," Simon answered. "There is, however, a solution."

Sebastian looked up from Isis. "What solution?"

"Well…" Reluctance filled Simon's tone. "The process would need to be completed."

Sebastian cringed. "You mean kill her then bring her back as a vampire."

"Yes. Otherwise, she will eventually stop breathing and never wake up. It may happen with the next seizure, maybe one after that. But eventually, she will run out of fight and not come out on the other side."

"And, from what we've seen," Sacha said, "those seizures could destroy this entire village."

"You understand we can't allow that," Paul stated, his eyes on Tia.

"Let her die or watch her turn," Selena said under her breath. "So, either way, she dies."

"But she can continue to exist," Simon shouted. "It will still be Isis, with all of her experiences, memories, and desires."

Sebastian and Selena exchanged a long, deep stare. Neither uttered a word; they didn't need to. Wiccan powers aside, they knew each other well enough to know one another's thoughts. It was clear they were deciding together. Selena was the first to nod her head.

Sebastian replied by doing the same.

"Simon," Sebastian said to the vampire. "Would you be willing to complete her turn?"

Simon shook his head back and forth. "I am sorry, my friends. I would if I could. But it doesn't work that way. It is only the vampire who started the process that can complete it. In this case, it sounds like you will need the vampire you fought in Las Vegas."

"The vampire we fought…" Sacha thrust her hand over her mouth. Her eyes became wide like watermelons. "We're talking about—"

"Valeria," Sebastian said with a defeated sigh. "We're talking about Valeria, who is currently exiled in the Other World for everyone's safety."

"The other world?" Tia asked. "What is the other world?"

"It's a planet from another dimension," Sacha explained. "It occupies the same space as Earth. Valeria was real powerful and totally nuts. She was sent there 400 years ago by the witches of the time—they named the place. She was sent back by us last year."

"So, it's like a prison." Simon returned to the examining table. He gazed down at Isis. "You will need her to complete the turn."

Man, Zack felt like his head was trapped in a vise. Of course, he didn't want to lose Isis; if they could save her, he was all in. But there had to be a way other than bringing back an all-powerful psychopath who wanted to reshape and rule the world with an iron fist. Hell, even if they did decide to knock on Valeria's door, why would she be willing to help her jailers? More likely, the witches would end up in another fight for their lives.

No, there had to be a better answer. But what? Zack was usually great at thinking outside the box. It was a gift that Isis on several occasions jokingly called his connection to the Wiccan energy. Right now, it was failing him; nothing came to mind. This wasn't even about witches. It was supernatural vampire stuff that was way out of Zack's scope. He couldn't remember a time he felt so useless.

Then again, the one actual vampire in the room didn't have any ideas either.

Selena shot to her feet. Her eyes narrowed. "Sacha and I can reopen that portal. We can use the same spell to create the rift."

Zack leaned forward. "What?"

"Selena, we can't bring her back!" Sebastian shouted. "She's there because she's insane. Not to mention, far more powerful than us."

"If we offer her freedom in exchange for saving Isis—"

"From what you're telling us," Tia interrupted, "Releasing her onto our planet is *not* a good solution."

"I agree," Paul said.

"We know her goals are to conquer," Sebastian said. "She sees us, and Isis, as obstacles. If anything, she'll kill all of us, and who knows how many others along the way."

"We can't just sit back and let our girl die."

"Hey," Zack called. "Before even having this argument, it's been a whole year. Do you guys even remember the spell?"

"Selena and I committed it to memory the next day," Sacha answered. "We never intended to use it, but with Luther over there, we decided we should have it ready just in case."

"Just because you *can* do this," Paul said, "doesn't mean you *should*."

"Doctor Mac, can you cure her of this?" Sebastian asked. "Believe me, we are open to any other options."

Isis moaned. All eyes focused on her. Her head rolled back and forth. "Is this going to be another seizure?" Tia asked the doctor.

Mac held his hand high above Isis. Static sparked from his fingers. "I don't believe so," he replied. "But that doesn't mean she won't have another one eventually."

Sacha grabbed Simon by the arm. "Simon, there has to be some other way." The desperation in her voice mirrored what Zack felt in the pit of his stomach.

"Actually, there is, but only if you know someone else this Valeria has turned. That vampire would be able to complete the process." Simon limped on his cane toward the medical table. "Any vampire created by Valeria would have her genetic material flowing through their bloodstream. It would connect with what is inside of Isis."

Simon's suggestion caused another awkward silence. Even if Valeria had transformed people before they met her, it certainly wasn't public knowledge. A lightbulb clicked on inside Zack's brain. He opened his eyes wide. "What about Luther?" he asked. "Luther turned Valeria. Right now, he's on that world with her. If we bring him back, isn't that the same genetic whatchamacallit as Valeria?"

Simon waved a finger. "It doesn't work that way, young man. The process is from the top down. The top, in Isis' case, is Valeria. Any vampire made by her can pass it along, but no one in the line prior to her can complete the process."

"What?" Zack slapped the palm of his hand against his forehead. "Who makes up these cockamamie rules?"

"Nature, young man," Simon answered. "Nature determines the rules."

A crackling sound issued from Tia's walkie-talkie. She snatched it from her belt and brought it to her mouth. "Go ahead." Her back straightened.

"I'm in the theater." Zack recognized the accent. It was Natasha. "Many of our people are here. They are demanding answers on our loss of gravity."

"Of course, they are," Tia said, without pressing the talk button.

"You're going to need to address this," Paul said. "Make a statement regarding the entire situation."

"Agreed." Tia spoke into the walkie-talkie as she strolled out of the room. "Tell our people I will be there momentarily to answer all their concerns." Paul followed her out the door.

"Zack," Sebastian called out. "Go with them. Keep an eye on that situation."

"You want me to leave right now?" Zack opened his eyes wide and glared at Sebastian. "You're about to decide what to do and you're kicking me out of the room for that conversation. Is this penance for not telling you right away about Isis' symptoms?"

"Zack, relax, it's not like that at all." Sebastian took a step forward. He was now chest to nose with Zack. Stress wrinkles filled his face. "The locals are riled up and many of them are witches," he whispered. "If Tia can't calm them and things go south, we may need to teleport out of here right away."

"Where would we go?"

"I don't know." Sebastian threw his hands up. "That's why I need you to assess the situation and see whether or not we're safe here. You have my word we will discuss with you our decision on Isis before we do anything."

As much as Zack hated to be left out of the conversation, Sebastian was right. Witches or not, they didn't know anything about these people. It was clear, based on the reactions to their arrival, that the villagers were suspicious of strangers. If that were the case, Isis' seizure side effect sure didn't help ease any concerns.

"All right, I'm on it." Zack followed Tia and Paul out of the room.

Chapter Fourteen

Zack stood in the back of the auditorium. It was the first time in a long time he could remember being on the floor of an auditorium as opposed to on or behind the stage. There had to be at least six rows in front of the stage, each with ten seats across. Less than half were filled with unhappy people, some louder than others.

It was interesting, although the people were one community, the divide seemed to be based on occupations. Three men and a woman dressed in mud-covered overalls sat together in the center of the front row. Those had to be the farmers. Zack had seen at least one of them working in the fields.

Two women and a man sat in the far left of the third row. They wore aprons and clothing that had Zack betting they either worked at or ran the marketplace. The waiter who served them, Maurice, sat in the second row along with an older man dressed exactly like him. Others were scattered throughout the auditorium sitting either individually or in pairs. There didn't look to be anyone under the age of thirty anywhere in the audience.

All eyes were on the oak wood podium in the center of the stage. Tia stood behind it with her back perfectly straight, taking in all the angry glares. She waited patiently for the noise to die down. Zack had spent most of his life on a stage, but never in front of an audience that was collectively pissed off from the start.

"Ladies and gentlemen," Tia said into the microphone. Her voice could barely be heard over all the shouting. "I want to address your concerns about our guests. However, it would be much easier to do so if you spoke one at a time. Raise your hands and I will call on you." The crowd chatter kept going. "Let's have order, please," Tia said even louder.

"Everyone, quiet down!" Paul shouted from Tia's left. His voice boomed with an authority that rivaled Tia's.

The chaotic talking from the crowd lowered in response. The room silenced after several "shushes" from different directions. Tia motioned to one of the farmers in the front row. Zack had seen him earlier when everyone floated in the air.

"Madam President, a number of the crops pulled right out from the ground," the man said with what Zack took as an American southern drawl. "That's weeks of work down the drain. All of us, but especially our witches, will be working a long time, day and night, just to regrow what we lost."

"What about the cattle?" Tia asked.

"They're shook up, but fine otherwise."

Tia folded her hands across the podium. "Farmer John, you have my full authorization to use anyone and any resources you need to rebuild our crops. I am confident you and your farmhands will face this challenge and rise above it, just as you have done so many times before."

"Well, we will do our best." Farmer John returned to his seat. The tension in his voice had dissipated.

"Madam President." A tall woman with short hair sitting by herself in the last row stood up. Her voice bellowed throughout the theater. "My son was doing his homework on the couch. Next thing I know, he, me, and the couch lifted in the air, then crashed onto the floor. We have no Wiccan powers. We could have been killed. As it is, we survived, but he sprained his wrist!"

"I presume he has been seen by medical?"

"Yes, one of the doctors healed his arm." The woman smacked her hands against her hips. "But what if something else happens? What if our village gets destroyed all because you allowed these strangers onto our land?"

"Yes," a man in the third row shouted. "What then?"

Chaotic conversation filled the crowd. It wasn't friendly or cordial. A few of the village residents twisted around in their seats and eyed Zack. Some of the gazes showed anger, others displayed fear. Zack turned his head away from the glares. If he were an actual witch, he would have teleported himself across the globe in a heartbeat. The people of this once-happy village were now at each other's throats. As the one who found them, their troubles were Zack's fault.

The talking became louder. Questions and remarks were shouted at the stage. Some of the audience broke into arguments with each other. Paul nodded to Natasha who was seated in the front row, unresponsive to the chaos around her. She raised a hand and pointed her forefinger at Paul. Zack caught the slight sparks around her hand.

"Everyone, *enough!*" Paul's voice boomed as if he had spoken directly into a microphone. The crowd silenced in response.

"People of New Salem," Tia said into the actual mic, "I am well aware of your concerns and I wish to address them by sharing with you what we know about these strangers and their story which influenced my decision. They have come here because we have the largest population of witches in the world. Their youngest has contracted an illness where she is suffering seizures that cause her to lose control of her witchcraft. It is a problem we haven't had on our land, at least not yet. And yes, we experienced damage because of it."

Heads nodded as Tia's voice boomed through the speakers. "It is important you all realize that these visitors are not an invading force. They were not sent by a neighboring power trying to take over our land. They are a family, who happen to be witches, and they need our help. Where else on this entire planet could they turn to for that help and understanding?"

"Madam President—" one lone female voice shouted from the audience.

Tia held her palm out to cut her off. The woman complied.

"We will help this family for two reasons. The second reason is that we want to know what, exactly, made the power of this young witch spiral out of control. We need to know in case it should ever happen to a witch here in New Salem. Yes, we realize it can happen because it happened to one of them. But that is secondary to the primary reason we agreed to open our home and help this family."

The entire auditorium was quiet. Every single villager in the room focused on each word Tia said.

Zack found himself doing the same. Tia spoke with a confidence Zack found impressive for someone so close to his age.

"We are a sanctuary for those blessed with the power of Mother Earth. It is here we can live freely and without fear among those who were not." Tia paused. Zack knew that pause well—it was used by performers, including himself, for dramatic effect. "*This* is the premise our village was founded on. It is the main principle of our origins that I, and each president before me, have governed."

Tia's head turned from far left to far right, making eye contact with each member of the audience. "I ask you all to be understanding as we work to save a fellow witch during a dire time of need. They are powerful, and if we can help her, I see in this family future allies, not to mention, a cure for a potential ailment one of our own may someday suffer."

After several moments of silence, Farmer John stood once again. "And if you can't cure her?" he asked. "If the damage to our village continues, or becomes worse?"

"Thank you, Farmer John." Tia leaned forward against the podium. "I assure you that New Salem is always my first priority. If the situation worsens, we will have no choice but to remove the threat from our village. This is my promise to you!"

The farmer exchanged a glance with his group, then back to Tia. "That is fair." The other farmers nodded their agreement.

"I must go now." Tia stepped away from the podium then shouted, "Thank you for your time."

She glided down the steps in front of the stage.

People shouted questions despite the president's request. Paul stepped behind the podium and leaned down in front of the microphone. "All right, folks, you all heard from our president and I believe she has answered all of your questions. This meeting is concluded. Please disperse through the side doors in an orderly fashion!"

Members of the audience stood. Some followed Paul's instructions and moved to the doors. A few still shouted questions. Tia strolled up the aisle where Zack was waiting. As Tia closed the gap, her wide eyes and smile intensified with a brightness Zack had seen only from Isis whenever she was excited to spend time with him…or when they were about to get intimate. He had never seen that look on the face of another, at least not aimed at him.

Zack was certainly flattered. How could he not be? Tia impressed him. At first glance, he envisioned her as one of the popular cheerleaders from his school. But he took back that thought. Tia had a maturity far beyond any of those girls. The idea that a girl like this would be interested in Zack threw him for a loop. Of course, despite his slight temptations, he wasn't about to betray the love he shared with Isis. But how could he tell the president of this village that he had to reject her flirtations right after she defended his new family to the entire population? It's not like he had any personal experience rejecting women even under normal circumstances.

"So, how'd I sound up there?" Tia asked once she was in earshot. Her hands pressed against her hips and a gleam in her eye that Zack took as a blatant gesture.

He took a deep breath, anxiously wiping the sweat

from his palms against his pants. Before he could answer, a deep voice spoke from behind him. "You handled it very well, as always, my dear."

Zack spun around to see a tall man—at least six feet in height—returning the president's smile with one of his own. His skin had the same tone as Tia's. He also appeared around the same age, maybe a year or two older. His arms, which were well toned, showed through the sleeves of his white dress shirt. Apparently, Tia's huge smile was for him. Oops.

"Zack." Tia placed a hand on his shoulder. "I'd like you to meet my fiancé Jasper. He is also part of Paul's law enforcement team. Jas, this is one of our guests, Zack."

Jasper offered a handshake, which, after a sigh of relief, Zack obliged. The man's hand engulfed Zack's. He had one hell of a grip. Jasper released Zack's hand and turned his attention to Tia. "You realize your speech was simply a bandage. Our people are still wary of these outsiders. Should another incident arise—"

"I am well aware of the situation." Tia playfully touched his chest. "I am not naïve."

"I know you are not," Jasper replied. "But you are taking a huge risk politically for strangers."

"Screw politics, I'm doing the right thing. *We* are doing the right thing." Tia threw a smile at Zack. "As I said, this is Jasper."

"Nice to meet you. Are you a witch?" Zack asked. It was the first question he had on his mind with everyone he met in New Salem.

"In the literal sense, I am, but not with a strong connection like others," he answered. "Certainly not like your witches."

"Jas has cognitive dreams," Tia explained. "He sees the future."

"That is true," Jasper said. "But they are only glimpses. I cannot control what I see in my dreams."

"He did see you coming," Tia added. "That's why Natasha was on hand to stop you from teleporting here. When she was unable, our witches created that illusion. We hoped it would make you turn back."

Zack nodded his understanding. It did explain a lot. "So, you two met here in the village?"

"No, our families were neighbors in Morocco," Jasper answered. "I was fifteen months old when Tia was born. Prior to that day, our families agreed to match us. That is why we immigrated here when I was seven, so we could become accustomed to one another and eventually fulfill our arrangement."

"Wait." Zack shook his head. Did he hear Jasper correctly? "The two of you were arranged when you were a baby and Tia wasn't even born?"

Tia grinned. "We were. I take it you and Isis are not an arrangement?"

"No! We chose each other." Zack raised his eyebrows. "Well, technically, we were matched by an evil witch with a love spell. She did that because she wanted to use me to kill Isis' family. But we beat the love spell. Then, we, um, chose each other."

The two eyed one another and laughed in unison.

"That sounds far stranger than our arrangement," Tia said.

Zack's cheeks went warm. "Yeah, I guess it kind of is."

"Is that always how arrangements work in your country?" Jasper asked.

"Not exactly." Zack snickered. Who knew this guy had a sense of humor? It was somewhere hidden behind that deadpan facial expression.

"Speaking of Isis," Tia interrupted, "I believe we should check on our patient."

Chapter Fifteen

Isis found herself floating near the ceiling of the medical room, staring down at her body which was unmoving on the examining table. Her Wiccan family huddled around her, Selena and Sebastian on one side, Sacha on the other. They glanced back and forth at each other, but no one said a word. It was as if they were all deep in thought, trying to figure out their next move. Isis wanted to call to them, get them to look up at her. She opened her mouth but nothing came out. For a moment she thought she was dead, but that couldn't have been the case. There would have been a lot more tears in the room had she actually died.

Isis' eyes were closed tight thanks to whatever liquid flowed through the tube attached to her arm. Her chest expanded and contracted. At least that confirmed she was still breathing. But if that was the case, how could she be looking down on herself? Did Isis' mind somehow project her consciousness out of her body? She had no idea witches could do that, yet that was exactly what was happening.

It did make sense though. Isis learned how to project her thoughts into another person's mind. So why not her consciousness while she was asleep? There was no limit to what a witch could do except for the limits of imagination and how much control they had over the planet's energy. Isis had spent the last seven years hearing about her "nearly unlimited potential." Maybe this was an example of it. It was just a shame she couldn't show her family what she was achieving right now, right above their heads.

God, she had never seen them so distraught. Mom squeezed Dad's hand to the point both of their fingers had become red. Sacha's eyes were wide, as if she hadn't slept in days, and where was Zack? Isis wanted to swoop down, wrap her arms around each of them and say that everything was going to be okay. But she wasn't sure that was the case. She also wasn't sure she had a body other than the unconscious one on the table. How was she supposed to get back in there, anyway?

"Selena," Doctor Mac said from across the room. "Your breathing is erratic. You need to relax. Bringing your stress levels up will not help your daughter—"

"Of course I'm stressed, dammit," Selena snapped. "How could I feel otherwise?"

"Sis, chill," Sacha shouted at her. "You know Doctor Dreamy Eyes is only trying to help."

"Yes, I do know that." Selena's tone calmed. Her eyes shifted to Mac. "I am sorry, Doctor."

"Think nothing of it," Mac answered. "As both a doctor and an expectant parent, I understand what you are going through."

"Not entirely." Selena leaned over the examining table and put a hand on the top of Isis' head. "We lost a child recently."

"Oh. If I may ask, what happened?"

Sebastian stepped behind Selena and rubbed the back of her neck. "I was thirteen weeks pregnant." Her attention never left Isis. "But something wasn't right, I sensed it. We went to a hospital where they tested the fetus and found he wasn't breathing. He died in my womb. They had to abort it."

"My condolences on your loss," Mac said with genuine empathy in his voice. "I know as witches we believe we have the power to fix everything. But that's not always the case. We can't reverse death."

"I can't lose Isis too, I just can't." Selena sniffled. "She wasn't born from my body, I didn't hold her as a baby, but she's still our child. We raised her for the last seven and a half years. We helped mold her into the young woman she is today. We lost our son. I don't know if I can handle losing our daughter as well."

"We won't lose her," Sebastian said. "We won't."

Isis stared down at her mom and dad. She wanted to cry in the worst way. If she were in her body, she most definitely would have been bawling. Actually, Isis wanted to fly down there and slap herself silly. She was so concerned about sparing other people's pain that she was willing to give up her own life. She never once considered her family's pain.

If she succumbed to this vampire virus and let it take her life, her loved ones would suffer emotional trauma to the point none of them would ever be the same. That included Zack. She'd only known him for a year, but they'd become close to the point a part of him would also die along with her. Isis couldn't allow that to happen to any of them. She had to survive, she had to hold on, at least until they could find a way. Isis saw in Dad's eyes—which were focused on Mom—that the wheels in his head were in motion. Dad was working out every possibility, which was what he did best. He would never let down his family, even in a near-hopeless situation.

"I know how we can save her," he said. Of course he'd figure it out.

Selena's head lifted. Her eyes turned into a gaze of hope. "H-how?"

"It's a big risk, but it is one I'm willing to take." He stood at attention like a soldier ready to go to war.

Selena's eyes widened. "What do you mean? What risk? How can we save her?"

"It's a solution I don't like," Sebastian answered. "You're definitely not going to like it."

"Then why even consider it?" Sacha asked.

"Because it's also the only answer we have." Sebastian threw his hands across the back of his head and took two handfuls of his hair. "I don't see any other choice."

Isis caught the determined glimmer in her dad's eyes. She sensed exactly what he wanted to do. He was right in thinking Mom wasn't going to like it. She didn't know it yet, but they were about to have a huge argument.

Chapter Sixteen

Although Tia's town hall meeting went well, the knot in Zack's stomach hadn't gone away. In fact, it was tighter than before the meeting started. As they walked through the village, several residents eyed him with suspicion. While Tia remained at Zack's side throughout the entire walk from the theater to the medical center, her boyfriend, Jasper, was always three feet behind. Zack questioned if he was more than just her arranged future husband but also her assigned bodyguard. If that was the case—and Zack wasn't sure either way—what was his mission right now? Was he looking to protect Tia from irate townspeople, or did he perceive Zack as the potential threat?

They stopped in front of the medical center. "We are here," Tia said. "Let your family know I will catch up with all of you soon."

Zack paused in his step. Tia was the first outside of the witches themselves to refer to them as his family. It was something Zack appreciated. He barely remembered his parents and, although he had an awesome uncle, it had been just the two of them. Now, he had an actual family that accepted him even though he was different. Ironic, because compared to the rest of the world, they were the ones who were different. Zack didn't share their connection to the Earth's energy, but he did relate to them better than anyone on the entire planet besides Uncle Herb. That was especially the case with Isis, which is why he would do anything and everything to help her.

Zack pushed the medical center's door open and entered the building. A hallway with three doors, one against each wall, faced him. The door to his left opened. Sebastian stepped out. His cheeks were red. His eyes blinked rapidly like they were trying to hold back either rage or tears. It was an emotion Zack had rarely seen out of the usually confident Sebastian. Something was wrong. Zack's heart dropped into his stomach.

"Isis," Zack gasped. "Is she…"

"She's resting comfortably, for now." Sebastian picked his head up and eyed Zack who breathed a sigh of relief. "We've made a decision. Well, I made the decision. It's the only way we can save her."

"I'm all ears," Zack said.

Sebastian looked back at the door to Isis' medical room. From the look of guilt on his face, it was a good guess that Selena didn't approve of their "only way to save her." Sebastian paced back and forth. "The sisters are going to open the portal to the other world and I'm going to step through. Valeria is our only hope to save Isis."

"I thought we agreed bringing Valeria back is bad?"

"It is," Sebastian replied. His pacing stopped. "We're going with a rendition of Simon's plan. I'm going to convince Valeria to turn me."

Zack's jaw clenched, biting his own tongue. No wonder Sebastian was worn out. He had battle weariness written all over his face, and understandably so. There was no way Selena was okay with this plan. Seeing Isis get transformed into an undead vampire would be hard enough. But for that to happen, Sebastian had to become one as well. Essentially, she'd have to see both her husband and daughter die and resurrect as something completely different. Zack could only imagine the emotions that must have poured out of that conversation. Sacha couldn't have been okay with it either.

It was practical suicide, even if the plan worked. Still, there was no point in trying to talk Sebastian out of it. Zack knew the man well enough to understand his mindset. Once Sebastian set his mind on a plan that he felt was for the betterment of the others in his coven, it was difficult to get him to change it. But Zack had to try anyway just to know that he did.

"Is that really the only option?" Zack asked. "Is there no other possible way to save her?"

"According to Simon, once the turn starts, it can't be reversed." A deep breath exhaled through Sebastian's nose. "Valeria's plasma is needed to complete the turn, or we lose Isis completely. I'm not willing to let that happen."

"There has to be something else we can do," Zack said. "What about taking Isis there? Valeria could finish the process herself without using you as the middleman."

"We thought of that," Sebastian replied. "Well, Sacha thought of it."

"And?"

"According to Doctor Mac, he's flushing the virus from Isis' bloodstream, but it returns instantly and, each time, stronger. It's trying to shut down her system. Isis should be dead already. Mac can only keep pace with the virus within the crystals, but he doesn't know for how much longer."

"So, we can't move Isis." Zack darted his eyes towards the ceiling. A lightbulb flashed in his head. "Unless you can take the crystals with you along with Doctor Mac—but he won't have his power over there and neither will the crystals. Damn."

"Even if that could work, I don't feel comfortable risking anyone else's safety," Sebastian said. "Isis is my responsibility. The risk is mine to take."

Zack formed a picture in his head of how this plan would work out. It was an exercise he and his uncle practiced with ideas for their magic shows. The picture of Sebastian sitting down and asking a favor from the vampire who tried to kill them and who they imprisoned in another dimension made his brain itch. No matter what game plan Sebastian had in mind, Zack couldn't get past the vision of Valeria scoffing at the idea, killing Sebastian, and then letting Isis die.

A dribble of sweat ran down Zack's forehead. He wiped it away with the back of his hand. "You realize you won't have the connection that makes you a witch here. But Valeria is still a vampire."

"I do realize that, yes." Sebastian shrugged. "I will convince her to do the right thing."

"And if Valeria is still holding a grudge?"

"If Luther is around, I'm sure he'll help me persuade her. If he's not, one way or another, I will find a way."

No, Zack couldn't see Sebastian finding a way, not by himself over there. It wasn't that he didn't trust Sebastian's judgment or ability, he did one hundred percent. But he didn't trust Valeria. She was a schemer who convinced Zack's uncle—the smartest man in Las Vegas—to let down his guard. Sebastian was a smart man as well, but, honestly, to Zack, the witches were all a bit sheltered from the real world. As performers, the only people they knew personally were ones who made money off their shows. For Sebastian to succeed, he'd need someone watching his back. A second set of eyes in case Valeria had a knife ready to stab him from behind.

"I'm coming with you."

Sebastian shook his head. "Absolutely not."

"What?" Zack exclaimed. "Why not?"

"I appreciate the offer, I really do." Sebastian placed a hand on Zack's shoulder. "But I need you here, keeping an eye on things and helping out in any way you can."

"That's bull! I can be a lot more useful over there with you!" Zack took a breath realizing his voice had raised two levels. "I can help out with whatever can come up."

"I hear you, Zack, but there lies the problem," Sebastian replied. "We don't know what sort of dangers are in the Other World."

"That's the point of bringing back-up!" Zack slapped a hand against his chest. "I'm a lot more experienced at being a human without supernatural powers than you are."

Sebastian nodded his head. "Everything you're saying makes sense. But this is the way it is. When we took you in, I made a promise to keep you safe. I'm not about to break that promise. I'm going in alone. Don't worry, I can handle this."

God, this was the problem with adults. They were so obsessed with protecting everyone younger that it made them stubborn. Zack wanted to grab a clump of his own hair and yank it out of his head. And then maybe shove them down Sebastian's throat. Well, maybe nothing so violent, but he needed to convince the man to change his mind. For Sebastian's sake and for Isis.

"Look, Sebastian..." Zack said while he worked on a convincing argument.

"I understand every point you're making," Sebastian said. "But my mind is made up. I can't put you in such a dangerous situation—"

The floor shook. Zack fell forward, dropping onto his hands and knees. Sebastian slammed against the wall. Somehow, instead of falling forward, he was pinned against the wall's surface, thanks to his witch powers, no doubt. A vibration resonated from the floor. Zack's hands, arms, and legs all shook. "E-e-earthquake?" he asked through a quivering jaw.

The vibrations came to a sudden stop. Zack held his hands in front of his face to make sure they were steady. "Was that—"

"Not an earthquake!" Sebastian stepped away from the wall. "That was Isis!"

He yanked open the medical room's door and charged in. Zack jumped to his feet and followed. Isis was unconscious on the medical table, her eyes shut. Selena sat in a chair next to the table holding Isis' left hand between her palms. Her eyes and cheeks were red and moist, much like Sebastian's. Sacha and Simon were staring out the window. Across the room, Doctor Mac held an empty syringe with a long needle in his hand. A drop of clear liquid fell from the tip to the floor.

"We were lucky," Simon said. "Apparently, Isis' seizure only affected this building. No damage out there as far as I can see."

"What happened?" Sebastian leaped over a box of gloves and stethoscope on the floor. He sprang to Selena's side, leaned down, and placed a hand on Isis' stomach.

Doctor Mac faced the corner, staring at the floor. Zack was sure he was using his power. On what, he had no idea.

"Doctor?" Simon said to him. "Are you all right?"

"She keeps moving my crystals." Mac nodded his head, then turned away from the wall. "I have to keep moving them back."

"I'm sorry about that," Sebastian responded.

"Oh, I'm not angry. I'm impressed. Isis has connected with my crystals in a short period of time. She's able to unconsciously override my connection. And I've been using them in this examining room for years."

"What did you do to her?" Zack asked.

"Once the signs of another seizure began, I administered another sedative," Mac explained. "I think at this point we need to keep her under."

"What are we going to do?" Zack shouted. "Keep her medically sedated for the rest of her life?"

"Zack." Sebastian threw him a warning to back off.

"I'm afraid that won't be for much longer," Simon sobbed. "Her lips are turning a shade of purple."

"We're not going to stand back and watch her die," Sebastian said. "It's time to enact the only plan we have."

Selena threw Sebastian a glare that lasted several seconds. To Zack, it meant they either disagreed on the solution, or that it was the only option and she still hated it.

The door leading to the hallway swung open. Paul charged in. "We saw the building shake. Is everything okay?"

"Everything is under control, at least for now," Mac answered.

Paul walked over to Isis. He touched her arm. "She looks weak. Her skin is ice cold. But I feel a pulse."

"Mac's treatment is a temporary fix," Simon explained. "She's being eaten from the inside out. If the turn is not completed soon, it will be too late."

Sacha pulled on Sebastian's arm to get his attention. She placed a hand on Selena's shoulder. "If we're going to do this, then we need to do it now." She gave them each a wide-eyed glimpse. "Are we actually doing this?"

Sacha and Sebastian locked eyes on Selena. After a moment that felt far longer, Selena straightened her back and nodded. She walked across the room to Paul. "We'll need room to open the portal."

"I'll clear the quad." Paul pulled his walkie-talkie from its belt clip, then marched through the open doorway.

Chapter Seventeen

The perspiration under Zack's armpits burned as if the hot sun above was setting them ablaze. The entire quad was empty of people, just as Paul promised, but they certainly weren't left alone. Zack was sure everyone from the village was watching them from the windows of the buildings or in crowds in front and to the sides of the buildings. Well, everyone except for Doctor Mac who stayed with Isis. Mac needed to help keep her alive or all of this was for nothing.

The reason for the crowds was clear. While being around witchcraft was still new for Zack, it was everyday life here in New Salem. People flying, making objects move, and creating illusions was as common to them as a car speeding down the highway to the rest of the world. Opening a portal to another dimension, however, was something new entirely. What The Witches of Vegas were about to do made them stand out and impress, even among their own kind.

For the moment, the attention of all the onlookers focused on the deep embrace between Selena and Sebastian. Selena's arms wrapped around his waist like an octopus. Zack's heart broke in half. He wanted to hold Isis in much the same way and with the same sense of dread, knowing that she'd never be the same again. Would Isis have any interest in him at all once she became an immortal vampire? Eventually, Zack would become an adult, then an old man, but Isis would stay sixteen forever. They would be as different to each other as Zack was to one of those farm animals. Selena had to be going through the same mental anguish for Sebastian.

"I don't like this either," Sebastian said to his wife. "But she's our responsibility."

"I know," Selena replied.

"You're sure you both remember the spell, word for word?"

Selena nodded. "We do."

"I will still be me when I come back," Sebastian promised her. "And Isis will still be Isis."

"I hope so." Selena pulled back her head. "Just make sure you do come back. No matter what."

"I'll do everything in my power to make sure of it," he answered with a slight grin.

"I know you will."

A ball of saliva got stuck in Zack's throat and made him cough. He was never the overly emotional type, but the relationship between Sebastian and Selena defined this entire family. The pure passion Isis had shown him mimicked theirs. Sebastian would do anything for his family, which included going alone to a world in another dimension.

No, Zack would not stand by and allow Sebastian to face this situation by himself. "I know what I have to do," he mumbled under his breath.

"And what exactly is that?"

The high-pitched voice from behind nearly made Zack jump out of his white sneakers. He spun like a top to find Simon standing behind him leaning on his cane in one hand and a long pointed wooden stick in his other. "What do you have to do?" Simon asked.

"Nothing!" The word shot off Zack's tongue. His eyes dropped to Simon's spear. "What is *that* for?"

"It's for Sebastian to take with him just in case he needs to protect himself over there." Simon tossed the spear straight up and caught it mid-air. "It's made of bamboo so it's incredibly light, but strong on each end."

"Protect himself." Zack's confidence dropped even further. Sebastian had never even walked down the street without having his Wiccan powers for protection. How would he survive in a strange land without them?

"I need to get this into Sebastian's hands," Simon explained. "I can't take the chance of a splinter."

"A splinter worries you?" Zack asked.

"Of course, it is one thing my deceased skin will not heal from." Simon held out the spear as far as his arm could stretch. "Luther and I used to joke about how a weakness to wood was the one folklore they actually got right about our kind."

"Luther joked?" Zack asked.

"Well, I did most of the joking. But it was one of the first lessons he taught me about being a vampire."

Zack rubbed his fingers along the spear's smooth surface. "It is impressive," he said. "You made it?"

Simon grinned. "My husband, Nikolas created this piece of artwork. He was quite the wood carver before arthritis took away his skills."

"Your husband?" Zack's eyebrows slanted. He glanced at Simon for what felt like an eternity. The reaction did not go unnoticed.

"Come now, Zack," the vampire snickered. "Does my sexuality make you pause?"

"Oh, no, it's not that at all," Zack said quickly. "It's just...you're an undead reanimated vampire and you're in a relationship? I didn't think you would be able to...well..."

"To love?" Simon tapped Zack's foot with the end of his cane. "There are feelings and emotions that stay with us through our memories, even long after death."

"That's good to know." Zack's mind focused on Isis. He truly hoped that was true for all vampires. Especially her.

"I'm surprised you didn't turn him," Zack said. "Didn't you want to be together forever?"

"Of course, I did. But Nikolas didn't want that," Simon replied. "As hard as it is seeing him age, I respect his wishes."

"His wishes are to grow old and die?"

"Yes, and I understand. For some mortals, that does hold meaning. Now, if you will excuse me?"

Simon waddled to Sebastian and the sisters with the spear clutched against his stomach. Zack couldn't imagine what it was like for this jovial vampire to watch his lover age to the point they were no longer compatible. But Simon did give him the choice. It was a choice no one was giving Isis. Did she want to walk the planet as a vampire for the rest of eternity? No one even considered that. Sebastian may have, he always thought of everything, but he didn't care. He had a single-minded focus to save the girl he and Selena raised as their daughter, no matter what that meant.

Sebastian and Selena stepped away from each other. The distress in each of them was obvious. Their relationship would change forever and only if everything went according to plan. There were so many unknowns in this, Sebastian might as well have been jumping out of an airplane and hoping to land on a single mattress in the middle of the wilderness to save his life. Yet he was ready to make that jump despite the trepidations he clearly had in his head. This was the definition of a great man. In that sense, Sebastian reminded Zack of his uncle.

Sacha clapped her hands, grabbing the couple's attention. "Okay, boys and girls, let's go over operation: save my niece." Her shoulders arched. The way Sacha took charge, it was clear that she understood their strife as well. "Selena and I will open the portal to the other world. Sebastian will go through and we'll reopen it in two hours and thirty minutes. Hopefully, you're still alive…well, you know what I mean."

"Sach." Selena's eyes narrowed at her sister.

"Sorry, you know I joke when I'm anxious."

"Two and a half hours," Zack said. "Is that enough time?"

"It will have to be," Sebastian answered. "Both Doctor Mac and Simon are sure Isis won't hold out much longer."

"Let's get this over with," Selena snarled. Sebastian took five steps back. She waved Sacha to join her.

"Sebastian!" Simon shouted, breaking the witch out of his narrow focus.

Simon held out the spear in both hands. "Just in case," he whispered. "You never know what you may face on the other side as you work toward your goal."

"Thank you." Sebastian clutched the spear in its center with his left hand. His focus returned to the sisters.

Selena dropped to her knees. Sacha stood behind her with hands planted firmly on her sister's shoulders. Selena pressed the tips of her fingers against one another near her chest. The two chanted in unison. Their voices were barely above a whisper and were so rapid that Zack couldn't follow a single word coming from their mouths.

One thing Zack learned about witchcraft was that chants—or spells as they called them—were used by witches to help them focus on a single idea. It was through that idea they were able to manipulate reality however they needed—in this case, opening a portal between dimensions. Whatever single-minded thought the two sisters focused on, it was what Luther had taught them to create that dimensional rift. The reasons they were doing this aside, it was so cool watching them create and execute such a huge spell.

After several moments, a small circle of blur appeared and hovered in front of them. To Zack, it looked like a soap bubble filled with water. At first, the circle was almost transparent. Then, it became clearer and solid. It expanded in size until it was wide enough to walk through. Sebastian took a deep breath, then marched forward with no hesitation in his step.

Sebastian placed his leg into the portal. Then, his right arm. Each body part disappeared as it went through a literal hole in space. He propelled his entire body forward. Within seconds, Sebastian was gone, now on the other side of the portal and in a completely different world. A murmur came from the circle of villagers that surrounded them. It was not unlike the one from audiences during the witches' shows. There was even some applause from the crowd, which also reminded him of their shows.

"Okay, Selena, time to close it up," Sacha said in a loud tone. Selena responded with a nod. They restarted their fast-talking chant.

That was the cue Zack had been waiting for. He propelled one foot in front of the other, running like an Olympic track star. His finishing line was the portal.

"Zack!" Sacha screamed, breaking her chant. "What are you doing?"

There was no time to respond. An instinct told him to stop or glide off to the side. He ignored it. Zack threw himself straight into the unknown.

His hands and feet tingled as he passed through the portal. The tingling engulfed his entire body. Everything went bright like the sun, forcing his eyes shut. The sound of Sacha shouting his name turned into an echo. Soon, he could no longer hear her screams.

His body slammed into something hard, knocking him off balance. Then, he hit what felt like a dry grassy surface.

Chapter Eighteen

Zack sat up and took a deep breath. The air had a hay-like smell to it that reminded him of a fresh cut lawn on a hot summer day. The grass, however, was unlike anything he'd ever seen on Earth. It had a gray hue, just like the sky. The grass was also long— almost like weeds—and it covered every square inch for as far as the eye could see.

There were also many trees in every direction. They, too, differed from any tree Zack had ever seen. The ones here were smooth surfaced with thin branches. The trees, along with branches that stretched up and out, had ones which curved inward like arms with their hands on their hips. None of the trees had leaves, but instead had thorns along the brown-tinted bark. This was definitely no longer planet Earth. Then again, according to the witches' theory, it rotated in the exact same position as Earth, just on a different frequency, whatever that meant.

Zack pulled himself off the ground and onto his feet. A circle of electric sparks snapped in the air. A moment later, they stopped. That meant their only doorway back had dissipated into nothingness. Now, the only connection left to the world Zack knew was the frustrated face glaring his way.

"You have got to be kidding me," Sebastian growled. "What the hell were you thinking?"

"That I could watch your back," Zack said through the lump in his throat.

"I told you I don't need you to watch my back. I needed you to stay there."

Zack had never seen Sebastian so enraged with nostrils flaring and teeth grinding. If not for the lack of powers in this "other world," the witch might have shot Zack dead with lightning bolts from his eyes.

"I…I'll be more useful here," Zack replied. "I couldn't let you come to this world alone."

"Dammit, Zack, you know what I have to do here." Sebastian climbed to his feet. "I won't be able to protect you from whatever dangers we face!"

"I don't need you to protect me, I'm not Isis!"

Zack stepped back. He really didn't mean to blurt that out. It was rude and nasty, especially to Isis' father while she was conceivably lying on her death bed. But it did reflect how Zack felt deep inside. From the moment they met Sebastian and Isis' relationship had always been about him being her hero. It was a role she still wanted from him, and one he was more than willing to fulfill. Still though…way unnecessary.

"I'm sorry, I didn't mean it that way," Zack said. "But I can help you save her. I think I've proven that I can be pretty useful, especially in a dangerous situation."

Sebastian let out a deep sigh. "I know, Zack. For the record, I have a lot of respect for you. That's why I trust Isis when she is with you. It's why I inducted you into my coven, even though you're not a witch. But, as the leader of this coven, it is my responsibility to keep the youngest of us safe. That's her and you."

Zack's gaze rose up. "Sebastian…"

"Don't get me wrong, I appreciate you, Zack," Sebastian continued. "Not just for who you are now but also for the man you will become."

"Sebastian—"

Sebastian raised a hand. "There will be time to finish this discussion later. Right now, we have to stay focused—"

"*SEBASTIAN, TURN AROUND!*"

Sebastian about-faced. A huge four-legged animal slinked their way. To Zack, it looked like a bull except it had long dark-gray fur like a wolf. It also had the height of a horse. Its paws were wide and solid with four long-nailed toes. The animal had a huge snout with wide black nostrils at the end that made heavy breathing sounds. Its head tilted sideways as its huge nostrils gave a loud sniff, first at Zack, then at Sebastian.

The animal stopped a few feet in front of him. "Zack, stay back," Sebastian said.

"It looks confused by us," Zack whispered while taking a large step backward.

A puff of smoke shot out of the animal's nostrils. Sebastian spread his legs into a defensive stance and pointed the sharp end of his spear at the creature. "Stay back!" Sebastian shouted.

The native creature's lips lifted, displaying its teeth. They were more like razor blades. A noise sounding like a deep horn blared from its open snout. It lunged forward, snatching the end of the spear in its mouth. With lightning quick reflexes, the beast yanked the weapon from Sebastian's hands. Its head shot up, tossing the spear high into the closest tree. The animal's upper body leaned down, showing that it was ready to pounce.

"Uh-oh." Sebastian gulped.

As if on instinct, Sebastian raised his left hand, pointing it at the creature. Nothing happened, it was a quick reminder that this was not the Earth they knew and he had no connection here.

The beast pounced, tackling Sebastian under its immense weight. Sebastian grabbed the throat, pushing with all his might to keep those sharp teeth from ripping his face off. It was a struggle he could only hold for so long as the creature had at least a hundred pounds on him. The animal hissed while closing the gap between its open mouth and the possible lunch which was Sebastian Santell's face.

Zack unzipped his fanny pack. He groped inside for something, anything, that could help. He found it. Flash paper!

Zack held the damp tissue and lit it at the end. No need to be subtle—this wasn't a magic act and his audience of one wasn't paying attention to him anyway. Zack tossed the paper at the creature's eyes. The paper ignited in a ball of flame which disappeared just as quickly.

The animal jumped onto its hind legs and flailed its front paws in the air. Standing vertical, it towered over Zack like a skyscraper. Sebastian rolled out of the way. The beast, apparently seeing fire for the first time, let out a screech that echoed all around. It galloped away, past the surrounding trees, and down a hill.

Zack let out a deep sigh of relief. "Well," he said between breaths, "I guess I'm useful to have around after all."

Sebastian sat up with eyes as wide as watermelons.

Zack expected either a humble apology or a reluctant thank you. Instead, Sebastian spoke in a nervous tone. "There's another one."

Zack peeked over his shoulder. Another creature strolled their way. It was of the same species as the first, only much larger. This one made slush noises through its nose with each breath it took. The creature stopped in its tracks just a few feet from Zack. Its head tilted with a look that spoke confusion, just like the first one had done. Zack stepped back as Sebastian rolled to his knees.

"What do we do?" Zack whispered.

Simon's spear launched from the top of the tree at a lightning speed. It stabbed straight through the beast's head, protruding out from its chin. Dark red blood gushed out the chin like a river down to the spear's end. Its lifeless husk tipped over.

"Holy crap!" Zack exclaimed.

At first, Zack thought this was Sebastian's doing. He quickly dismissed that thought. Even if he had his Wiccan abilities —which he didn't—he'd never kill an animal so mercilessly. But if it wasn't him, then who?

Zack and Sebastian's attention darted to the top of the tree. Between the branches, a pair of dark eyes gleamed back. Her hair was longer and dirtier than Zack remembered. Her black blouse and pants looked worn and shredded by the knees and stomach. Still, he recognized her immediately. The corroded teeth when she smiled proved a dead giveaway.

"Valeria," Zack said.

"Well, well." Her thick rhotic accent bellowed. "I certainly did not expect to see the two of you today. This *is* quite a surprise."

Valeria leaped from the tree. She landed on her feet in front of Sebastian. While he stood his ground, Zack stumbled back. Man, even after all this time, seeing her again, being so close to this four-hundred-year-old witch who almost destroyed humanity…it sent a chill down Zack's spine. Maybe this wasn't such a good idea after all.

Valeria threw a quick glance at Zack, a reminder how when last they met, she wanted to murder him. She also tortured and tried to kill Isis. For many nights after, the thought of it woke Zack in a cold sweat from reliving the events in his dreams. A few times, it hit him even when he was wide awake. A year had passed since that confrontation. It took a while, but Zack had convinced himself that he had processed and mentally dealt with it. Now, seeing her again in the flesh, his jaw quivered, and his entire body went cold. Which meant he wasn't over it at all.

"You brought fire," Valeria said. "Quite helpful. These cactus-like trees do not create it and the animals fear it."

Valeria yanked the spear out of the dead animal's head. She held it in front of her face. "Did you bring this with *me* in mind?" she asked. "It wouldn't have helped you anymore than it helped you against those animals."

Zack's eyes popped back to the top of the tree. How long had Valeria been up there watching them? Obviously long enough to see their struggles with that four-legged alien monster. Yet she stayed back and observed rather than swooping down with an immediate save. That didn't bode well considering they came for her help.

"Valeria, where is Luther?" Sebastian asked.

Valeria tossed the spear over her shoulder. "So, you're here for him," she said. "Of course, you would be." The vampire grinned. Her eyes went dark. The fangs on either side of her mouth showed. It was the face that had spooked Zack in those nightmares. "Luther is dead. I killed him. And now I will kill you!"

Sebastian's eyes narrowed. Zack couldn't tell if it was due to anger or fear. "We are not here for a fight," Sebastian growled.

Zack wanted to chime in as well. But when he tried to speak, his jaw wouldn't cooperate. His heart fluttered like a rabbit on speed.

Valeria burst into a high-pitched cackle. "I joke with you." She tapped Sebastian's shoulder with the back of her fingers. Her eyes were once again pure white. "Luther is hunting for blood. I was doing the same. Then I smelled human blood, so I came to investigate. And here you are."

"I see you haven't lost your sense of humor, Valeria," Sebastian said with a deep sigh of relief.

"Can...can we see Luther?" Zack asked, his jaw refused to stop shaking.

"Come, I will take you to our home. I am sure he will be surprised to see you." Valeria waved an arm, telling the two to follow. "Surprised and quite curious as to why you are here."

Chapter Nineteen

Isis wasn't sure how long she had been awake, only that she could hear every movement and discussion around her. Much of the talk was between Doctor Mac and Sacha on how long Isis could survive. Her mom, who hovered next to Isis' examining table, added little to the conversation except for the occasional sniffle. Isis hated seeing her so upset. "Don't worry about me, I'm okay," she wanted to say. But best not to bring attention to herself or Doctor Mac would put her back to sleep.

In between dozing, Isis heard something about how her power had caused everything around her to float. Simon described it as if the air changed into helium. The effect spread far beyond the building. Isis had the ability to make her body float. She also made another person float, but only once. It was Valeria and it helped her family send that evil hag back to the Other World. But to do it to everyone and everything around her? God, she hoped no one was hurt when that happened. The Vegas earthquake that did kill someone still lingered in her head.

"Let me adjust the needle," Doctor Mac said. Soon after, a set of strong fingers wrap around Isis' wrist. The needle in her arm moved. It made her elbow jerk. "You're awake, aren't you?" Mac asked.

No point hiding it anymore. Isis opened her eyes to

see Mac's distinguished eyes staring down at her. She tried to sit up, but her body wouldn't cooperate. Mac turned his attention to the clear bag on the pole next to the bed. A liquid ran from the bag through a tube and into the syringe.

"Amazing. The anesthesia has lost its effect," Mac explained. "I'm guessing that's because your body is instinctively channeling the energy."

"I thought you were blocking her connection with your enchanted crystals?" Sacha asked.

"Once I realized Isis is using her connection to fend off the virus, I shut them down," Mac explained. "In this case, the crystals were only hindering her, and my efforts."

Selena's head lifted. "Maybe she can beat this vampire virus the same way?"

"Doubtful," Mac answered. "The vampire virus is as natural as our connection to the planet. It's also a hell of a lot more powerful."

"Like cancer." Sacha grabbed Isis' left ankle and squeezed.

"At this stage, I would say that is an accurate depiction." Mac's eyes locked on Selena. "I have to put her back under."

"You said the anesthesia isn't working," Sacha said.

"It's not." Mac walked to the bed. "I have to inject a stronger dose or use other means."

"No," Selena responded.

"I'm sorry, Selena, but I have to think of the people in this village. In the likely event another seizure occurs, without the crystals blocking her connection—"

"I understand that!" Selena sat at the edge of the

bed near Isis' waist. "Let me take care of it."

"Very well. I leave it in your hands." Mac turned away.

Selena leaned in, bringing her lips near Isis' ear. "How are you feeling, sweetie?"

Selena's hand wrapped around Isis' wrist. "Cold. Tired." Isis' voice croaked like a frog. Her throat felt dry. "I'm scared."

"I know you are," Selena replied. "We all are. But have faith. I swear we are going to get you through this."

Selena placed her palm against Isis' forehead. It was time for her to go back to sleep. "Wait, please," Isis pleaded. "I…I need to tell you something."

"Of course."

"I want you to know, you were my role model. The woman I wanted to be. The witch I wanted to be like." Isis' eyelids drooped. She forced them open. "I…I know you all call me 'Daddy's little girl' but I love you both so much—"

Selena shushed her. "I know you do. I've never once questioned our relationship."

"I learned a lot from you. How to be strong—"

"Isis, stop!" Selena's hand moved to the top of Isis' head. "Do not say goodbye. We have a plan—let's give it a chance."

Isis took a deep breath. "T-turn me into a vampire."

"Yes. It's the only way to save you."

"I know. I've been listening."

An image formed in Isis' head. It was of herself leaping from one building to the next with two fangs hanging from her mouth while searching for blood. The image disappeared, replaced by a sudden pain. It felt like her head was clamped between a pair of giant pliers.

Isis shut her eyes tight, then reopened them. It did little to relieve the pressure. "Valeria won't help," she mumbled.

"You know your dad, our coven leader," Selena said. "He can convince anyone of anything."

Isis felt a tear roll down her cheek. "I…I don't want him to go. It's dangerous. She'll hurt him. Maybe k-kill him."

"Don't bet on that, kiddo," Sacha said from across the room. Her voice cracked. "We have two of the most resourceful men in the world working together. They will find a way."

"Two." Isis tried to lift her head, but to no avail. It felt like a weight was holding it against the pillow. "Zack went?"

"We couldn't stop him," Selena answered.

"You know that boyfriend of yours," Sacha added. "He's sneaky like a squirrel."

"N-no. I don't want them to go." Isis felt her eyelids fluttering. "It's too dangerous. D-don't risk their lives. Not for me." The vision of Selena looking down on her went dark. That was a bad sign.

Another voice, filled with concern, echoed the name, "Selena." It belonged to Mac. "Do it now."

"M-mom, please." Isis' words slurred. A chill ran through her body. "St-stop them—"

"Shush! Right now, don't speak, just listen to the sound of my voice." Selena's hand squeezed Isis' forehead and massaged her temples. A tingling began between Isis' ears. "I want you to think back to when you were nine years old and you first came to live with us. It was about two months before you felt comfortable and safe."

Selena's voice was soft, rhythmic. It was barely above a whisper, yet Isis heard every word. "That was when your dad and I would wake up in the middle of the night and find you in our bed lying in between us."

The memory formed in Isis' brain. Everything Selena said was true. Isis didn't know if she could trust this new family, not after all the bad experiences she had with other foster families. It's not like they went through an agency; they just picked her up off the street. But it wasn't long before she realized they were genuine and caring. They were exactly the kind of family she had yearned for. Well, minus the part about them being witches, of course, but that was the reason they entered her life in the first place.

"You would roll back and forth, wrapping your arms around each of us, resting your head on our shoulders until you fell asleep. That's when we knew you were our child, ours to raise. Ours to protect with our lives. The next morning, you were ready for your lessons, to discover your power and learn to use it."

"Learn to use it," Isis said, but did she say it out loud or in her head? She couldn't tell anymore.

Isis realized that her eyes had completely shut. They had stopped fluttering. Her body no longer shivered. Her mom kept talking but Isis could barely make out the words.

Perhaps this was for the best. Sleep was exactly what her body craved, at least until she turned into a vampire. Then she'd never sleep again. God, she hated the idea of her dad and Zack going face-to-face with Valeria. But this was Dad's plan to save her. Isis trusted they would succeed. They had to. If Valeria killed them, then Isis would lose the two men in her life, and then she would still die a slow and uncomfortable death.

And what if they did succeed? Becoming a vampire was an even scarier thought, but at least she would still be around.

Mom's lips touched Isis' forehead. Her eyes popped open. She was now sitting on the floor of their Vegas penthouse suite. Isis was nine years old again. For some reason, that made sense.

Isis was in the middle of what was the most amazing living room she'd ever seen. They had just moved into the hotel's biggest suite, their new home. It was fancy, like what she thought a king and queen's castle would look like on the inside. It even had an old Roman look to it with circular designs on the walls and long pillars in all four corners.

Isis knelt next to Selena who had an arm over her shoulders. Sebastian sat on the carpeted floor as well across from them with his hand stretched out. A pencil hovered in the air inches above his palm. "Okay, Isis, I want you to focus on the pencil," Sebastian said. "Right now, it's mine. Focus on the energy around the pencil. Make it come to you."

Isis tightened her fists and focused all her attention on the pencil. An aura of colors formed around it. In her mind, she asked the pencil to come to her. The colors around the pencil were bright, like a rainbow. Slowly, it responded to her by moving through the air. She wrapped her fingers around it as a wide smile spread across her face.

"I did it, I did it…" Suddenly, the pencil snapped

in half. "Oh no," Isis cried. The smile left her face.

"That's okay," Sebastian said with a chuckle. "It's going to come. I promise you it will."

Selena gave Isis a huge hug. "You're going to be a powerful witch someday."

Isis wrapped her arms around Selena's waist and hugged her back. "I am going to be a powerful witch someday," she repeated.

At this point, Isis had been with her new family— her new Wiccan family—for four months and a week. She already sensed that they cared, and they loved her so much. If only they knew how at sixteen years old, she was going to die. Or she'd die and be reborn a vampire. Isis still wasn't sure which fate was worse.

Chapter Twenty

Zack and Sebastian followed Valeria for what must have been miles. The vampire kept an amazing stride, paying no mind if her followers could keep up or not. Despite the mugginess that made his clothes stick to his skin, Zack forced his legs to keep pace. Sebastian, from what Zack could see, did the same while periodically checking his watch.

On the way, Zack peeked around, taking in their surroundings. He couldn't be sure if the place consisted of more forest or grassland. There were certainly plenty of those weird-shaped trees—in fact, there were more and more the further they traveled—but the entire ground was carpeted in that long grass for as far as his eyes could see. Amazing that any of this nature could survive in a heat that even rivaled Las Vegas' famous summer temperatures.

This was the moment Zack realized a scary, yet exciting truth—he was walking on an alien planet. Okay, according to the witches' explanation, it was the same planet as Earth, but in an alternate dimension, but to Zack, it still counted as a different planet. He also became one of the first humans to interact with an alien being…even if it was an animal.

A slight grin crossed his face. He just accomplished an impossible trick that no other magician in history could claim. What a shame he couldn't share this experience with any of them. This was the ultimate non-reveal, an oath they all had to take. Still, he would have snapped a few pictures to keep as a personal souvenir if he still had his phone.

A rustle from behind snapped Zack out of his thoughts. He stopped and circled around. There was nothing for miles, just trees and grass. He couldn't shake the feeling they were being followed. But how could that be? Except for a bunch of animals—and the two vampires—they were the only beings on this world. It had to be paranoia…didn't it?

"Zack, come on," Sebastian called. "No time to dawdle."

"I'm coming!" Zack turned and caught up with Sebastian.

"Is everything okay?" Sebastian asked.

"Yeah, I think so." Zack took another look behind them. Once again, he saw nothing. They continued the journey with Valeria several feet ahead. "Sebastian," Zack whispered along the way. "Are we sure this is smart, following Valeria blindly like this?"

"No, not at all," Sebastian answered with nonchalance. "But I have a hunch we will need Luther to convince her."

"Are we even heading to Luther?" Zack's whisper jumped up an octave. "The first thing she told us was that she killed him, then she laughed and said she was joking. That tells me she's still insane. For all we know, she's leading us to her feast and we're the main course."

"I also have impeccable hearing," Valeria stopped in place and shouted. She flashed a narrow-eyed glare at Zack. It made him stop as well. His tongue jumped to the back of his mouth and tried to retreat down his throat. "Rejoice," Valeria said, "for we have arrived."

She waved her hand at a crudely built cabin. There were four walls of tree logs, all of which were stacked and tied together with long, thin layers of sod. The "cabin" had a doorway but no door. There were square cutouts for windows on each side. It even had a roof made with logs just like the walls. One word came to Zack's mind. "Wow!"

"That is impressive," Sebastian said. "How did you build this?"

"I had over three hundred years with no one to talk to and nothing to do." Valeria flashed a prideful grin. "When I was not hunting, I needed a project to keep myself busy. During the day, this is what I worked on. At night, I stalked those mangy mutts for their blood."

"The structure is impressive, Valeria," Sebastian said. "I see your ability to create is as strong as your ability to destroy. Perhaps it is even stronger."

Valeria bellowed, "You flatter me because you need something. Let's find out what." She strolled toward the cabin. "I do believe Luther is home. Let's see if we can shock him back to life with your arrival."

****

The inside of the cabin was bare except for two stacks of logs running across the floor and facing each other. The vampires used the logs as something to sit on, which was evident by Valeria waving to Zack and Sebastian to, "Have a seat." The cabin was nothing but light brown, except for the red bloodstains all over the logs and grass-covered floor. Zack could only guess that the stains were left over from the vampires' feasting on those animals.

Valeria was right about one thing; Luther was more than surprised to see Sebastian and Zack enter the cabin. Of course, she didn't give him the slightest warning before they walked through the doorway. The elder vampire, however, did not need long to regain his composure.

"I did not explicitly tell you to never re-open the portal," Luther said. "But I thought it was implied. Tell me why you are here, Sebastian."

Sebastian opened his mouth to answer. Valeria cut him off. "Clearly, your witches are in some sort of trouble, Luther," she said. "Why else would they venture to this world looking for you?"

"Actually, we're here for *you*," Zack shouted at Valeria.

Her head tilted with confusion.

"We're here because of Isis," Sebastian said. "She's in trouble."

"Why am I not surprised?" Luther rolled his eyes and shook his head. "After Sacha, Isis was my second guess. Tell me what happened."

Once seated—vampires on one set of logs, witch and human on the other—Sebastian explained the reason for their arrival. He laid it all out on the table. As Sebastian spoke, Valeria took Luther's hand. The thought of what these two fossils were doing to occupy time in this parallel dimension made Zack throw up in his mouth.

"So, let me understand what you are asking of me." Valeria's smile disappeared for the first time since their arrival. "You want to return me to our world so that I may complete the girl's turn and save her continued existence. How interesting."

Zack's eyes shifted to Sebastian, then to Valeria. "We didn't come here to bring you back," he quickly responded.

Sebastian waved a hand at Zack. It was a clear message to stay quiet and let him do the talking.

"Valeria." Luther threw her an accusatory glare. "You started the turn but left her incomplete. Why? Was it simply for the sake of torture?"

"Not at all. I truly wanted to take her on as my apprentice, so I began her turn," Valeria explained. "But her defiance forced me to put additional thought into that decision. I did intend to finish what I started, after a valuable lesson on obedience." She pointed a long-tipped fingernail at Sebastian and Zack. "But their interference, and yours, prevented me from completing the process."

"We need to complete it now," Sebastian said. "But Zack is right. We cannot take you back."

Valeria leaned forward, coming eye to eye with Sebastian. "Well then, how do you propose we accomplish this task?"

Sebastian hesitated, but then responded, "Turn me. Once you do, I can finish turning Isis."

"So, you are willing to die and be reborn like us to save your charge." Valeria let out a loud and lingering cackle. "I see you have thought this through."

"How do you know about secondary turns?" Luther raised a hand as he spoke. "I am sure I never taught you this."

"From a friend of yours, Luther," Sebastian said. "A vampire named Simon."

"Simon." Luther's eyebrows arched. "He sought you out?"

"No, we went to him."

"And you found him?" Luther leaned forward after Sebastian nodded. "Simon left the village, or did *you* find *it*?"

"You know about New Salem?" Zack asked.

"I almost forgot its name," Luther replied. "I am the one who sent Simon and his mate there for their own safety. The world can be a dangerous place for a vampire who has difficulties being inconspicuous." His eyebrows rolled. "Which is an accurate depiction of Simon."

"Who is Simon?" Valeria asked. "What village do we speak of?"

"It was after we sent you here the first time," Luther answered. "The coven gathered witches and those accused of witchcraft. We took a ship across the seas, seeking out uninhabited space. The swampland in Swedeland called to the witches. It was well hidden, and I recall they said something about the area being the nexus for the planet's ley lines.

"They cleared land for miles within its center, leaving enough swamp around it for secrecy and protection. Once the work was complete, I was no longer needed, nor did I see it as a life I wanted to live. I waited until they were settled, then I chose to return to America."

"Hold on!" Sebastian shook his head. "You knew about New Salem all this time? You never mentioned it once."

"In my time, I have relocated many witches, and one vampire, to the village." Luther leaned toward Sebastian. "Madeline did not want her daughters raised there nor did she want *you* sent. Believe me when I say she made her wishes abundantly clear. There was never a reason to discuss it with any of you."

Zack stood from the log. He wanted to get everyone's attention, but also, the bark was pressing against his cheeks. "I hate to interrupt your story, but we are on limited time. We need to get back while Isis is still able to be saved."

"He's right." Sebastian stood as well. He took a deep breath, perhaps the last one he expected to ever take. "Let's do this before I change my mind."

"There is but one problem with your plan," Valeria said.

"Which is?"

Valeria now stood. She stepped toward Zack, who quickly moved away. She peered into Sebastian's eyes. "I have not agreed to participate. No, I will not turn you."

"What?" Sebastian gasped. "But why?"

"You did this to her," Zack exclaimed. "You have to make it right—"

But it was too late. Valeria had stormed through the cabin's doorway, never looking back.

Chapter Twenty-one

Zack exited the cabin as Sebastian and Luther spoke. It sounded like Sebastian was pleading their case, which may have been his plan all along. Zack didn't understand why; this wasn't Luther's decision to make. It was Valeria's. Doubtful Luther could convince her even if he tried. The persuasion had to be put directly on her.

He found Valeria leaned against the wall with a long stem of grass hanging out the side of her mouth. Her eyes were pointed at the gray-tinted sky. A sly grin crossed her lips. "Funny," she said. "You were the last of the three men in the cabin I expected to follow me out."

"Can I ask you something?"

"This should be good." Valeria sneered. "Go ahead, ask away."

Zack could tell from the look on Valeria's face that she was waiting to see who would follow her out and offer their best argument just so she could shoot it down. Her rejection of any argument would most likely follow an arrogant scoff. He decided to throw out a different topic.

"How did you escape this world?" It was the one question that lingered in Zack's mind since learning that Valeria had pulled off the ultimate escape trick. "How did you get back to our world?"

Valeria's face grimaced. "That is not the subject I expected you to ask about."

"The magician in me desperately wants to know. You have no connection here yet you opened a portal that brought you back." Zack leaned against the wall next to Valeria. "How did you pull it off?"

Valeria's head pointed up. After a moment, she shrugged her shoulders. "It took quite a while, over three hundred years, but it finally happened," she explained. "A group of four irresponsible teenage witches in Mayong, experimenting with the energy, opened a portal to this world. I stepped through before they could close it."

"Mayong. That's in India, right?"

Valeria nodded. "You know your geography. I am mildly impressed."

"Are any of those witches still alive?" Zack asked, blowing off Valeria's condescending remark.

"They needed to learn a lesson on abusing the gift Mother Earth has bestowed on us, but they were not my enemies," Valeria replied. "The witches were still alive when last I saw them."

"You really didn't kill them?"

Valeria chuckled. "I am not the monster you think of me."

"I hope that's true because Isis is suffering," Zack said. "She's losing her fight to live."

"I'm sure she is." Her eyes glanced back to the sky. "Frankly, I'm surprised she has lasted this long. Her connection is strong, indeed."

Zack's foot shook inside his sneaker as he took a step towards Valeria. "She won't survive much longer. You have to do this."

"Do I?" Valeria removed the stem from her mouth and balanced it on her forefinger. "What incentive do I have to cooperate?"

"Because it's the right thing to do?"

Valeria's slanted eyes sent a clear message to Zack. It let him know that appealing to her better nature would not work. She wanted something in return and Zack knew exactly what. "You want a trip back to Earth in exchange for saving Isis' life."

"That is exactly what I long for," Valeria answered. "I am sure Sebastian will never agree to those terms."

"You're right. He can't and he won't."

"Then my answer to him, and to you, remains the same." Valeria crushed the stem in her hand and let it fall to the ground. "He will have to watch his young charge die."

A deep voice grabbed both their attention. "And what if I ask this of you?"

Zack and Valeria were no longer alone. They had been joined by Luther with Sebastian walking through the doorway behind him.

"This is my family, and they are in peril," Luther said. "Therefore, I would like you to do as they ask. For me."

Valeria scoffed. "Never forget, Luther, that *you* are the one who dragged me through that portal and stranded me here. It is *you* who prevented me from fulfilling my destiny. In fact, you have done so twice."

"On the contrary," Luther replied. "I helped you achieve it."

Valeria's face scrunched. "In what way?"

"Look around you, Valeria." Luther motioned at

their surroundings. "Your goal was to be the center of a world at peace. You will never have that on Earth, but it is exactly what we have here, with all of eternity to enjoy it together."

Luther took her hand. "All you need to do is tie up one loose end from the world we left behind. Be a hero to them, and then we can live in eternal bliss."

"Your sentiments touch me, Luther," Valeria responded. "I will consider it."

"We don't have the time for you to consider it." Sebastian stepped between the two vampires and stood face-to-face with Valeria. "But if what you have to gain by helping us doesn't convince you, then let's talk about what you have to lose if you don't."

Valeria snorted. Her shoulders rose. "I am stranded here. What more could you possibly take from me?"

"The sisters are opening that portal in…" Sebastian peeked at his watch, "eighty-three minutes. If I am not returning as a vampire created by you, then I will drag Luther through that portal with me and leave you behind. You will be alone. Again."

Valeria studied Sebastian with a careful eye. After several moments, she snarled. "You do not have the horns or the tail to pull such a ploy."

"Ordinarily, you'd be right. But my kid is suffering. Her life is on the line because of *you*." Sebastian poked Valeria in the chest to emphasize his point. "If Isis has to die, you stay here in isolation for all of eternity."

The two locked eyes, refusing to blink. Zack had seen Sebastian during intense negotiations with the hotel manager, negotiations he almost always won thanks to his confident stare. After a year in his presence, Zack was sure he could tell when Sebastian was bluffing. But could Valeria?

"What say you, Luther?" Valeria never removed her eyes from Sebastian's. "Will you truly leave me here in isolation if I do not agree to their demand?"

"I am fond of our life here, Valeria," Luther replied. "But they are my family. Please do not ask me to choose between them and you."

"Those are our terms," Sebastian said. "What do you say?"

Valeria's eyes shifted over Sebastian's shoulder. Her eyebrows touched. "I say we have another visitor."

Zack peeked behind him. Luther and Sebastian did the same. One of the animals stood several feet from the cabin with an intense look on its face. Its eyes were pointed at the group.

"Has it been listening to us the entire time?" Zack asked.

Another animal stepped from the trees and stood behind the first. Two more came out. They stood next to the second animal. Soon, dozens scurried out from all sides of the cabin.

"What are they doing?" Sebastian asked.

"Their motivation is clear," Valeria answered. "When you returned me here, this time with Luther, they found the predatory threat to their species doubled in number. They were murdered at twice the rate. Now, it would seem they believe their threat has doubled once again. They are going on the offensive."

"Sebastian and I are not a threat to them," Zack exclaimed. "We don't drink blood."

"Clearly, *they* are not aware of that," Valeria said.

More of the animals came out from behind the

trees, enough that a circle had formed around the entire cabin. The leader remained within the circle. Its attention stayed on the four of them.

"What are they going to do?" Zack felt his heart pounding through his chest. His nerves had jumped into overdrive. "Are they going to eat us?"

"From what I've seen, they have never eaten meat. Their palate consists of this planet's grass," Valeria answered. "Regardless, my best guess is that they will rip us to shreds and leave us for dead."

"Everyone, get back inside the cabin!" Luther commanded.

"Will that protect us?" Zack asked.

"Hardly," Valeria answered.

More of the animals filled the circle. Without another option, the four scurried through the doorway.

Chapter Twenty-two

"What the hell do we do?" Zack shouted as he stared out the cabin's back window.

The animals marched, single file, leaving a good amount of space between the cabin and the circle they had created. There were at least fifty of them moving around the cabin and leaving no path for escape. The leader hadn't moved an inch. It stared a hole through the cabin as the horde passed behind it.

"Seventy minutes," Sebastian growled. "We don't have time for this."

Luther twisted away from the side window and faced the group. "We may have only one option," he said. "We will need to take the fight to them. These beasts are in no rush. They could wait outside this cabin for days. Since we do not have that luxury, I suggest we make our move before they make theirs."

"What are the chances we'd get past *all* of them?" Zack asked.

"None," Valeria snapped. "There is no chance we would get past this many working in tandem."

"I don't understand. They're animals, aren't they?" Zack cried out. "They're acting like an army."

"Yes, an army with a single-minded focus." Valeria walked up to Zack. "Eliminate the threat to their species. Save themselves from extinction."

As Valeria peered down at him, Zack found his

back pressed against the wall. If the vampire was trying to assert dominance by intimidating him, it worked all too well.

"There is no other option. We will need to fight our way past them." Luther cupped his fingers together and cracked his knuckles. "Valeria and I will take point. The two of you follow from a distance."

"That tactic will not get us far," Valeria replied.

"Wait, you're saying our only option is to go through them?" Zack asked. "Is there a way we can go over their barrier?"

"Valeria and I could leap over them," Luther answered. "You and Sebastian cannot."

"We are not here for a needless battle." Sebastian stared out the doorway. "Valeria, you said they're doing this because they think Zack and I are as much of a threat as the two of you. We need to let them know that's not the case."

"Is that all?" Valeria snorted. "How do you propose delivering the message? Do you plan to go out there and explain it to them?"

Sebastian spun his head to Valeria, then back to the doorway. "Yes, that's exactly what I'm going to do. I will speak with their leader."

"Sebastian, there is no one for you to converse with out there." Luther clutched his arm. "These are simple-minded creatures."

"I don't think so," Sebastian replied. "They are working together against a perceived threat." Sebastian peeked out the window. "The first of these creatures that met us was confused. It knew something was different about us. Right now, they're using a well-thought-out strategy that does not strike me as instinctual. They also clearly have a chain of command. I suspect their minds have evolved enough that they are capable of reasoning. Anyone with a reasonable mind can be persuaded. Persuasion is my Wiccan strength."

"Sebastian, you don't have your connection here," Luther said.

"No, but I've been using that connection to influence audiences of thousands for a long time. Perhaps some of that over the years has enhanced my natural skills."

"That's a really huge perhaps," Zack exclaimed.

"When in packs, they do all follow the leaders," Valeria said. "If it backs away, the rest will as well. But if it chooses to rip you into shreds, they will be on top of us before we know it."

"It's a risk, but we don't have the time or the resources for a war we can't win." Sebastian stepped through the doorway. "We also don't have any other options, not when they have us hopelessly outnumbered. This is our best plan of action."

Zack held his breath as Sebastian began his slow stroll to the lead animal. It stared him down with wide eyes and mouth hanging open. The animal's sharp teeth showed. Sebastian stopped his motion. He looked the animal in the eyes, then dropped to his knees.

"I see why you are impressed by that one," Valeria said to Luther. There was a veiled smirk in her tone.

The leader tilted its head at Sebastian's actions. It snarled, then walked to him. Whatever happened now would determine their fates. Peace or war. To think Zack and the witches all believed Valeria would be the biggest threat here in the Other World.

The circle of creatures stopped their movement as

if an unspoken command had been sent. The leader sniffed Sebastian's face, then the rest of his body. Sebastian dropped his head then slowly brought his left hand in front of his chest with his palms facing out.

"Be careful," Zack whispered to no one in particular.

The leader roared. It echoed all throughout the area. It was followed by several roars at random from around the cabin. Sebastian brought his open right hand under the animal's snout. He had a heap of grass on his palm. The creature slurped it off Sebastian's palm through its nose.

Sebastian's mouth was moving, but from the distance, Zack couldn't make out any words. Sebastian spoke in a low and slow pace. Zack was sure the creature couldn't understand either, but its head tilted even more.

"I don't believe it. He's actually doing it."

Zack glanced back to Luther who stood behind him, observing Sebastian and his new friend with an intense eye. He then scanned the entire cabin. It was empty. "Where's Valeria?" Zack gasped.

Luther's head shifted from left to right. His eyes and mouth opened wide. "Oh no," he moaned.

The beast sniffed Sebastian's stretched hand. The plan was working. A trust was being formed between two species from different worlds. The circle of animals focused on the interaction. So did Zack and Luther. Not a single sound issued from the pack. For the first time, Zack believed that Sebastian's plan could work...but where the hell was Valeria?

The cabin's wall shuddered. Zack's head lifted. Valeria stood on the roof's edge. Her eyes were pitch black. She squatted, then smiled. "Valeria, please, don't!" Zack shrieked. But it was too late.

With a scream, she leaped high in the air like an Olympic star. Her body sailed, clearing an amazing distance. She landed with her knees across the small of Sebastian's new friend's back.

The animal screeched as its stomach slammed into the ground. Sebastian fell over. "What are you doing?" he shrieked.

Valeria swung her body around. She wrapped her hands around the animal's neck and yanked. Zack cringed at the sound of the loud snap. "My God, why did she—"

"Wait!" Luther pointed. "Look."

Valeria stood and raised the lifeless corpse high up by its throat. She let out a loud growl that put the animals' roars to shame. All at once, the beasts scurried in different directions. The rumble of so many animals frantically running at once shook the ground so hard Zack had to brace his feet.

"Why?" Sebastian shouted from all fours. "I had this. There was no reason!"

"The plan worked." Valeria tossed the dead animal aside. "Without their leader, the animals lost their direction. They have left to regroup. We now have time."

"That was not the plan!" Sebastian climbed to his feet. He marched up to Valeria. "You didn't need to jump in. You certainly did not need to kill this creature!"

"Relax, my dear." Valeria slapped her hand against Sebastian's arm. "The battle is over. We were victorious. You showed amazing bravery, Sebastian. It made for an excellent distraction. Now, I am ready to grant your request."

"You are?" Sebastian asked. Zack was sure he could still see steam pouring out of his ears.

"That, I am." Valeria locked her fingers and cracked her knuckles. "Come, let's make you a vampire."

Chapter Twenty-three

"Are you sure you want to do this?" Luther asked. "Once you are turned, you will be exactly like us. There is no going back."

Zack eyed Sebastian who faced him and the two vampires. The threat was over. They were alone, except for the carcass several feet away. That meant it was time. Sebastian nodded. His jaw trembled ever so slightly. He fully understood what he was sacrificing, and what that sacrifice would cost him. Immortality would never make up for it.

"I understand." Sebastian breathed deep, cupped his hands together, then stepped forward. "Okay, so how does this work?"

"First," Valeria answered, "I will make you my own. My blood must flow through your body, changing all that you are."

"Like what you did to Isis," Sebastian snarled.

"Exactly." Her huge grin offered no apologies. "I believe I shall go through your neck. I will then immediately kill you."

"During this process," Luther added, "she will cut off your air supply until your heart stops. At that point, you will, for all intents and purposes, be dead. Before your brain functions can cease, her blood inside you will take over your functions. Then, Valeria will breathe her essence into you, which will make you self-aware."

"You breathe through his mouth," Zack said, remembering Simon's explanation. Simon also explained that it was the plasma in the blood, not the blood itself that made the transformation, but this didn't seem like the right time or audience to argue semantics.

"The boy is correct." Valeria's eyes stayed on Sebastian. "When you wake up, you will no longer be alive, but you will still exist."

"Is that it?" Zack raised his eyebrows as he looked back from Luther to Valeria. "That's all there is to it?"

"My immortality connecting with his, changing his physiology, and reanimating his corpse is hardly a case of 'that's all there is to it'," Valeria hissed.

"Sebastian, listen carefully," Luther said in a calm tone, like a parent speaking to his child. "When you wake up, be prepared. You will feel different, you will be different—"

"I get it, Luther." Sebastian sucked in a deep breath. "And I'm ready."

"Wait." Zack gripped Sebastian's wrist. "I need to speak with you first."

"Zack, there's no time and nothing to discuss."

"Please. This is important. It can't wait until after—we need to talk first."

"Go ahead," Valeria said. "The process can be exhausting. I will need a few moments to prepare."

Sebastian checked his watch, then sighed. "All right, Zack, out with it."

"In private." Zack yanked Sebastian's wrist. "Come with me. Please."

While keeping a tight grip on Sebastian's wrist, Zack led him into the forest of trees that surrounded the cabin's grounds. Sebastian tried to yank his wrist free, but Zack wouldn't release his grip. Once Zack was satisfied they were far enough away, he turned Sebastian around so they'd face one another. Zack purposely sandwiched his confused "coven leader" between himself and one of the trees.

"Let me save you some time, Zack," Sebastian said. "You are not talking me out of this. I am doing what I must to save my daughter, your girlfriend. This is the reason we came here in the first place."

Zack leaned in so his nose almost touched Sebastian's chin. "You know Isis won't be the same. But she can adapt. What about you?"

"I'll do what I must, as I've always done for those in my coven." Sebastian pulled back his head. "We should return—"

Zack wrapped his arms around Sebastian's waist. He pressed his forehead against Sebastian's chest. The surprise forced him back against the tree. It was exactly what Zack wanted to happen.

"Hey, it's going to be okay," Sebastian whispered to him. "I'm going to be just fine, and so will Isis."

"I know you both will."

Zack released his grip and backed away. Sebastian's head swung to his left wrist and the metal shackle around it. Sebastian tried to pull his arm forward, but the other end of the cuffs was wrapped around the tree's thin but strong branch. It was the first time Zack used an emotional embrace as a sleight of hand distraction. He also purposely cut the circulation off around Sebastian's wrist. It kept Sebastian from feeling the cuff slip around his wrist.

"Zack, what do you think you're doing?"

Sebastian's eyes dropped to Zack's fanny pack with the zipper wide open.

Without a response, Zack ran through the forest and back to the cabin.

"Zack Galloway, get back here and free me!" Sebastian's shouts were panic filled. "*ZACK!*"

Zack returned to the cabin's grounds. From the suspicious glances, it was clear the vampires suspected something was amiss. Luther stepped forward which stopped Zack in his tracks. "Where is Sebastian?" he asked, although it sounded more like a demand.

"Um, there's been a change of plans."

"Meaning *what*?"

Zack tossed the handcuff key at Luther, who caught it in mid-air. It's not like the key was necessary to free Sebastian—the cuffs had a latch that unlocked them. It was an easy escape, so long as the captive knew where it was located. Luckily, Sebastian didn't. He never paid much attention when Zack discussed the secrets of his magic.

Luther ran to the forest. Zack, meanwhile, approached Valeria. "I would like you to turn me, instead of Sebastian." He peeked over his shoulder. "And if you could do it before they get back, that would be great."

"Well, aren't you the brave boy," Valeria replied. "Making the ultimate sacrifice for the sake of your sweetheart and her coven."

"Let's do this, now," Zack snapped. "Um, please?"

Valeria shrugged. "By all means. Better you than allowing that annoying witch to live forever."

Zack's throat went dry. He realized that when he tried to swallow. His saliva burned the entire way down. No changing his mind now, right? Well, technically, he could, but he wouldn't. This was his plan all along, from the moment he ran through the portal. It had to be him, not Sebastian.

Valeria stared Zack down for several moments. He wasn't sure if she was assessing him or simply trying to intimidate him. If it were the latter, he wouldn't show it. Zack kept his back straight and looked her right in her purple irises.

After several tense moments, Valeria opened her mouth showing two long fangs. She ran her knuckles across those two sharp teeth, cutting the skin. Valeria pointed her hand downward. Dark red goo—her four-hundred-year-old blood—dripped along her fingers until it covered her claw-like fingernails. Zack wanted to gag, but he'd rather not embarrass himself in front of the undead vampire.

His body tensed. "So, should I hold my breath or something?"

Valeria grinned. "No, just stand still."

"All right, then wha—"

Valeria lunged forward. Her hand clutched Zack's throat like a metal vise. His neck stung from the skin getting pierced on opposite sides by Valeria's fingernails. By instinct, he tried to suck in a mouthful of air, but couldn't. It was like being under water without a surface to swim for. Zack's arms flailed. It took every ounce of concentration to keep them from grabbing Valeria's wrist. He wanted to struggle for his life, but his brain reminded him not to try. This was what needed to happen. Yes, Zack was about to die, but not for long.

His arms and legs went numb, meaning struggle

was no longer an option. The pressure he felt in his throat engulfed his entire face. His vision faded to the point he could barely make out the image of Valeria in front of him. His hearing still worked. Her loud cackling confirmed that. It hit him at that moment, the last breath of air he took was his last. Even without feeling in his body, his brain yelled at him to fight, to stay alive. He blocked out those thoughts by focusing on Isis. He couldn't lose her and this was the only way...

Everything went dark. Including the sound of Valeria's laugh.

Chapter Twenty-four

Zack opened his eyes to see gray sky staring down at him. At first, the color confused him. Had he gone color blind? Where was the blue? Then, through the grogginess, he remembered where he was. The Other World. Man, he felt as if he had been asleep for days. He tried to take a breath. Nothing happened. Not a drop of air sucked through his mouth. It was like being under water except he wasn't drowning.

"What…what's going on?" Zack placed a hand against his chest. He couldn't feel a heartbeat. In fact, there was no movement in his chest at all. How was this even possible? Oh, right, vampire.

"How…how long have I been out?" he asked.

A deep male voice responded, "You were unconscious for approximately twelve minutes after resurrection." It was Luther's voice.

Zack sat up. The odor from the grass was stronger than before. It was a combination of wood and garlic. The stench made his nose itch. "Yuck," he mumbled to himself.

"Drink," Luther said.

Zack rubbed his eyes. His vision cleared. Luther kneeled in front of him, hands out. He held them under Zack's chin. A thick red liquid filled his cupped hands.

"What is that?" Zack's voice echoed in his head. Was that something he'd need to get used to? Forever?

Valeria, who stood behind Luther, answered. "That is blood." Her face had red stains around her lips.

"Right now, your body is weak after enduring the process," Luther said. "Fresh blood regenerates you."

Zack wanted to ask where the stuff came from until he remembered the dead animal laid out a few feet away. Don't think about it, he told himself. Just don't.

"Drink," Luther repeated.

Zack sipped the pool of blood from Luther's hands. It tasted like a thick syrup but without the sugar, flavoring, and everything that made syrup taste delicious. He expected it to be too vile to swallow, but it actually didn't taste like anything at all. "Finish it," Luther demanded. Zack complied.

"You will need to add new blood into your system every twenty-four hours without fail," Luther explained. "To wait will leave you weak and lethargic. Eventually, your body and brain will stop functioning. Once that happens—"

"I know. Gone."

"Yes." Luther swatted the remaining blood from his hand. He stood and offered the same hand for Zack to take. "Isis will need the same once you turn her. Do you understand the process?"

"I believe I do." Zack wiped the blood from his mouth with the back of his forearm.

Zack took Luther's hand and was yanked to his feet. At first, his body wobbled. It took a moment to gain his equilibrium. He held his hand in front of his face. Unlike Luther and Valeria, Zack's fingernails weren't long enough to puncture anything, let alone skin.

But he wouldn't have to puncture Isis' skin.

Valeria's plasma was already flowing through her bloodstream, just like in his own. That meant step one of the process was already done. Now, he just needed to kill, then revive her. Zack didn't like the thought of murdering his girlfriend, but ironically, it was the only way to save her life.

"My skin," Zack said while staring at his hand. "Wasn't it supposed to turn pale white like yours?" Ugh, did Luther and Valeria's voices echo in their heads all the time? Did Simon's?

"That will come as your skin ages," Valeria answered. "Give it another two hundred years or so."

Zack rolled his tongue along his upper jaw. Then he felt his mouth with his fingers. "Where are my fangs?" He looked up at the two vampires. "Shouldn't I have fangs?"

"Those, too, will grow," Luther said. "Be patient, the time will pass quickly."

Valeria chuckled. "Right now, you are a baby vampire."

To Zack's left, a pair of narrowed eyes glared back at him. They belonged to Sebastian. So far, not a word had come from his mouth. That was always a sign he was pissed. "Sebastian, I'm sorry—"

"It's done." Sebastian dropped his head and rubbed his temples. "Let's just make sure this wasn't for nothing, okay?"

"Okay," Zack answered.

Sebastian breathed deep. His back straightened. "We have twenty minutes to get back to where we started before the portal reopens. It took us over twenty to get here. We have to move fast."

"I'm ready," Zack responded.

"Then allow me to show you the way," Valeria said.

****

This time, Zack had no problem keeping pace with Valeria and Luther. He never found himself out of breath as he never once needed to inhale air. That was because, technically, he was dead…well, undead. There were advantages to it, but there had to be disadvantages as well. He'd find those out soon enough. Lucky Zack would never need to sleep again because the thought of that would keep him awake every single night.

Of the four, the only one huffing and puffing the entire way was Sebastian. To his credit, he kept up with the three vampires like a man possessed. In a way he was possessed in his single-minded focus on saving Isis. Zack and Sebastian hadn't exchanged too many words on the trip back. That wasn't a good sign. Zack stopped in his tracks to let Sebastian catch up to him. Might as well get the confrontation out in the open.

"Are you angry?" Zack asked.

"No, Zack, I'm not angry," Sebastian said after a deep breath.

"Okay, because you seem angry."

Sebastian's walk slowed. Zack also slowed down to match Sebastian's pace. "Answer one question for me," Sebastian said. "Was that your plan all along? When you jumped through the portal to 'watch my back,' was it always with the intention of taking my place and having her turn you?"

"Yes," Zack answered. "It was the only way I could think of to save Isis and keep this family together."

"As the leader of our coven, those tasks were both

my responsibility," Sebastian replied.

"You would have saved Isis," Zack said. "But it would have ended up destroying your coven."

Sebastian stopped in his tracks. Zack did the same. "Meaning what?"

"Selena needs you," Zack said into Sebastian's light-blue eyes. "She needs you at her side so you can grow old with her. You promised you would be there for her."

"That promise wouldn't have changed. I'd still be by her side—"

"As a vampire, you couldn't keep your promise to Selena." Zack had never interrupted Sebastian before. He never needed to. "You'd be an undead immortal while she ages until her natural death. Your relationship wouldn't have survived."

"Is that why you did it, Zack?" Sebastian's said with an accusatory glance. "So *your* relationship could survive?"

"I did it for all of us, Sebastian, for your family and our coven. For all of us to move forward, it couldn't be you making this sacrifice."

"It wouldn't have been easy." Sebastian's tone calmed. "But I believe this coven can survive anything. We would have figured it out."

"You're wrong. Selena needs you to be her husband just as much as Isis needs you to be her father. They need you alive. So does Sacha." Zack held his hands out and grinned. "If we get back in time, you've kept your promise to everyone."

"And what about the promise we made to your uncle?" Sebastian hollered. "We told him we'd take care of you and keep you safe. Instead, all we did was get you killed!"

Zack's head dropped. "I'll...I'll be okay."

Luther shouted at them. "I thought the two of you were in a hurry to return!"

Luther and Valeria were looking back at them from several feet ahead. Luther waved them along. "Sorry," Zack shouted.

"This conversation is not over," Sebastian whispered. He and Zack resumed their pace.

Finally, after several silent minutes, Valeria stopped mid-step. "We are here."

Zack's eyes flashed in all directions at all the same brown trees and gray grass they had seen throughout the entire journey. "How can you tell?" he asked.

"She's right," Sebastian said between deep breaths. "This is the spot." He motioned to the ground where Simon's wooden spear rested a few feet away from the animal it was used to murder.

"That, and the long cliff not far away." Valeria pointed to the east. The grass-filled ground came to an end several feet ahead. After getting attacked by those animals, then confronted by Valeria, Zack hadn't even noticed the cliff.

"We are just in time." Luther pointed to sparks forming ten feet in front of them.

The sparks grew into a circle of static large enough to step through. Sebastian motioned Zack to walk forward. Zack complied.

"Despite the circumstances, it was good to see you." Luther patted Sebastian's back. "Save the girl. Then, give her and the sisters my best wishes. May the rest of your lives bring you joy."

"Thank you, for everything." Sebastian looked up

at Luther, then to Valeria. "I wish you both the same here."

Zack studied the portal. He could still see the forest on the other side, although it was blurry through the static. He glanced back where Valeria's eyes were wide. "I can feel it," she mumbled. Her eyes went dark, as if the proximity of the portal to home triggered something inside of her. Zack thought his heart skipped an anxious beat, but that couldn't have been the case.

"Sebastian, we have to go!" Zack shouted. "Now!"

Luther nodded Sebastian's way, then stepped back. Sebastian moved toward the portal.

"Mother Earth's energy." This time, Valeria's words were clear. "It connects to me even through the rift." Her black eyes focused on the portal. Two sharp fangs protruded from under her top lip.

"Valeria." Concern crossed Luther's face. "We should leave them." He sounded anxious. "Will you join me on another hunt?"

From the corner of his eye, Zack caught the spear vibrating against the ground. "Sebastian!" he gasped.

The spear levitated upward, then flew through the air as if it had been fired from a cannon. Sebastian spun from the portal. The wood spear shot through Luther's back and straight out his chest. Luther's eyes rolled to the back of his head and he fell over. Zack stood frozen in shock.

"Luther!" Sebastian screamed.

"The energy is once again *MINE*!" Valeria threw her arms forward. A wind engulfed Zack and Sebastian, yanking them through the portal. Zack hit the ground hard, face first, as did Sebastian. The two rolled along familiar green grass.

"Selena, close the portal!" Sebastian lifted his head and shouted. "Close it now!"

"What the hell?" Sacha screeched, her hand gripped around Selena's.

Valeria stepped through the circle of blur. "Oh my God!" Selena gasped.

"Selena, let's get her the hell back in there," Sacha shouted. "Now!"

The sisters pointed fingers at Valeria. Whatever they wanted to do, Valeria didn't give them the chance. "*Separatum!*" she chanted and threw out her hands. Selena and Sacha lifted in the air, then flew in opposite directions.

From all fours, Zack felt helpless, completely unsure of what to do. Those feelings mirrored the open-mouthed expression on Simon's face. With the two sisters separated, the portal evaporated into a series of sparks, and then it was gone completely. Valeria eyed Tia, who was frozen in place just a few feet away from the immortal witch.

"What do you want here?" Tia straightened her back and threw her hands on her hips.

"Natasha! Get the president away!" Paul shouted in mid-run. He whipped out his pistol.

Natasha wrapped her arms around Tia. They faded away. Paul fired three bullets. One hit Valeria in the shoulder, the other two in her chest. All the bullets did was turn the Wiccan-vampire's attention his way.

"Paul, she's a vampire. Bullets won't work," Simon shouted.

"*En aire!*" Valeria raised an arm.

The gun flew out of Paul's hand. He was pulled off his feet. He dangled inches off the ground. It was as if an invisible hand hung him by his ponytail.

"Pesky human mortal," Valeria roared. Her black eyes and fangs showed.

"Force blast!" Selena charged and threw her hands forward.

Valeria fell onto her face as if hit from behind by a truck. She rolled across the grass, ending up in a seated position. Paul fell from the air. He landed on his feet.

"I am not ready for this battle. Not yet," Valeria said.

Sacha ran to her sister's side. "She's disoriented. We have to finish her off!" She grabbed Selena's hand just as Valeria disappeared. "She's gone!" Sacha gasped, looking back and forth from Selena to Sebastian and Zack. "I don't understand. The two of you flew through the portal. What happened over there?"

"Valeria felt the power from the other side of the rift," Zack said. He and Simon helped Sebastian to his feet. "She hitched our ride."

"I take it that was Valeria?" Paul asked. "She *is* powerful."

"What about Luther?" Selena screamed.

"She killed him." Sebastian's voice croaked. "She impaled him with Simon's spear."

The answer made Simon shriek. "She killed him with *my* spear?" Zack replied with a nod.

"Zack, go!" Sebastian said to him. "We went through this for a reason. Go save Isis."

Zack gave Sebastian a quick thumb up, then ran for the medical center. Simon followed.

Chapter Twenty-five

Isis woke up to find two hands wrapped together, pushing on her sternum. At first she thought she was dreaming, but her head didn't pound in her dreams. The pressure against the center of her breastbone, and the pain she felt in the ribs forced Isis to cough—it sounded like a dry heave. Once the pushing stopped, Isis opened her eyes to find Doctor Mac hunched over and staring down at her.

"Welcome back." His voice was kind, but it sounded like it came from a bad phone connection. The machines humming in the room sounded as far away as the doctor's voice. It had to be because of the cloud that covered Isis' brain. "How are you feeling?" he asked.

"N-nauseous." Isis wanted to grab at the pain in her stomach. Her arms wouldn't move. Neither would any of the muscles in her body. "Wha' happened?"

"You stopped breathing," Mac answered. "I had to resuscitate you."

"You...you woke me." Isis' eyelids closed. "Another seizure, everyone...in trouble..."

"I realize that." Mac clutched her wrist with one finger and thumb. "But keeping my patient alive is always my priority. Now that you're breathing normally again, all things considered...you know what has to happen."

"I know, back to sleep." She would have protested,

but maybe sleep was best. No headache when asleep—

Frantic footsteps ran into the room. "Doctor Mac, he's here," Simon's high-pitched voice announced. "We can proceed."

Isis let out a sob. Simon's words meant Zack and her dad were back and the mission was a success. If she had the energy, she would have protested their plan, or even used her powers to stop them from going in the first place. Isis wasn't worried about being turned, especially if it was the only way to save her. But the idea that Dad had to become a vampire in order to turn her into one…it wasn't fair. Not to Mom and not to their family. Certainly not to Dad.

"So I see," Mac responded. "Are you all right?"

"Yeah, and I'm ready to complete the turn." Isis heard the answer, but it wasn't Dad's voice as she expected. It was Zack's. She knew Zack went with him to the Other World, but to watch Dad's back, not to be the one that was turned. What happened over there?

Isis forced her eyelids open. Energy around the room blinked, then evaporated. The steady humming ceased. Isis hadn't even noticed the hum until it just stopped.

"What did you do?" Simon asked.

"I shut down the crystals," Mac answered. "I was using them to enhance Isis' natural connection so she could fight off the vampire virus. Now, you don't want her to fight it off. Work quickly. Without the crystals, she won't last long."

"Then I guess it's time." Zack approached the examining table. "I know what to do after she's…gone. But how should I go about, well—"

"Try this," Mac said.

Through sheer force of will, Isis tilted her head enough to see Doctor Mac hand Zack a huge syringe. It was filled halfway with a silvery-white liquid. Zack held it in front of his face and stared intently at it. "What is this?" he asked. Isis wondered the same thing.

"It's a concentrated dose of potassium and carbon monoxide." Mac placed a finger in the center of Isis' chest. "Stick the needle here as far as it will go and empty the contents. It will stop her heart without affecting her brain function. After the syringe is empty, remove it from her chest, wait sixty seconds, then do your thing."

Zack's eyes widened. "You're not going to inject her?"

"No, I will not." Mac stepped away from the examining table and moved to the door. "I'll give you some privacy for the procedure."

"Doctor Mac, could you bring us two full cups from my emergency supply?" Simon asked. "They will both need it once the process is complete."

"Understood."

The sound of Doctor Mac's shoes squeaking along the tile floor faded through the doorway. It was time for Isis to die. While everyone kept saying it was necessary, no one asked if she wanted to live as a vampire, or if she wanted someone else to make that sacrifice for her. Guess it was inevitable now. The guilt gnawed at her when she thought it was Dad coming back as a vampire. But Zack? She couldn't even process that yet.

"You said you know what to do," Simon said from the opposite side of the examining table. "Are you sure you have been educated in all the steps involved in a turn?"

"Luther described the process to me before Valeria stabbed him through the chest." Zack's voice was different. He spoke slower and without his usual excitement. He sounded reluctant, which made sense. It wasn't an easy thing he had to do, killing his girlfriend and all. Plus, Zack did just go through a rather intense lifestyle change. He could have still been recovering... Wait, did he just say Luther was killed?

"I appreciate your experience in case something goes wrong," Zack said.

"I'm here for you, Zack," Simon assured him. "But I don't really have any actual hands-on experience to offer. I've never turned anyone."

"Never?" Zack's jaw dropped as he stared across the table. "In all this time?"

"I lived in a small apartment in Manhattan. Then, I came here, to this village. Who was I turning?"

"Great." Isis heard Zack's eyes roll.

Zack stared at her over the medical table. Their eyes locked. Isis was used to seeing such bright green eyes that were upbeat and caring. Now they seemed distant and almost empty. They reminded her of Luther's eyes. His lips had a slight tint of purple. Seeing Zack's face like this caused a small lump to form in her throat. This wasn't what she wanted for him.

"Zack?" Isis mumbled. "Are you...?"

"I'm sorry." His eyes went wide. He looked like he wanted to cry except he couldn't. "I'm so sorry for having to do this."

Zack held the syringe with the needle pointed down. After a moment's hesitation, he jammed it into her chest. Isis felt the syringe's contents shoot into her. A cold chill went through her entire body. Zack closed his eyes and counted from one.

So far Isis didn't feel any different, but that would soon change. Her heart would stop long before Zack stopped counting. Isis always saw herself as a survivor no matter what life threw at her. That especially became the case once realizing she was a witch. This time, there was no stopping the inevitable. She had no fight left in her.

Isis let her eyes close. There was no dream waiting for her. Just darkness.

Chapter Twenty-Six

The deed was done. Even though Zack's heart no longer worked, he still felt it break when the monitor next to Isis stopped beeping and gave off a flat tone. She was gone. He had killed her, as he meant to do. Then, he let out a deep exhale—even though he didn't need to inhale prior—and blew into Isis' mouth. He couldn't feel air leaving his mouth, but he followed Luther's instructions to the letter.

After another exhale into her mouth, Isis' eyes popped open. Zack called her name. She didn't respond.

According to both Simon and Doctor Mac, she needed time to heal. Her body had been through a lot, draining much of her energy fighting the vampire virus for the last twelve months. Where it took Zack about fifteen minutes to become self-aware as a vampire Isis would need a lot more time. Mac had to give her the blood intravenously through her right arm.

Zack exited the examining room, then out the door of the medical center. He cupped his hand over his eyes like a visor. The sun blinded him more than it ever had before. Was that the first side effect of being a vampire? He took another look at the medical center's door before willing his feet to walk forward. Leaving Isis' side was the last thing he wanted to do, but Doctor Mac insisted he leave and give the patient time to rest and recover. Zack reluctantly deferred to the doctor's orders.

He joined The Witches of Vegas in the middle of the quad. They were deep in conversation when they caught his approach. He made eye contact and nodded to let them know the turn was successful. Zack expected some sort of jubilation, or, at the very least, sighs of relief. But the stressed-out facial expressions barely changed. Zack knew why.

Selena was the first to approach him. She wrapped her arms around his neck and offered a passionate hug. "Thank you," she whispered in his ear. "For saving them both."

Zack noticed they were alone in the quad. Normally, there were dozens of villagers on all sides watching every move they made. "Where is everyone?"

"They're holding a town hall meeting," Sebastian answered. "It's a vote on whether or not the people of New Salem—specifically their witches—want to help us when Valeria returns."

"It seems all these people do around here is have town hall meetings," Sacha mumbled.

Zack threw his arms in the air. "I don't understand. Why would they not help us?"

"It's not their fight, it's ours," Sebastian responded. "We are the ones who released her. It's our mess to clean up."

Zack wanted to object, point out that Valeria was a threat to the entire world, including New Salem. But Sebastian was right, as usual. "I still can't believe we let this happen. If we just left her behind and let Luther show us the way to the portal, she wouldn't have been there, she wouldn't have connected."

"I'm sure that was her plan all along," Sebastian said through clenched teeth. "Valeria played us. She did what we wanted in order to gain our trust. I'd bet anything Valeria knew she'd be able to connect with the Earth's energy through the rift."

"I agree." Selena gripped Sebastian's hand. "You were both focused on returning and saving Isis. Valeria took advantage. It was a smart ploy on her part."

Zack appreciated both of their sentiments, but he still kicked himself. As a magician, he should have seen through Valeria's set-up. It wasn't a smart ploy, as Selena said, it was an obvious one. But the idea that Valeria would regain her Wiccan power just by being near the portal never even dawned on him. And it should have. He felt really stupid right now.

"Heads up, everyone," Sacha said with an eye on Tia and Paul marching their way. Jasper followed. Whatever the decision, their facial expressions and body language weren't giving anything away. Should they all survive, Zack promised himself he'd never play poker with any of them.

Tia stopped in front of the group. She folded her hands and cleared her throat. "I'm sorry to inform you, the majority of New Salem has voted that we do not engage."

"There were several who wanted us to ask you all to leave our village immediately," Paul added.

"She knows about New Salem," Sebastian said. "She is coming, whether we are here or not. I am sure of that."

"We came to that conclusion as well," Tia replied. "That is why we are keeping the quad clear and our people will be on lockdown. Better the battle should take place here where we can contain it from the rest of the world." She offered her political grin. "We wish you good fortune, but we also ask that once your war is settled and should you be victorious, you leave New Salem forever."

"We understand," Sebastian said.

"I sure don't understand!" Sacha stepped next to Sebastian and faced Tia and Paul.

"Sach," Selena warned.

"They need to hear this," Sacha snapped. "Valeria's mission—the reason she was exiled to another dimension in the first place—is to take over the world. She wants to enslave mortal humans, and she'll kill any witch who doesn't join her in what she thinks is a holy crusade. Valeria is determined and psychotic. If she kills us, your people, witch and otherwise, are all in big trouble."

"That is true," Selena jumped in. "However, this is your home, and we will respect your wishes."

"Do you have the power to defeat her?" Paul asked.

The three witches exchanged glances. Finally, Sebastian answered, "Possible. She's powerful, but with the right strategy, I believe we can beat her and send her back to the Other World."

"We beat her the last time," Sacha added, showing a stance of confidence that Zack did not share.

"There is something you need to hear," Tia said. She focused her attention on Jasper. "Let them know, Jas."

"I had a dream about a week ago," he said. "Consider it a forewarning of your battle to come."

"You want to tell us about your dream?" Sacha's

eyebrows rose. "Seriously?"

"He sees the future in his dreams," Zack said. "Jasper, what did you see?"

"It was the aftermath of a battle that took place here in New Salem. Most of the details remain hazy, but one phrase stayed clear with me long after I woke. 'The immortal witch has won the day.' If this was a glimpse into future events—"

"We get it," Selena cut Jasper off. "But we still have to stand our ground and try to stop her. If we run, it could be devastating for your village."

"We understand," Tia replied. "I wish we could assist you. But my people have made their decision."

"I will stand with you."

All eyes shifted to see Simon waddling their way with his left fist clutched to his chest. As he came closer, Zack eyed the older vampire from head to loafers. There was no way this guy had ever been in an actual fight, before or after his death.

"Simon, are you sure?" Tia asked.

"Luther was my mentor, Madam President," Simon responded with a look of purpose Zack didn't expect out of him. "This Valeria ended his existence with a weapon I supplied. I am partially responsible, and I need to make amends." Simon walked up to the witches. He held out his left fist and opened it. Five small diamond-like crystals shined. "Doctor Mac is unable to enter the conflict directly, but he thought these would help."

"Enchanted crystals." Sacha's eyes opened wide. "Ooh, I can feel they are even more powerful than my set."

"Yes," Selena said as Simon poured the five

crystals into her palm. "Especially considering ours stopped working the moment we transported ourselves to the village."

"Simon," Zack said. "Are you sure you want to be out here when Valeria arrives? With her power, she can end your existence just like she did to Luther." Not to mention, Zack couldn't imagine what Simon could do to help, anyway.

"I appreciate your concern, young vampire, but I assure you I will not be totally useless." Simon reached into the seam of his pants. He pulled out a wooden stake. Its tip was sharpened to a perfect point. "If your witches can counter her power, I can exploit her vampiric vulnerabilities."

"We appreciate your help, Simon," Selena said. "And I'm sure we can utilize you. Do you agree, Sebastian?"

"We could have used the combined connection of every witch in this village," Sebastian answered. "But we'll take what we can get."

Sebastian and the sisters fell into conversation with Paul and Tia. They went back and forth, from discussing the best way to limit the damage to the village when Valeria arrived, to The Witches of Vegas' immediate exit once the battle was over. Zack took a few steps back. His head still pounded from the realization that he was no longer the normal human being of their coven. He was now more of a supernatural being than they were. Well, Isis was going to be one as well...if she recovered. But what if she didn't? Everything they'd just gone through, everything they'd done, and that included releasing Valeria onto the world. It was all to save Isis. She had to pull through.

Zack realized that he wasn't the only one who left from the huddle. Simon had wandered away as well. That's when Zack noticed. "Simon, where is your cane?"

"I don't really need it," the vampire answered. "I use it more so as an accessory."

An accessory? "But I saw you limping earlier."

"Of course I limp." Simon pulled up his right pant leg. "A limp is inevitable when one must rely on one of these."

Zack inspected the thin, brown bar that ran from his thigh to his foot. His brows pulled together once he realized what he was looking at. "It's made of wood?"

"That it is," Simon said with a clear sense of pride. "As I told you earlier, Nikolas was quite an expert in his whittling abilities."

"Your prosthetic leg is made out of the one material that can kill you?"

Simon tapped the side of his right thigh. "The leg has not killed me yet, dear boy. In fact, it has proven to be a close friend."

"Sure it has." Zack took a step back. Of all the supernatural types in the village, this was the one they had to rely on as an ally in what would most certainly be a battle to the death.

Simon let out a chuckle. He put a hand on Zack's shoulder. "You find me odd, don't you? I see the discomfort across your face."

"Um, no, not at all," Zack lied.

"No need to lie to spare my feelings." Simon grinned. "Oh, I recognize that look. Nikolas had it on his face almost every time we were at a social gathering." His head tilted. "Actually, Luther made that same face as well. But rest assured, you and your gaggle of witches can count on me."

"On behalf of me and my gaggle of witches," Zack said as sincerely as he could, "we appreciate your help."

Zack focused on the sky, an attempt to avoid the most awkward conversation he'd ever been involved in, especially with an adult. This wasn't just an adult, but an immortal one as well. That's when he realized, unlike moments ago, they were no longer under a bright yellow sun. A black cloud covering had formed directly above the village—and only over the village. The horizon in all areas away from the village still had a clear sky. The cloud covering spiraled in its center. The sound of wind intensified.

"Sebastian!" Zack shouted. "It just got darker."

"Yes, she's here," Sebastian said.

"It's time to put the village on lockdown," Paul announced.

"Agreed." Tia pulled her walkie-talkie from her right pants pocket and brought it to her mouth. "Sound the alarm, we are officially under lockdown." She turned to the witches. "I wish you all the good fortune Mother Earth will give you today."

Tia moved briskly to the auditorium. She was followed by Paul and Jasper. Paul stopped midway, looked back at them, then resumed his journey. An alarm like a school's fire drill, from speakers on the roof of all four quad buildings, blared throughout the village.

"Okay, let's go over the plan!" Sebastian, said, his mojo taking over. "Selena, Sacha...combined, you have the power to match Valeria. This time, I'm going to need *you* to keep her distracted. Meanwhile, I'll get the crystals in place around her. We take them over before she can, then use them to bind her powers. Simon, keep a safe distance but be ready to drive that stake into her heart if necessary. If we can't trap her, and you see an opening, take it."

Simon clapped his hands together. "Go, team!" he shouted with far too much enthusiasm.

"Sebastian, what about me?" Zack hoped his omission wasn't meant as a slight.

"Be ready for anything, Zack," Sebastian said. "Keep that clever eye of yours on the battle. If you see any advantage we can exploit, pass the word."

Selena poured the crystals into Sebastian's hands. "Whatever happens, we can't let Valeria get to Isis in that medical center."

"You got all that, Zack?" Sebastian asked.

"I understand." Zack didn't care for his role of lookout or guard dog. But Sebastian was right. Isis was vulnerable, and Valeria had an obsession prior to her imprisonment. Only problem with the plan was if she did get past the witches, and then came for Isis, Zack didn't have a clue how he could stop her.

The spiral in the black cloud circled faster and faster. With it came a heavy wind. It was like a controlled cyclone that surrounded them. Sebastian stepped forward. "We are here, Valeria! We are waiting for you!" His voice could barely be heard over the heavy wind. "Show yourself!"

A red and orange ball erupted in the center of the cloud. The cloud evaporated around it. The sphere slowly moved downward, growing in size as it descended. Smoke poured out all around. Sebastian and the sisters were visibly sweating from the heat as it moved closer. The center of the sphere became a dark red.

"Is that...fire?" Sacha asked.

The fireball expanded until it covered most of the sky. "Oh God, it's big enough to destroy this entire village!" Selena shrieked.

"Is that what she's looking to do, burn the village and everyone who lives here?" Simon gasped.

"Not if we can help it." Sacha reached out with her left hand and grabbed Selena's right. "We have to shield the village."

"Shield the village," Sacha and Selena chanted, "Shield the village, shield the village." In response, a clear dome of energy sparked and crackled. It covered the entire village from one end to the other. The fireball slammed against the top of the dome. Flames shot out in all directions, but none penetrated the dome.

"Oh wow, they actually did it!" Simon shouted with glee.

The fireball smacked the dome again and again. With each bounce, the intense struggle on the sisters' faces increased. They were engulfed in a battle of wills with Valeria and it was one they had to win. Sixty-eight lives, plus their own, depended on them. The top of the dome exploded into a ceiling of fire.

"It's not going to hold," Sacha grunted.

Selena let out a scream, pushing upward with her left hand. But it wasn't enough. The fire melted through the dome and sped up. The heat intensified the closer the blanket of flame fell to the ground. Zack wanted to shout something helpful, an idea they could use to stop it, but this was way out of his sense of reality.

"You have to contain it," Sebastian yelled. "Contain it or we're all done!"

"We…we're trying," Selena groaned as her knees buckled. "It's too powerful."

"Only one chance now," Sacha said with the same pain in her voice as her sister.

Sacha pulled her left hand from Selena's tight grip. "Away!" she screamed. The wind shifted knocking Selena off her feet. Her sister dragged against the ground, away from Sacha.

"What are you doing?" Selena screeched. "You can't stop it alone, Sacha!"

"I can't let this thing destroy the village, or you!" Sacha raised her arms high in the air. "*Fire, to me!*"

"Sacha, you can't take in the fire!" Sebastian shouted. "If you do, you won't survive!"

Zack started toward her. He wanted to somehow stop her, maybe yank her away before the flame hit. Simon grabbed his arm before he could get near. Sacha glanced at Sebastian. Her expression said she knew what she was doing and accepted that fate. She screamed again, "*Fire, to me!*"

As if heeding her command, the fireball folded and wrapped around Sacha like a giant hand of flame closing its fist. Zack called out her name. He couldn't see or hear Sacha beyond the inferno. Was there a chance she teleported just in time to save her own life?

The fire closed in on itself as if it were being sucked in by a vacuum somewhere in the center. The flame had dissipated leaving Sacha in its wake. Smoke discharged from every pore in her body. Her skin was red like a sunburn that covered every inch of her body.

Zack dropped to his knees. With all their power, he thought The Witches of Vegas were invincible. Until now.

"My goodness," Simon cried out.

Sacha's body fell over like a tree that had just been chopped down. Her eyes were wide-open, but it was clear she was no longer there. Selena screamed out to her sister, but there was nothing she could do. All anyone could do at that moment was watch in horror as Sacha's body burst into flames.

Chapter Twenty-seven

Selena ran to her sister. She dropped to her knees. "Fire begone!" Selena shouted and waved her hands frantically over Sacha's body. Zack wanted to help—if only he had a bucket of water to throw on Sacha. But all he could do was look on with a feeling of helplessness in the pit of his stomach.

The intense flames fanned out leaving Sacha's charred body in its wake. Although Selena had stopped the fire, the aroma of charred flesh stayed behind. It had a charcoal-like smell mixed with a coppery stench. Heavy white smoke still rose from Sacha's body. Everyone kneeled around her, Zack and Simon on one side, Selena and Sebastian on the other. Her body shook but Zack was sure Sacha was gone.

He wrapped a hand over his eyes. As much as he had come to love Sacha, it was too much for him to see her this way. The sight of her red and charcoal colored husk made Zack want to puke, if he was still capable of doing that. But if seeing Sacha's skin burned off her body was hard for him, he couldn't begin to imagine the devastation Selena and Sebastian must have felt. Or Isis once she found out.

Zack forced himself to uncover his eyes. He had to put his feelings aside and be strong for everyone else's sake. As bad as this was, he had a feeling their problems had only just started.

Selena took her sister's limp hand. "Her skin is hot and there's...there's no pulse." Her eyes were wide like grapefruits. Her lips moved, but no other words crossed her tongue.

Sebastian cupped his hand on Selena's shoulder. "She's gone."

Zack didn't need Wiccan power to know the thoughts going through Sebastian's mind. The man took pride in the responsibility of keeping his family safe, and their unit had just been destroyed beyond repair.

"My goodness," Simon gasped. "The power...the cruelty..."

Sebastian's head popped up. There was a slight gleam in his eye. "Simon, you can bring her back. Turn her."

"And force her to walk eternity like this?" Simon shook his head. "I wouldn't curse my worst enemy that way."

The grass rustled. Zack whirled around. They had company in the quad. Valeria stood dead center with darkened eyes glaring their way. The dirty rags had been replaced by a black overskirt dress. Instead of bare feet, she wore green high-heeled shoes. Her head rotated from far left to far right, taking in the village surrounding her. A huge grin formed across her face as she pointed her open palm their way.

"Guys, heads up." Zack didn't know what Valeria had in mind, but it wouldn't be anything good.

A breeze came from Sacha's body, rustling Zack's hair. It moved in Valeria's direction. The witch raised her arms, offering an inviting embrace. Valeria grinned. Her cheeks flushed.

Zack remembered the lessons he learned about

witches, particularly on how a witch could absorb another witch's connection if their body were set ablaze. That had to be what Valeria did with Sacha's connection. By right, that connection should have gone to her sister, but Selena was still too shellshocked to fight for it.

Valeria took in her surroundings and spoke. "Witches of this village!" Her voice boomed across the entire quad. "You may feel safe here in your self-imposed prison, but beyond these walls, humanity still fears and despises our kind!

"They fear us because we were chosen by Mother Earth as her planet's dominant species. We are meant to lead, not just this small, hidden patch of land, but the entire world! Our connection to the planet deems us her true masters!"

"Sebastian, what do we do?" Zack whispered. He didn't get a response. Sebastian's eyes were glazed over, staring down at Sacha's corpse. It was as if he had come to the realization that he couldn't fix this. Zack reached out and pulled on his arm. "Sebastian!"

"I offer you this one chance to correct history," Valeria continued. "Stand by my side as we take our rightful place at the front of the evolutionary chain!"

Sebastian opened his hand, exposing the five crystals across his palm. "We have a plan," he said. "Selena!"

His wife wrestled her attention from her sister and shifted it and her gaze to Valeria. She nodded.

"Stay with me, Selena. We can still do this." Sebastian jumped to his feet and tiptoed away, veering to Valeria's left. Selena's head, however, dropped back down to Sacha.

Sebastian stared at his palm and blinked his eyes. An enchanted crystal left his palm and flashed on the grass several feet behind Valeria.

"The choice is yours!" Valeria announced, her head facing up as if she were under a spotlight. "But understand the paths in front of you. If you stand with me—with your kind—you will reap the benefits. However, stand against me and your defiance will be met with force beyond your imaginations!"

With another blink from Sebastian, a second crystal disappeared from his palm. This one appeared on Valeria's right side. The third appeared across from the first at equal lengths from the two. The fourth fell the same distance from the previous. The pentagon was almost formed.

Valeria focused on Sebastian, who looked back at her and blinked his eyes one last time. The final crystal stayed in his palm, refusing to follow his instructions. "No!" Sebastian gasped. He closed his hand around the crystal and ran for the fifth spot. The one chance they had of ending the battle before it began relied on Sebastian's speed.

"*Crurem adflictas.*" Valeria waved an arm in the air.

In response, Sebastian's right leg twisted at the knee. He fell to the ground. He reached out, stretching his left hand as far as it could go. With a wrinkled nose and clenched jaw, Sebastian opened his palm. The crystal slowly floated for the finish line.

"*Brachium confractus!*" Valeria shouted.

Sebastian's arm twisted at the elbow. Zack flinched at the snap evident even from a distance away. With a finger-point to the sky by Valeria, the enchanted crystal flew up and over the medical center. Valeria waltzed over to Sebastian's unmoving body. Her heavy boot dangled inches over his head.

"Selena, snap out of it!" Zack grabbed the witch by the shoulders and shook her. But her stare stayed downward on her younger sister's charred remains. "She's in shock," he said to Simon. "I don't know what to do!"

"Then I guess it is up to me," the vampire responded.

Simon stood up. His narrowed eyes focused on Valeria. He held the wooden stake in his right hand and pointed the sharp end. Then, with a war-like scream, he charged, wobbling at a rapid speed. Valeria raised a hand. Simon slammed into what Zack guessed was an invisible wall. The vampire flew backward and rolled across the grass. The stake fell from his hand. Somehow, Simon's prosthetic leg stayed in place.

"Ooh, I felt that," Simon mumbled. His head fell back against the ground.

Valeria turned back to Sebastian. She raised her foot over him. With a demented smile, she slammed it down. Her foot went through his head, hitting the ground. Sebastian's body faded away.

"What?" she screeched.

Zack let out a relieved sigh at the sight of him rolling along the ground. Even hurt, the man found a way to save himself...at least for the moment.

Valeria peered down at Sebastian. His broken arm still hung straight out. "You fooled me with an illusion." Valeria laughed. "Very clever ploy, albeit a temporary one."

Zack needed to do something. But what? His first

instinct told him to grab that piece of wood and charge. Maybe he'd get lucky and catch her off-guard. But Simon already tried that tactic and it ended badly for him. Zack wasn't a witch, while Valeria was a powerful one. If he tried anything, she'd crush him before he got anywhere near her. In fact, she'd probably shove that stake straight down his throat. To have any chance, he needed Selena back in the game. She was their only hope.

"Selena!" Zack shouted just inches from her face. "Your husband needs you! Valeria is about to kill him, too!"

"No." Selena's head picked up. "I won't let her."

Selena's eyes narrowed with determination. "Through the heart," she whispered. The wooden stake on the ground slid across the grass, making a beeline for Valeria. The stake propelled upward and torpedoed into the Wiccan vampire's chest.

"Speed," Selena chanted. She jumped to her feet and ran at Valeria like a windstorm that barely registered with Zack's eyes. She grabbed the end of the stake and shoved it deep into Valeria's evil heart. "For Sacha!" Selena screamed.

"Yes!" Zack pumped his fist.

Selena got her. The battle was over. Now, it was just a matter of seeing Valeria fall.

But Valeria stayed on her feet. Her head lifted. With a fierce black-eyed glare into Selena's face, she grinned. "As witches, with enough will and experience, we can warp the fabric of reality around us."

Selena lifted off the ground. Zack's excitement disappeared. She clutched her throat with both hands, gagging and wheezing.

"I removed my body's vulnerability to wood centuries ago." Valeria ripped the stake from her chest. It was covered in red goop. She let the weapon fall from her hand. "Your misguided rebellion is now over."

"Screw this," Zack whispered. He could no longer sit around like a punk and watch everyone else get manhandled by Valeria. With Selena struggling, Zack had to make a move. Charging at her directly didn't work for Simon. Neither did that stake through her heart. But what about the throat? Even if it didn't kill her, would it distract her long enough for Selena to unleash the full brunt of her power?

A plan formed in Zack's head. If he could ram his body into her at full force—hit Valeria before she saw him coming—he would only have a moment to grab that stake near her feet and attack. But maybe that would be enough time. If he could drill it directly into her windpipe before she could regain her balance... It wasn't the best plan, but he had nothing else at his disposal.

Zack jumped to his feet. He was ready to ram his body into her as hard as he could. But his feet wouldn't move. Neither would any part of his body. This time, it wasn't nerves keeping him from moving. It was Valeria, who stared directly at him.

"L-let me go." Zack could barely get his mouth to move.

"So you may attack me?" Valeria replied. "Your intentions were clear, my kin, so consider this your one and only warning. Stay out of matters that do not concern you."

Valeria still had Selena levitated in the air. As she dropped her hand, Selena slammed—face-first—into the hard, grass-covered ground. Selena's body didn't move, but at least she was still breathing. Zack couldn't tell if she had been knocked out, or worse.

Either way, The Witches of Vegas had lost.

Chapter Twenty-eight

Isis' upper body shot up from the examining table. Her head darted around the room seeing everything through new eyes. Her brain felt cloudy as if she were waking from a long, brutal nightmare. She tried to take a deep breath but realized that the air wouldn't enter her lungs. She no longer needed to breathe.

"So this is what it's like." Isis held her hands in front of her face. They looked the same, but nothing about her existence would ever be the same again.

Isis couldn't remember the last time she ate, yet she didn't feel the slightest pang of hunger. An empty IV bag hung on a pole with a tube running to the needle in her arm. The bag was stained red on the inside. Isis yanked the needle from her flesh. A sound from nearby brought her alert. It sounded like a throat clearing. She wasn't alone. Doctor Mac, leaning on the counter across the room, watched with a studious eye. Beside him, a monitor hummed. A flatline raced across the screen.

"Welcome back to the living," the doctor said. "Well, in a manner of speaking."

Isis grabbed a handful of her hair. For some reason she thought it would feel like old straw, but it didn't feel any different than before. Maybe a bit matted down—and terribly unwashed—but it felt real.

"How are you?" Mac asked.

"I think I'm okay." Isis shook her head. She covered her ears and said it again. "I'm okay." She uncovered her ears and said it a third time, "Okay. Wow, this is weird."

"I'm sure you will notice many changes in your physiology," Mac said. "It will take time to adjust."

"I have some idea. Luther used to tell me what being a vampire was like." Isis pinched her arm. She was able to feel it. "Hey, where is everybody?"

"It's a long story," he answered. "Right now, you need to rest. At least I think you do." He turned off the monitor. "Your condition is uncharted territory for me, although your healing process appears to be similar to how the Wiccan healing works."

"Something's going on." Isis closed her eyes. She connected with Zack's mind faster than she'd ever been able to do before. At one time she promised him she'd never read his mind unless it was an absolute emergency. An instinct assured her that wherever he was right now, it had to be an absolute emergency. Otherwise, he and her family would have been in the room waiting on her to wake up.

Zack was a vampire just like her. She almost forgot it was him that made her into one. She could now see everything through his eyes. Oh, God, it really was an emergency. "Valeria is here," Isis shrieked. "She's kicking their asses. Sacha? She's…No!" Isis gasped. The connection with Zack broke. "I have to help."

"Your coven requested I keep you here so you'd be safe." Mac folded his arms and looked his patient over with a slight smirk. "Any chance you will comply with their request?"

Isis threw the doctor a backward glance.

****

Valeria had taken out The Witches of Vegas in a matter of minutes. Even Simon was still down, not that he put up much of a fight. Valeria's warning ran through Zack's head. It was one he'd happily ignore if there was anything he could do to turn the tide. So far, nothing had come to mind.

Selena was still unconscious. Valeria stood over her and held out a palm. A flame appeared above her hand. It expanded from her thumb to her pinky finger. The determination in her narrowed eyes spoke volumes. They said she was about to burn Selena alive. It was exactly how she killed Sacha. Zack was finally able to move his arms and legs, but he still couldn't get himself to charge in and attack Valeria. This time, the reason was nerves.

"Valeria, please!" Zack shouted. "You don't have to kill her!"

Valeria's angry glare beamed Zack's way. "How I wish that were true," she said. "I'd prefer this witch fought by my side. But she can still assist me in my mission. I will take her connection just as I did her sibling's."

Valeria's attention dismissed Zack and returned to the fireball in her hand. He had to do something. Zack could never live with himself if he just stood by and watched Selena get burned alive. Every possible strategy at his disposal scrolled through his head. As a vampire, Zack was sure he had some sort of enhanced strength and stamina. But Valeria was a vampire too with an advantage in size. Not to mention, her experience being a vampire for hundreds of years. Zack had only been one for a few hours. None of that included the fact that she was a powerful witch as well.

The last time they faced off, he used magic tricks to distract Valeria. To say he got lucky was a huge understatement. His antics bought just enough time for The Witches of Vegas to arrive on the scene and make the save. This time, magic tricks wouldn't work. The witches wouldn't be able to make a last minute save. Zack peeked at Sacha's corpse. He could not allow Selena to suffer the same fate, but how could he stop it? He was even willing to sacrifice himself, if that sacrifice wouldn't be in vain.

A familiar roar grabbed Zack's attention. It was one he never expected to hear on this side of the dimensional portal. One of the beasts from the Other World stared down Valeria, an unexpected ally in the fight for their lives, and one that came in the nick of time. As if on instinct, Valeria threw her fireball at the beast. It leaped over the flame. The fire hit the ground. The green grass and brown mud absorbed it with ease—a product of Wiccan design, no doubt. The animal kept its distance but let out that high-pitched roar once again.

"How are *you* here?" Valeria screamed. Then a knowing grin formed across her lips. "Ahh, I should have known!"

Her glare locked onto Sebastian who had pushed his upper body off the ground with his unbroken arm. His eyelids were wide and red, expressing the pain two broken bones caused. Of course, the animal from the Other World was one of Sebastian's illusions. If the point was to give his wife time to regain her senses, it failed in its purpose. Selena was still groggy. She may have even suffered a concussion.

Valeria pointed her chin. Sebastian's arm yanked out from under him. His upper body dropped back to the ground. The illusion of the alien animal faded away. Valeria glanced back and forth from Sebastian to Selena. "I remind you," she cackled, "you and your coven brought my wrath onto yourselves."

"It's time," Zack said to himself. "Man up. Attack." But he still couldn't push himself to charge the powerful Wiccan vampire, not without a plan. Otherwise, it wouldn't accomplish a damned thing.

Silence filled the air. Then came a loud bang. A bullet caught Valeria in the right leg. Perhaps it was surprise more than the impact, but it caused her to stumble. "Now who dares?" she screamed.

From several feet away, Paul lowered his pistol which was wrapped in his right hand and leaned against his left palm. He wasn't alone. Natasha hovered on his left, holding her hands high in the air. Carolyn stood to Paul's right with a grenade in her palm. She pulled out the pin.

"Valeria, you have just endangered every single life in this village," Paul announced. "Therefore, you are deemed a danger by the New Salem Law Enforcement team! You are a threat to our citizens and must be neutralized!"

Valeria pointed an open hand at Paul. Before she could act, a bullet hit her in the chest. She jolted under the impact. It was followed by a second one. A third bullet shot through Valeria's left leg. Zack's gaze raced to the tallest of the four buildings surrounding them— the school. Jasper stood on the roof with a sniper rifle pointed at Valeria. Damn, Zack suspected there was more to Jasper than he let on, but he didn't think the guy was an expert marksman.

Another bullet dropped Valeria to all fours. Paul shouted to his crew, "NOW!" Carolyn tossed the grenade so it landed in front of Valeria. It was followed by Natasha yelling, "*Kupol!*"

Zack covered his ears. The grenade exploded. It became trapped within a clear dome that surrounded Valeria. The dome filled with a mushroom of black smoke. Carolyn let out a scream of victory. Wow, if Zack's jaw weren't attached, it would have fallen off his face. These four New Salem protectors worked like a well-oiled machine. More so, they took Valeria down with ease, and only one of them was a powerful witch.

Zack ran to Selena and kneeled at her side. He put a hand on her shoulder. "Selena, they got her," he whispered. Her body flinched from Zack's touch.

"Paul, I no longer sense her presence," Natasha said.

"We blew her to pieces," Paul responded. "Open the dome."

The smoke cleared. The celebration ended. There was a circle of scorched grass, but no Valeria. Not even her remains. "Where is she?" Paul raised his pistol.

Valeria reappeared behind him. "Look out!" Zack shouted. But his warning came too late. Valeria slapped her right hand against the back of Paul's head. His eyes went white. His body fell forward like a rubber doll.

"Paul!" Carolyn spun around, whipping her pistol from its holster. The gun dropped from her hand. As Valeria stared her down, Carolyn grabbed her left shoulder gasping for air. She fell next to Paul.

A bullet from the school's rooftop hit Valeria in the back. She faced the building and whipped her arm in its direction. "Enough from you!" she roared. "A*edificium fatiscit*."

Zack looked in horror while the entire top floor crumbled. Jasper ran from the edge as everything around him collapsed into the floor below. Sight of him was lost in the demolition. Valeria turned back to Natasha and smiled. All the confidence had been sucked out of the young witch's face.

"What of you?" Valeria asked. "Will you stand with me or die with these lesser beings?"

Without a word, Natasha dropped to her knees between her fallen comrades. She placed a hand on each of them. All three disappeared. Zack had no doubt her destination was the medical center.

"Now," Valeria said. "Back to you."

Next to Zack, Selena stirred. She pulled herself to her knees. Her face was bruised along the right cheek and forehead. A smile crossed Valeria's face. Zack scanned the entire quad. There was no one else left to make a save, just him, with no plan and no way to stop her.

Zack looked to the ground. That's when it hit him. He knew exactly how they could have beaten Valeria, except it was too late. Damn, if only he had thought of it a lot earlier. But with all the witches down, his solution was no longer an option. Not without a miracle. Selena grabbed her head. Valeria's smile grew.

From a distance, residents of New Salem peeked from behind the buildings surrounding the quad. With so many witches, together they may have had the power to overwhelm Valeria. But none of them made a move to get involved. Although New Salem's law enforcement found a legal loophole to intervene, apparently the villagers were abiding by their vote and staying away.

"Screw this!" Zack stood and faced Valeria. Wiccan power or not, it was up to him to do something. It was time to stop looking for help from others, find his backbone, and take a stand, even if it was suicide. He could not just sit there and watch Valeria murder the family that took him into their lives.

Zack jumped between Valeria and her intended victim. Valeria's hand shot up with a finger pointed out. He snatched her wrist in mid-rise with his left hand and punched her in the chest with his right. As a vampire, Zack had enhanced strength, yet all his might didn't back Valeria up a step.

"Z-Zack, run," Selena groaned.

But he refused to budge. He stayed in place, in front of Selena. "You want to get to her—" Zack straightened his back and clenched his fists. "—you'll have to go through me."

"I did warn you, didn't I?" Valeria's head tilted. She made a fist to match Zack's. Her fist, however, was covered in smoke. "You may be my creation, but I will not hesitate to kill you if I must."

"Like you killed Luther," Zack shot back. "The one and only being in the world that genuinely loved you. Yeah, I saw it in his eyes. I saw it in both of your eyes, you loved each other. And you killed him, anyway."

"I do what I must and without hesitation. I am on a divine mission from Mother Earth herself. I will not be hindered by *anyone*!" Valeria swatted her left hand in the air. Zack flew to the side. The impact with the ground let him know that, even as a vampire, he could still feel pain. He looked to Selena but it was clear she had no fight left in her. Across the way, Sebastian had passed out. Valeria stood over Selena with a proud grin on her lips.

Zack pushed his arms against the ground, lifting his upper body. "We're not done!" He pulled himself to his feet. "You can't kill me, Valeria. You already did that, remember?"

Valeria's angry eyes narrowed. "You are not a threat to me, but you are a nuisance." She raised a hand. Zack was yanked off the ground. He hovered, unable to move his arms or legs. "If I suck your brain out through your nose..." A look of curiosity crossed her face. "You will cease to exist. I believe it will be very painful. Shall we see?"

A throbbing pain formed in Zack's forehead. It was like a hot spike digging through his temple. Zack wanted to scream but he couldn't even speak. He couldn't close his eyes. So much for a last-second miracle. They already had one of those in Paul and his team. Valeria went through them just as easily. She was like an unstoppable hate-train tearing through anyone in its way. But Zack wasn't ready to say goodbye to the world, as a human or as a vampire. Unfortunately, there was nothing he could do except...say goodbye—

The medical center's door ripped from the hinges and flew across the quad like a giant Frisbee. The edge slammed into Valeria's back, staggering her. Zack dropped to the ground. The throbbing in his brain stopped.

"Now what?" Valeria growled, regaining her composure and turning to the medical center. "Well, I've been waiting for you."

Isis stood in the doorway. She had recovered. The

blackened eyes said she was also pissed off. Her fists were clenched. The miracle Zack hoped for had just arrived.

Chapter Twenty-nine

Isis felt it in her bones; everything about her was different. The Earth's energy flowed through her body like water gushing through an open dam. She'd never felt so connected like this in her entire life. Maybe that was because she was a vampire? Right now, she couldn't contemplate the why, not with a much older and angrier Wiccan vampire staring her down.

"I will give you one chance to join me, Isis," Valeria said in a semi-calm tone. "I know you think we need to be enemies. But you also understand why I do what I must. You have experienced the horrors humanity has inflicted on our kind. Do what you know is right and stand by my side as my apprentice and we drag this world down the path it was meant to follow."

Isis peeked around. Her family and Simon were out of the fight. Poor Sacha—she wasn't ready to wrap her head around that. From the corner of her eye, she caught Zack running off. His thoughts were vague and erratic, but Isis picked up the essence; he had a plan. A weapon that would turn the tide. But what weapon could stop Valeria? No time to dig deeper, Isis had to stay focused on the psychotic immortal witch in front of her. For now, she was on her own.

"Let's take your first step," Valeria said. "I will allow you to absorb your adopted coven's connections so you may add them to your own."

Was she serious? Isis didn't even need to ask, but the offer offended her. "You killed my aunt! You hurt my mom and dad! Now you want me to kill them?" Isis locked darkened eyes with Valeria's from across the quad. "The right path for me is not with *you*!" Isis put as much bravado into her statement as she could. Her tone didn't even intimidate herself.

"Disappointing," Valeria replied. "But not unexpected." Valeria's sharp fangs flashed. She lifted her arms over her head. The ground shook like an earthquake.

Isis shifted her body with every shake, barely keeping her balance. "What am I doing?" she asked herself. She was a witch and she needed to act like it.

Isis focused on her lighter than air spell. Her body lifted inches off the ground. Valeria dropped her arms, stopping the earthquake. Isis let her feet touch the grass.

"Are you truly foolish enough to challenge me?" Valeria shouted. "You think you can harm, much less defeat me?"

Feeling the power, Isis took a step forward and sent a force blast directly at Valeria, who countered with one of her own. Although neither budged, the grass and dirt for yards around ripped from the ground.

Isis' arms went heavy, like iron weights hung from them. They dropped to her side. Her energy blasts stopped. Luckily, so did Valeria's. Isis' entire body felt like one big charlie horse. She wouldn't give up, not against the monster that destroyed her family. Isis pulled herself to her feet just in time to see Valeria in the air. She rocketed down at Isis with her long claws aimed for her victim's throat.

"Teleport!" Isis shouted, focusing on the energy

coursing through her body. The image of the lunging Valeria faded. When everything became clear, she was now several feet away, behind Valeria. One shockwave should stagger Valeria and take her out. Isis focused on the idea and threw her hands together. But before they could touch and trigger the shockwave, Valeria twisted like a whirlwind and whipped her hand in the air. Isis' feet yanked upward. Gravity dropped her on her backside.

To the left, Mom sat up with a hand clutching her forehead. From the glazed-over look on her face, she was still out of it. Across the quad, Dad was on his face, out cold. Isis was in this fight alone, and there was no way she could beat Valeria by herself. "Zack," she whispered. "Whatever you're planning, now would be a real good time."

Zack's voice echoed in her head. "Hang tight, I'm looking for it."

"You are strong, little witch." Valeria's eyes once again went dark. "But you are a fool. You face one who is far more familiar with the power than you."

Valeria strolled across the field, stopping in front of Isis. "I see now that neither I, nor Mother Earth, can count on you to make the right choice." Valeria shook her head. Her eyes narrowed. "I wonder, although I cannot end your immortal existence, if I were to set you on fire, would that allow me to absorb your Wiccan connection? I believe we should conduct this experiment."

Isis pushed herself back using her elbows and feet. She didn't want to seem intimidated, but that was all she did feel. It was the same fear Valeria brought out of her one year ago. She had promised herself never to feel that way again. Damn, even though this was the most powerful Isis had ever felt, she was once again on her backside, backing away from Valeria. Her best shot wasn't enough.

"You insist on standing in my way," Valeria said. "And now, you are an immortal. I will not have you pestering me for all eternity."

The wooden stake lifted off the ground. It hovered in front of Isis with the point aimed for her throat. "Zack!" Isis shouted. God, she hoped he really did have a brilliant plan.

"Foolish girl, no one is going to save you," Valeria crowed.

Zack's voice popped in her head again. "I have it," he said. "Just keep her busy. Trust me."

"Okay, I understand," Isis said out loud.

Valeria laughed. "No, unfortunately, I do not believe you do." The point of the stake pressed against Isis' throat. "And I don't think you could ever understand."

Selena was back on her feet. "No, I won't let you hurt her." The words barely came off her tongue. "Not again."

"*Vis bucina*," Valeria shouted. An energy blast shot from her hand. It knocked Selena down like a bowling pin hit by the ball. Isis grabbed the stake. She tried to yank it out of the air. It wouldn't budge. For that matter, she couldn't move her legs either. Valeria's attention was once again focused her way. Smoke emanated from her fists. The heat made Isis' face sweat.

"I was willing to share this path with you." Valeria's hands ignited. "Take solace in knowing that your sacrifice will improve our world for witches everywhere."

"Valeria!" Zack shouted from the medical center's rooftop. He held over his head another of Nikolas' wooden spears. This one was just like the first, but older and less polished.

Zack, what are you doing? Isis focused the thought to Zack. She didn't receive a response. After reading his thoughts, Isis understood his plan. But it was risky, especially the way he expected to execute it.

Zack charged and leaped off the roof. With the spear pointed forward, he flew through the air in an arc he could never have made prior to his death. Valeria twirled like a top to face him. The fire extinguished from her hands. With a wave of her arm, the spear disintegrated in Zack's hand. Wood chips filled the air. With one hand, Valeria caught Zack by the throat. His body dangled from her tight grip.

"What do you think you're doing, boy?" Valeria pulled him close so their noses nearly touched.

Zack squeezed an answer through his throat. "M-misdirection, witch."

His left hand fell to his side, fingers open. The fifth enchanted crystal dropped to the ground, lined in perfect symmetry with the other four crystals. *Do it now!* His voice shouted into Isis' head.

Valeria tossed Zack aside and twisted back to Isis. "*Push!*" Isis shouted. With all her focus and willpower, she fired pure force at Valeria. The energy pushed Valeria a step back. Just a step. But it was enough to knock her within the circle of the five enchanted crystals. Isis focused on them just as she had been taught by Sacha. Isis knew this set of crystals well as she had relied on them in Doctor Mac's medical room to keep her alive.

Five lines of electricity shot from each crystal and came together at the top forming a pyramid of energy. It surrounded Valeria. Isis jumped to her feet. Valeria pointed both hands at Isis and mumbled. She reeled back in panic when nothing happened.

"I stopped your connection with the planet's energy," Isis explained. She willed the crystals to move in, shrinking the barrier around Valeria. Within seconds, the old witch was trapped in an invisible coffin of energy. Her arms were now wedged at her sides, unable to move.

"What now, Isis?" Valeria snarled. "Banish me and I will find my way back. You know you cannot kill me. Wherever you imprison me, I will find a way to be free."

"I know that." Isis dropped her head. "You won't ever stop."

She had an idea of how to end Valeria's threat. It was one she had thought about several times over the year in case Valeria ever returned. She didn't like it and she couldn't ever see herself doing it. Plus, she never had a strong enough connection to pull it off, anyway. But now she had the strength, and there was no other way. Valeria was right—she couldn't be detained and certainly not convinced to see the error of her ways. She was relentless when it came to her life's "mission." And this was the only chance to end the threat.

Isis looked up to the sky, then to Valeria. "I know what I have to do."

At Isis' mental command, she and Valeria floated straight up. Valeria struggled, hitting the barriers with her elbows and knees but there was no escape, not while she was disconnected from the energy. That's why Isis made sure the crystals followed them into the sky, keeping their perfect symmetrical pattern.

Chapter Thirty

Isis took herself and Valeria straight up and through the clouds. The blue sky which had surrounded them turned pure white. Soon everything went pitch black except for sunlight shining off the stars from great distances away. They were still within Earth's atmosphere, but the planet was far below them. Isis created a glow which illuminated around her body.

She expected to see an enraged Valeria glaring at her with daggers of death. Instead, to Isis' surprise, she saw clear purple irises and a tempered demeanor. "What exactly is your plan?" the much older Wiccan vampire asked.

"I wish there was another way, I really do," Isis said with a slight sob. "But I know there's not. I can't kill you and I can't stop you. You said you fight for witches around the world, but how many have you hurt? How many have you killed—"

"Is your plan to talk me to death up here?"

"No," Isis answered. "I'm going to send you away. Far away."

"To where?"

"Nowhere." Isis motioned forward with her forehead. "I'm going to give you a push through space. So you will keep floating far away from Earth."

Valeria shook her head. "Hurtling through space. Well, I guess you do intend to murder me. Even a vampire cannot endure the freezing temperatures of space. I very well may float for all eternity. I would never even be aware of it." Valeria burst into a loud cackle. "I was right about you after all, young Isis. You would have made an excellent apprentice. We could have changed the dynamics of this planet together and ruled throughout all of eternity."

"I don't want to do this. That's why we're different. You like hurting people," Isis said. "I don't want to rule the world. I have to save it from you."

"And once the deed is done, what happens with you, young witch?" Valeria slammed her forehead against the energy surrounding her. Isis held her focus, if the act was meant to shake her and lose concentration, she wouldn't take the bait.

"Do you travel back to Las Vegas and hide your true self behind the cheers of mortals as you play the part of circus jester?" Valeria shouted. "Or will you hide in that quarantine for witches directly below us? I offer a path to all witches in which you no longer need to hide. A world where the people will embrace who you are. If not me, who will correct humanity's historical error? Certainly not *you*."

"Your path is filled with death!" Isis shouted. "Your way hurts innocent people. I know what it's like to be an innocent person and be hurt. To suffer for no good reason…"

"Innocence is a fairy tale, child," Valeria responded. "You will learn this over time. Especially once you experience humanity through a long-term perspective."

"You're not my teacher and I'm not your student." Isis' tone calmed. "You're evil. Maybe you don't want to be, maybe you don't mean to be, but it's what you've become. You're obsessed and blind. This is the only way to stop your evil."

"If you're going to do it, then do it," Valeria snapped. "But do not lecture me. You haven't lived long enough to realize the horrors humanity has brought onto our kind will never stop. That is why I must not, either." Valeria's face scrunched with anger. "You know nothing of what you speak."

Isis stared at Valeria, knowing that she was dead wrong. Yes, Isis had experienced firsthand the cruelty of humanity. But she'd also seen enough kindness in people to know that it outweighed the evil. Zack and his uncle represented the best humanity had to offer. So did Isis' family. Witches or not, they were still part of the humanity Valeria despised. From what she had seen, New Salem embraced the best of humanity as well. They lived in harmony…a harmony that Valeria would only destroy.

After several moments, Isis' nostrils flared. "I have no choice. The world is better without you. I'm sorry."

Valeria shook her head and scoffed. "You are sorry. Small comfort for one you are about to damn for all eternity."

"I know."

Isis pointed forward. Valeria, and the crystals, floated backward and away from Earth. Valeria once again banged her head against the shield around her. The energy sparked but thanks to the power of the crystals, it held. Valeria moved farther and farther back until Isis could barely make her out. Once the crystals were out of range from Earth, their power would no longer work. They, and Valeria, would no longer be connected to Earth's energy. Within moments, the coldness of space would freeze Valeria's body straight through.

Isis leaned her head forward and focused on enhancing her vision. The crystals floated away into five separate directions. Valeria's body kept moving out of the planet's range. She was now yet another frozen projectile surrounded by ice and traveling through the vast emptiness of outer space.

Isis allowed herself a sigh of relief. She hated stooping to Valeria's level of heartlessness to stop her, but this was one time it was justified. How many deaths had just been avenged? More importantly, how many more lives would have been lost had Valeria continued with her "divine mission?" Well, technically, Valeria wasn't dead, she lived on, but frozen and floating far away from the planet she tormented. Still, a better fate than she forced on so many, especially Sacha.

Isis glared down at the planet. With her eyesight enhanced, she could see the village. Her body shook with frustration, and she knew exactly who to fault for that. It was time for one more confrontation. Isis let out a scream, then chanted, "Return me to the village," with her eyes closed. Isis focused on her body, letting it float back down.

Chapter Thirty-one

Chaos filled the quad. The moment Isis and Valeria disappeared into the sky, residents of New Salem came out from hiding and formed a crowd. Two witches with the power to heal—they introduced themselves as Doctor Mac's medical assistants—treated Sebastian's broken limbs. Selena insisted that they both heal him first before worrying about her scrapes. Another group of villagers covered Sacha's body with a brown blanket and removed her from the quad. Zack had no idea where they took her; he couldn't bring himself to watch.

Instead, he kept his attention on the black cloud which had re-formed over the medical center. Isis had Valeria trapped at the point they went up. But Valeria was powerful and manipulative. Even if Isis could hold her, what could she do to end the threat? Valeria couldn't be killed, so what did Isis do with her? And why hadn't she come back down yet? A dozen paranoid thoughts ran through Zack's head.

Simon limped up to Zack and gave him a friendly slap to the arm. "Are you okay, my fellow immortal?" Convenient that Simon was back on his feet now that the conflict was over. Maybe he was helped off the ground by some of his neighbors?

"I'm fine." Zack kept his head pointed up.

"That was one hell of a battle we just endured. We

233

may not have come out unscathed, but we stood our ground and overcame near-impossible odds."

"Yeah." Zack bit his tongue out of respect to his elder.

Simon lifted his gaze to the sky. "I'm sure she is okay."

"I hope you're right, Simon. I really do—"

Zack's hair ruffled as a wind out of nowhere blew through the quad. No one reacted to it. It was the first sign of any sort of weather he had noticed other than warmth and sunshine since their arrival to the village.

"Simon, do you feel that?" Zack asked.

Simon's head cocked. "The breeze does seem to be picking up rather fast. Unusual."

The wind pushed against Zack's back, almost knocking him over. It lifted him in the air. So far, it was only happening to him. Simon called out. Before he could respond, Zack found himself floating upward like a balloon after a child lost a grip of its string. No way this was Valeria's doing; she wouldn't have singled him out. If anything, her attack would have hit the entire village. But if it wasn't her, there was only one other with that sort of power.

Zack hovered over the quad. He then froze in mid-air. The wind shifted and carried him over the medical center. Then, it stopped. Zack dropped onto the roof. It wasn't enough of a drop to hurt him, but it was enough to make him fall to all fours.

He found Isis hovering in front of him. Her eyes were dark as night. "Hey, what is it?" Zack asked. "What are you—" A rumble came from the cloud. Rain poured on their heads.

"Why did you do this, Zack?" Isis' eyes were dark,

her teeth clenched. He had seen that look before, on Valeria when she was enraged. The whole area trembled with deep thunder. Jagged bolts of lightning zigzagged around them.

"Why did I do what, turn you?" Zack's head shot up. "It was the only way to save you."

"Not me, I mean *you*! I knew this was your plan the second Mom told me you went, too! I knew you'd come back…" She motioned both hands at him. Static spread from her fingers. "Like *this*!"

"I had to!" Zack shouted over the thunder. "I couldn't let it be your dad. He needed to stay human. For your mom and for you!"

"I know that! I didn't want him to be turned, either!"

Another thunderbolt exploded like a nearby firecracker. It was so loud that the rest of the village must have heard it as well. The rain intensified into a downpour. It was only happening over the medical center. All around, thick sunshine blanketed the area.

"It was him or me!" Zack wiped the rainwater from his face. "What else was I supposed to do?"

"You could have let me die!" Isis screamed, clenching her fists. "You were the only normal in my life, Zack! The only normal I had!"

The rain intensified. Zack flinched from the drops pelting against his skin. "Now look at you!" Isis yelled through the storm. "Now you're…"

"Now I'm what, Isis?" Zack shouted, his own anger starting to boil. Everything darkened. It must have been from his eyes blackening.

Isis' eyes shut tight. "Now you're like us."

Her body floated down until her feet touched the

roof. Her clenched fists opened. The rain stopped as fast as it started. So did the thunder. He'd have thought it all an illusion if not for the fact he was soaking wet. Isis' head and shoulders slumped. She looked like she wanted to cry except that wasn't something she'd ever be able to do again.

Zack pulled himself to his feet. He thought he knew Isis better than anyone else outside her family. But he now realized how much he misunderstood her all this time. She always showed such pride in being a member of The Witches of Vegas. The smile on her face when her folks trained her lit up the room. Zack was sure she loved being a witch and part of a family of witches. But it was the family part that she loved. For Isis, the witchcraft was secondary. How did he not get that until this moment?

"Isis, you're the most normal person in my life, too." Zack walked toward her. "Nothing changes that, not even this."

Isis' head popped up. Her eyes and mouth opened wide. Zack took her hands. Both dropped to their knees.

"Zack," Isis whispered after several moments of silence. "We're vampires."

"Yeah, we are." Zack let out a sigh. It was a weird sensation exhaling without breath. "Any idea what that means?"

"Only kinda-sorta," Isis answered.

"I guess we're going to have a lot of time to figure it all out." Zack leaned in. He wanted to kiss her just to see if he could still feel, and make sure they still had a connection even after death and rebirth.

"I hate to interrupt." The high-pitched voice sent both Zack's and Isis' attention to the edge of the roof where Simon was perched. "I came to check on you," he said. "By the way, sweet rainbow."

Zack's eyes shot up. The black cloud had been replaced by a rainbow that ran across the sky above the building. "How are they?" Zack asked Simon.

"Sebastian was healed to the point he can be moved to the medical center," Simon answered. "Selena's head wound is healed. At her insistence, the other injuries have yet to be treated. There are others in need of our medical staff's expertise first."

"What about the school?" Isis asked. Across the quad, the roof had collapsed into the top floor. "Please tell me there was no one in there."

"Is Jasper okay?" Zack asked. "Did he get off the building in time?"

"Someone *was* in the building?" Isis gasped.

Simon waved his hands to signal them both to stay calm. "The quad buildings were all empty. Yes, that includes the children who were all in their homes with their families." He folded his hands and smiled. "Jasper avoided the brunt of the collapse. He suffered some injuries, but nothing that cannot be healed by our powerful Doctor Mac and his medical team."

Zack stood up. He offered a hand to Isis, who took it.

Simon limped their way. "There is a lot the two of you need to learn if you are to survive as vampires. It is not the easiest of existences, especially at the beginning. I can tell you that I am still here only because Luther took me under his wing and passed along all that pertinent information. I wish to do the same for you. That is why I have requested to our president that the two of you be allowed to remain here in New Salem."

"What about my family?" Isis asked. "Will they stay too?"

"The conversation was only about you and Zack. It did not extend to the rest of our guests. I know earlier they were asked to leave. The president has not said if her mind has changed on that request."

Zack and Isis exchanged a glance. Isis cupped a hand over her wide open mouth. Even without that look, Zack knew exactly how she felt about this.

Her head dropped. "My folks...they're still teaching me about being a witch—"

"There are plenty in this village who can finish your Wiccan training," Simon responded. "But there are very few in the entire world who can teach you how to exist, and continue on, as vampires."

"I think we can figure it out." Zack put a hand on Isis' shoulder. "We'll have each other to lean on."

"You need to learn to hunt for animal blood while ignoring the temptation of human blood."

Zack raised his eyebrows. "What do you mean by temptation?"

"Human blood has an enticing aroma, and we have an amazing sense of smell." Simon slapped a finger across the side of his nose. "Over time, I have learned to ignore it. I am no longer tempted. When I first turned, being around people was like walking through a bakery when everything has come fresh out of the oven. And that's just one aspect of our existence you need to learn about."

"I was just around people," Zack said. "I didn't smell their blood. I certainly wasn't enticed to open anyone up and slurp out their insides."

Simon waved his hand in a dismissive fashion. "You also just recently had blood. Believe me, when the previous dose has run its course and your body craves another to survive, the temptation to 'open someone up and slurp out their insides' can take you over."

"But… we can resist it?" Isis asked.

"Well," Simon replied, "there are tricks of the trade, so to speak."

Isis placed her hands over her face. Zack thought her fatigued—but fatigue was something they could no longer feel—she was just overwhelmed from everything they had just been through. Zack spoke up. "Can we take some time to think about it?"

"Of course, the decision is yours." Simon waved them along. "For now, let's get off this roof and join everyone in front of the medical center. I wish to show you something quite charming. It is just one of the many ways the people of New Salem come together."

Chapter Thirty-two

New Salem had a unique tradition when it came to their residents who were injured and receiving treatment at the medical center. According to Simon, the tradition was reserved for those hurt while defending the village from threats. Valeria's attack was by far the worst they had ever faced. The New Salem villagers all waited outside the medical center so they could greet the patients once released.

Isis would have appreciated the tradition if her mind weren't preoccupied with guilt. The lack of a door to the medical center was evidence of the battle that stared her in the face. They didn't even have Valeria to blame for that. To get Valeria's attention, it was Isis who telekinetically ripped the door from its hinges and propelled it into the mad witch. If she had time, she would have found another way. In that moment, it was the only projectile that was available and strong enough to get the evil witch's attention.

Isis knew—even if others didn't want to say it— that everyone getting treated in that building had her to blame. That included her parents and the village's law enforcement who had to fight a threat that should never have been here in the first place. No one around Isis was throwing her dirty looks. But if they did, she would understand why.

"Hey," Zack said, snapping Isis out of her

thoughts. "I'm sure your folks are okay. Most of their wounds were healed before they were taken inside."

Zack was right, at least about her mom and dad, but what about everyone else in there? How would the people of this village recover? Isis' gaze darted to the damaged school. God, everything Valeria did here fell on her shoulders.

Jasper was the first to leave the medical center. The villagers cheered. He took a bow and stepped forward where he was greeted by village president Tia. The two exchanged a passionate embrace. Zack had mentioned they were in a relationship. Whatever injuries Jasper sustained, Doctor Mac healed him completely. It gave Isis hope for the rest of the patients. With that hope, she allowed herself a moment of ease.

Another figure walked through the doorway. This time Paul stepped out to the cheers of his fellow New Salem residents. Paul, however, did not walk out unscathed. He was hunched over, leaning on a brown cane. He was immediately hugged by a tall blonde woman and a teen girl with similar hair color. The girl was about Isis' and Zack's age. Paul kissed the girl on her forehead, then gave the woman a long smooch on the lips.

"She caused a minor stroke," Paul said to them. "Mac healed me as best he could, but the brain is the hardest muscle to restore. He's preparing me for weeks of physical therapy. I may walk with a limp for the rest of my life."

"We'll get through this," his wife replied. "It's what we do, right?"

Paul straightened his back as best as he could. He took another step using his cane for balance. Tia was waiting for him. "Madam President," he said. "I'm sorry to report Carolyn did not make it. The heart attack Valeria induced was too much for her to overcome. Mac couldn't save her. He had to make an immediate choice so he wouldn't lose us both. Because of my position of authority, he chose to heal me first."

"I understand." Tia wiped her eyes. "We will make sure her sacrifice is remembered."

Isis sobbed. Her insides couldn't take it anymore. She ran to the president and vice-president. "I'm sorry. It's all because of me and I'm so sorry about all of this."

"No one is blaming you, Isis," Tia said to her. "I can promise you that."

"I'm blaming me!" she shouted. "We never should have come here. My family wanted to save me, and it brought nothing but fighting and death. None of you deserve this."

"Isis!" Zack placed a hand on her shoulder. All eyes were pointed their way.

Paul hobbled past everyone. "I can use a walk. Isis, why don't you join me?"

Paul's question did not sound like a request. Isis walked with him, staying by his side in case he lost his balance. He led her across the quad to a quiet area between the school and the marketplace.

"I never found out what happened to Valeria," Paul said.

"She's gone," Isis answered. "Valeria can't hurt this village ever, or anyone else, again."

"That's good to hear," Paul said. "I understand Simon wants you and Zack to remain as part of our community, so he can teach you."

"We're going to turn it down," Isis replied. "I shouldn't be here, not after everything I caused."

"What you caused?" Paul asked. "What do you think you caused?"

"It's because of me we came to your village. It's because of me Valeria was here. Your village was a happy place before we entered your lives with our problems."

"Tell me something, Isis. Did you ask Valeria to make you a vampire?"

"No. Of course, I didn't." Isis threw her arms out. "I never wanted this."

"So, she infected you against your will."

"Yes!"

"Then how is any of this *your* fault?"

"Because I wasn't strong enough, or brave enough, to fight her." Isis shook her head. "My family should never have taken me here in the first place."

"They brought you here because they were looking for help to save you," Paul replied. "I know if it was my daughter's life on the line, I'd go anywhere and do anything to save her. It was Valeria who infected you. Then, it was she who nearly destroyed our village. None of that happened because of your actions. You are not guilty of her rampage. In fact, it was you who stopped it. An action which, by the way, was quite brave."

Isis looked up at Paul. His words didn't take away all the guilt, but she did feel a little better. It was a relief that the village didn't see her as a monster. Well, at least Paul didn't. "Thank you," she mumbled.

"With that said, there are concerns which go much farther than just New Salem."

"What concerns?"

Paul leaned forward on his cane, bringing himself as close to eye level as possible. "Valeria was an immortal witch. That sort of power and longevity corrupted her. I saw it all over her face. The woman was intoxicated and consumed by the power."

"That's how Luther described her." Isis shut her eyes. Luther…another loved one taken by Valeria.

Paul poked Isis in the stomach with his finger. Her eyes shot open in response. "Isis, *you* are now an immortal witch. You won the day, but don't let that get to your head. With that sort of power, it can be easy to forget your morals."

"No matter how long I go on, I will never be like her. I don't hurt people!"

"I can see that in you, Isis." Paul pushed himself upright. "But who can say what will happen hundreds of years from now? We all change. In the medical center, Sebastian told me some of Valeria's history. He also told me how in each generation, groups of witches like your family, were trained and ready in case Valeria ever returned. It's a good thing that safeguards like your coven were put in place."

"What are you saying?"

"I believe similar precautions must be put in place for you." Paul's tone became stronger. He was no longer speaking to Isis like a child. "That responsibility should fall on New Salem's witches to make sure you never become like Valeria. And to be ready in case someday you should ever lose your perspective on humanity."

Isis took in all of Paul's words. "Are you saying you're forcing me to stay here?"

"No, this is a community, not a prison," Paul replied. "It's still your choice, but it is your best choice. I agree that you're nothing like Valeria. That means you could become a strong asset to the people of New Salem. I believe that could be your future, Isis. Still, I'd rather hope for the best and prepare for the worst, wouldn't you?"

She couldn't argue with Paul's rationale. When Valeria was turned by Luther, she could have been as much of an unassuming type as Isis was today. Did Valeria always think so little about human life that she'd kill anyone who got in her way without the slightest bit of compassion? Or did that happen over a long period of time? If it was the latter, after hundreds of years, could Isis also become that jaded toward the living as well? The very thought made her head hurt.

"I get it, I really do," Isis said. "The only thing is…I just don't want—"

The crowd in the quad cheered again. This time, it was Selena and Sebastian who stepped out. They seemed well. Zack greeted Selena with a hug and Sebastian with a handshake. Then, Simon shook their hands. It was a relief to Isis that the crowd applauded her folks as opposed to throwing rotten tomatoes at them. It meant Paul and Tia were telling the truth when they said no one blamed them for their recent troubles.

Isis threw a wide-eyed look to Paul, who smiled. "Go ahead. I'll be fine getting back on my own."

"You're sure?"

"Go!"

Isis ran across the quad, zigzagging between the people in front of the medical center. She gave her folks one huge bearhug around their waists. "Are you okay?"

she asked. "Please tell me you're both okay."

"We're okay," Sebastian said.

"What about Sacha? Is she really…"

"I'm afraid so," Selena whispered. Isis tightened her squeeze.

"Valeria, she's gone?" Sebastian asked.

"I sent her into outer space," Isis answered, letting them both out of her hug, but keeping a grip of each of their hands. "She's frozen and floating far away from Earth."

"Really?" Sebastian asked.

Isis nodded. "It was all I could think to do."

"It was good thinking," Selena looked to the sky. "I hope she rots up there forever."

"How are you doing, Isis?" Sebastian asked with concern.

"I don't know." Isis threw her hands against the sides of her head. "I'm still me, I think. But I feel different."

"You are still you, Isis," Sebastian said. "You will always be you. Even if we're not here helping you grow."

Simon stepped forward. "Ahh, then we are in agreement?"

"No, we're not." Isis faced Sebastian and Selena. "You always said we are more than a coven—we're a family and we stick together. I still need you."

Selena put her hands over Isis' cheeks. She leaned her face in so their foreheads touched. "Isis, we don't want to lose you either, but we can't teach you to survive as a vampire. They didn't include us in your invitation. We're not happy about this, but if we can't stay here, you need to."

"I don't understand," Zack chimed in. "You lived with Luther for most of your lives. He must have shared with you what a vampire needs to survive, right?"

"You would think that," Sebastian muttered. "But Luther was the textbook definition of a private person."

"Where will you go?" Isis asked. She couldn't hide the frog in her throat.

"We haven't figured that out yet," Selena answered.

"I don't think Las Vegas is an option," Sebastian added. "I'm sure we're under investigation over there for your abduction. That would especially be a problem if we went back without you."

Simon slapped his hands together and held them against his chest. "My friends, I am sorry my invitation could not include you. I am offering to train these new vampires out of necessity, but I could only make that case for them. I do promise, they will learn everything they need to know to exist for the next thousand years or longer. Plus, they will always be safe here in New Salem. I'll make sure of it."

Before Sebastian could answer, Isis cut him off. "I'm sorry, Simon, but I won't stay, not if it means breaking up our family."

"I don't think that is a good plan for you," Simon responded. "Are you sure?"

Isis nodded. "I am."

"Regrettable." Simon waved a hand at Zack. "What about you, my friend?"

"Isis speaks for both of us," he said with his hands pressed against his hips. "I know there's a lot you can teach us, but we stick together, whether it is here or anywhere else."

Simon nodded. "I can, perhaps, speak with Tia on the subject once more."

"Speak to me about what?"

Isis whirled to see Tia approaching their huddle with Jasper at her side. Even with enhanced vampire senses, she didn't notice the president's approach. Apparently, neither did Simon and he was more adept at using those senses.

"We were discussing our arrangement to bring Isis and Zack to New Salem as citizens," Simon explained. "And how the offer does not extend to their guardians."

"No, it does not," Tia replied. "We do have protocols here. Simon has good reason to sponsor our two young vampires. However, it is not his place to make that offer to you."

"Madam President," Sebastian said with the look in his eye Isis knew well. It came out whenever he was about to be persuasive, and not always with just his natural charm. "We are not here to question your ways, but they are right, we've been through too much together to split up—"

Tia raised a hand, cutting off Sebastian. She offered a huge smile. "So, allow me to make the offer directly to you. Selena and Sebastian, the two of you have an amazing connection to Earth's energy. Plus, we have all seen firsthand how well you handle adversity."

"Thank you," Selena said.

"I can see the two of you playing important roles in New Salem. Therefore, I invite you to remain here as citizens." She looked back at Jasper. "When the dust settles and we have mourned, our law enforcement team will need new members." Jasper nodded his agreement. Tia returned her attention to Isis and her family. "We could use you in that role. Would this be acceptable to all of you?"

"What about my sister?" Selena asked.

"With your permission, we would like to hold her funeral here and then bury her among our honored ancestors," Tia answered. "She did, after all, give her life to save us all."

"I have a question." Sebastian raised a finger. "You clearly planned for us to stay. Why not make this offer initially along with Isis and Zack? Why make us think we had to leave, and without them?"

"Originally, we did decide it was best that you left," Tia answered. "But recent events have given us a change of perspective. That aside, as I understand, you are celebrities in Las Vegas. I had to know for sure you want to be here."

"Was this a test?" Selena asked.

"I guess you could say that." Tia shrugged. "We've had…experiences with witches who were not fully committed in their relocation to New Salem."

"Boy, have we." Simon laughed.

"We understand Isis and Zack need to be here. With you, it's a choice," Tia said. "There are laws and there are customs everyone in our village must follow. If you are willing to acclimate, we would be honored to have you among our citizens."

Selena and Sebastian exchanged a look. There wasn't much of a decision to make since staying was the only way to keep the family together. They had to want that, too. Still, Isis loved how they rarely needed a verbal conversation to reach a decision. It was the type of connection she wanted to someday have with Zack. Of course, she also thought she and Zack would have a normal relationship and grow old together. Some things were just not meant to be.

Sebastian extended his hand. "We accept and we thank you."

"Good." Tia shook his hand. "When you are ready, the first thing we will ask of you is to put your power toward assistance in rebuilding our school."

"We can certainly do that." Selena displayed a surprising grin.

Chapter Thirty-three

After living a life as a magician, and then with powerful witches, Zack was hard to impress. But the cohesiveness of the New Salem villagers, he had to admit, was remarkable. Witches and non-witches alike worked together in groups. Each group worked on a different task. Within an hour, two graves were dug six feet apart and the caskets were levitated into the air, then lowered. Tombstones were engraved and placed at the head of each burial place. During this time, another smaller group reattached the doors to the medical center.

Once the work was done, villagers gathered in front of the two new graves for what would be a somber funeral. Everyone had come out to pay their respects. Paul, his family, and Natasha were directly in front of Carolyn's grave along with a few people Zack didn't recognize. Even Doctor Mac made a rare appearance outside of the medical center to attend the service.

"I want our new arrivals to know that New Salem has a specific design," Tia said while facing the mourners from between the graves. "Our cemetery is circular and surrounds our land so the souls of our fallen still play a role in our community. They watch over us through sickness and in health. They keep our children safe. They guard our borders from outside threats. For hundreds of years, our ancestors have protected our village from evil spirits and will continue to do so for all eternity.

"Today, our village came under attack. Although the threat to our lives has been neutralized, it was not without cost. Our lost souls now join the spirits of our ancestors. Carolyn was born and raised here. She trained under Paul and became a member of the New Salem Law Enforcement team. I've known Carolyn for most of her life, and I can tell you that is the role she has wanted since childhood. She always put the safety and security of our village first, and she did so without hesitation. Carolyn, a beloved daughter and younger sister. We will miss her."

Tia dropped her head and took a deep breath. She returned her attention to her fellow villagers. "We also pay our respects to one of our new friends, Sacha. She was not a resident of New Salem. But today, she heroically sacrificed her life to save our village. Sacha, a beloved sister, sister-in-law, and aunt. In one day, she earned our admiration.

"In life, these two fine women brought joy and security to their loved ones. In death, they join our family, friends, and neighbors in watching over us and our future descendants. Ladies and gentlemen, I ask you all to take a moment of silence as we remember our fallen."

Everyone stood in thought or prayer. Zack was sure if he dropped a pin, he would hear it fall. It wasn't until this moment that he realized how many children of various ages lived in New Salem. How many of them had Wiccan power or would once they were of age? It wouldn't be all of them—just like with the adults—but enough that this community made up the most powerful group of people in the world. That they kept it secret for hundreds of years was a miracle itself.

Isis, a few feet in front of him, had her head buried in Sebastian's chest. Selena stood on Sebastian's other side with her arms wrapped around his waist. Sebastian held them both tight. Selena's sob was loud. When Sebastian turned his head, Zack saw the water in his eyes. Somehow, Sebastian held it together for the sake of his wife and daughter, but only by a thread.

A hand grabbed his shoulder and squeezed. Zack jumped out of his thoughts. "Why are you not standing up front with your family?" Simon whispered in his ear. He was once again using his cane.

"I'm devastated about Sacha's death and that's after only knowing her for a year," Zack answered. "Selena and Sebastian grew up with her. Sacha helped raise Isis. Since I'm new to the family, I thought I'd give them the time to mourn together."

"I would think they'd prefer to have you at their side." Simon threw him a grin. "That's not vampire advice, that's human nature advice."

Damn, Simon was probably right. Zack did belong at their side, not avoiding the only people left in the world that he cared about. He stepped forward but quickly pulled back. What could he possibly say to make them feel better? Sacha was the spirit behind The Witches of Vegas, and now she was gone. There were no magic words Zack could pull out of a hat to make them feel better about it.

"Simon, can I ask you a vampire-related question?"

"Of course," the older vampire replied. "I am here for any vampire-related questions you may have."

"That's good because I have about a billion of

them." Zack rotated back to face Simon. It was also to get Simon to release his shoulder grip. "I get that, technically, we are dead, which means we can no longer feel. I think I can sense that happening in me but with Isis that's clearly not the case. How can she feel? Are those just instinctual memories or something?"

Simon glanced over at Isis who still had one hand against Sebastian's back and the other holding Selena's arm. Her face was red despite being dry from a lack of tears. "Some of us think with our intelligence," he answered. "And others think with our emotions. Most of us are a combination of both, but we lean in one direction or the other." He returned his gaze to Zack. "I take it Isis is an emotional young lady?"

"Deeply. Yes."

"As I told you before, our emotions stay with us, some long after death." He slapped Zack playfully on his back. "You should go to her. She can use you right now."

"What about her skin tone?"

Simon's eyebrows shot straight up across his forehead. "I'm sorry, what?"

"I know my skin is going to look like paste after a while. But Isis' skin is a few shades darker. Will she also become as pale?"

Simon's slight eye roll didn't go unnoticed. "I couldn't answer that, Zack. My skin was the same shade as yours before I died."

"I know, but what about vampires that have her complexion or darker?" Zack asked. "How do they look after a few hundred years?"

"Perhaps that is a question you can ask when we go to the vampire club next week," Simon answered. "That is where we share vampire stories and compare experiences. They even keep all types of blood on tap."

"Are you joking?" Zack's head tilted. "There is really a vampire club?"

"Of course, there's not a vampire club, Zack," Simon snapped. "Until recently, the only other vampire I've ever known besides myself was Luther." Simon spun Zack around and shoved him hard against his lower back. "Now stop stalling and be there for your family. Jeeze."

Well, damn, so much for the teacher's philosophy of "there are no stupid questions." Apparently, his new "mentor" had a low level of patience and a high use of sarcasm. Zack made a mental note then took a slow walk to Isis and her folks. He was still unsure of what he could say or do. Maybe Simon had a good point, that being there was enough. Once in front of them, the three looked his way.

Selena was the first to speak. "How are you doing, Zack?" she asked.

Zack peered into their sad eyes. They were all waiting for him to say something, anything. Unfortunately, nothing brilliant came to mind. Even though his heart no longer beat, Zack decided to speak from it anyway.

"Last year, when I lost my uncle, Sacha went out of her way to make me feel better. I mean, each of you did too, but Sacha really said a lot of the right things that worked."

"She thought the world of you, Zack," Sebastian said.

Zack nodded. "I want to do the same for all of you. I've been trying to come up with the right words to make you feel better today." Zack shook his head. "But I think there are no right words that can be said. Maybe I shouldn't even try because you have a right to feel sad. Maybe all I can do is stand here and be sad with you."

Selena offered a slight smile. "I think you just said the right words."

Isis wrapped her arms around Zack's neck and gave him a tight, passionate hug. Turned out Simon was right; he should have been by their side from the beginning. They needed him as much as he needed them.

At Carolyn's grave, Tia exchanged sad hugs with an older couple and a younger adult woman. Zack was sure they were Carolyn's family. Tia did the same with Paul and Natasha before walking across to Sacha's grave. Isis quickly stepped away from Zack like a student about to get caught misbehaving by the teacher.

"Hey," Tia said, grabbing each of their attention. "No rush, but when you're ready, we can discuss your relocation to New Salem."

"We are ready," Selena responded.

"Good. Then I would like to offer you a nice cottage. It has three bedrooms, two bathrooms, and it's fully furnished with a mid-century theme." Her head darted to Zack and Isis. "Oh, unless you would prefer two smaller cottages. I do have a few of those available as well."

"Two cottages could work." Isis grinned. She paused at the double glare she received from Selena and Sebastian. "Or maybe not." Her teeth clenched.

"One will be just fine, thank you." Sebastian's eyes never left Zack and Isis. "At least for now."

Zack wanted to argue that he and Isis should have a place of their own. Neither needed to sleep, which would only become annoying to those in the cottage who did. Besides, it wasn't like he could get her pregnant, right? They were dead, after all. For the first time in his life, he decided to keep his mouth shut and refrain from speaking his mind.

"The three-bedroom cottage it is," Tia replied. "The faster you gather your belongings, the faster you can get settled in."

"That's appreciated," Selena said. Her eyes shut and her lips turned downward. "Unfortunately, our belongings are in Las Vegas. Without my sister, I don't know if I have the power to teleport us such a distance."

"Isis does," Zack announced. "She teleported us a few times from Vegas to my uncle's grave on that Caribbean island."

"That's right, on your birthday," Sebastian responded. "I didn't know the two of you had gone back any other time."

"I can do it," Isis said. "Can I just…have a few minutes to say goodbye to Sacha?"

"Of course." Sebastian wrapped his arm around Selena's waist. "Take all the time you need."

Isis took Zack's hand and walked to Sacha's grave. The look on her face as she stared down was blank, like she just didn't have any more sadness left in her. Her eyes shut and she squeezed Zack's hand.

"Hey, can I try something?" Zack asked.

"Try what?" Isis faced him.

Zack planted his lips onto Isis'. The kiss was passionate and longer than any kiss they'd ever shared. It was a reminder that they no longer needed air. Their lips touching gave Zack a warm feeling inside. It could have been an unconscious memory of what their kisses felt like, but either way, it was real to him.

Zack's biggest worry about being turned into a vampire was that over time he would lose his humanity. That he would someday forget how to feel. Now he knew it wasn't a worry at all. With Isis at his side, that would never happen.

Chapter Thirty-four

Tia folded her hands across her desk. So far, she had served only two years as president of New Salem. She had eighteen months as vice-president under her belt prior to being forced into the big chair. Despite this, her residents still saw her as the one who should have all the answers and be able to accommodate any request they made.

Her grandfather—the former president—was right when he told Tia that many of the requests that came across the desk would be similar in nature. There was a good chance he never had one like what the village's newest residents had just asked. Especially from a family with such strong connections and who had just become residents of New Salem less than four hours ago.

She eyed the faces staring her way. Sebastian and Selena sat on the wood chairs in front of her desk with Isis and Zack standing behind them. When they asked for this meeting, Tia thought there was a problem with their new accommodations. They hadn't yet transported to Las Vegas to retrieve their belongings. Sebastian had said there were issues with that trip due to a misunderstanding over Isis' guardianship. Tia thought they would ask for assistance in reacquiring their belongings. She certainly called this one wrong.

"Okay, let me see if I'm following." Tia leaned

back against her beige leather chair. It was the widest chair with the biggest backrest in the entire village. It certainly wasn't meant for someone of her lean physique. It was originally designed by Nickolas for Tia's grandfather, who had far less than a lean physique. "You wish to reopen the portal to that other dimension so you can bring your family mentor's body back for a proper burial."

"We wish to bury him next to Sacha," Sebastian explained while Isis leaned against the top of his chair. "We know she would want that. He would as well."

"It was Isis' idea," Zack added.

Tia glanced over her shoulder where Paul leaned against his cane. Even in his new habilitated condition, he refused to sit. He felt standing behind Tia's chair and peering down at whomever sat across the desk provided Tia an edge in terms of stature. Normally, Jas stood behind her along with Paul. But he just fractured his right leg by leaping off a five-story building to save his own life. Once healed, Tia and Doctor Mac insisted he get at least a day's rest.

Then again, look at what this family sitting in front of her had just gone through. They lost a beloved family member, Selena suffered a concussion, and Sebastian had two limbs broken. Add to all that their two youngest had to die and be resurrected as vampires. All this just to save the world. Immediately after suffering such trauma, they were leaving their lives behind and relocating to a new land that was unfamiliar to them. Now they were ready to get back out there and take another risk that required an amazing exertion of power. Perhaps that was the life of big-city people. They were movers and shakers.

Looks of resolve crossed Zack's and Isis' faces. It mirrored the look on Sebastian's. He opened the meeting by saying they had one loose end to tie up. Selena, however, came off far more reluctant. She was slumped in the chair with her head pointed down.

"What about you, Selena?" Tia asked. "Do you not share in your family's request?"

"Luther was like a father to us," Selena replied. "So, of course, I would want to bury his remains here. It's just...I know how to open a rift to the Other World, but without Sacha, I don't think—" Selena paused and wiped a hand across her moist eyes. "I know I don't have the strength to make it happen."

"Can you teach another witch how to do it?" Zack asked Selena. "Maybe Isis?"

Paul slammed his cane on the ground. "Absolutely not!" His enraged tone made Zack spin back and almost jump out of his chair. "That knowledge cannot spread under any circumstances."

"I'm sorry, but I must agree with my vice-president," Tia said. "I do not believe this is something that should be taught to any witch in New Salem, or anywhere else. If you do not have the power to do this, Selena, then I'm afraid it cannot and should not be done."

Isis' face lit up with excitement She grabbed Selena's shoulder. "I can give you the strength," she said. "I can make your connection stronger."

"How can you do that?" Sebastian peeked back and asked.

"I don't know how. But I did it before when Mom and Sacha couldn't take us here. I shared my connection. That's how we got through."

"Oh." Selena's eyebrows rose. "That explains a lot," she said directly to Sebastian.

Tia kept a firm posture to go along with the friendly grin she had practiced for years in the mirror. It was something her grandfather taught her early on. The smile displayed confidence and hid nervousness that may have been in the pit of her stomach. She felt that uneasiness around Isis. From what Tia knew about witches—and that encompassed a lot—the more connected a witch had to the Earth's energies, the younger they were when that connection manifested. The most powerful witch Tia knew that was born in New Salem was Natasha. She manifested at twelve years old. Isis was three years younger when it happened to her.

Isis' outer appearance was one of a scrawny and slightly immature teenage girl. But inside she had a wealth of potential in her Wiccan abilities. That was on display when she single-handedly defeated Valeria. At sixteen Isis was a powerful witch and she would only become stronger. Now that she was a vampire, even old age would never kill her. Her level of experience in controlling the energy would grow forever.

Initially, Tia had her reservations about Paul's proposal. It was a long-term commitment to make on behalf of generations that hadn't even been born yet. But now that she had time to think about it, Paul was right. Isis' guardians instilled a good set of morals and values in her. They taught her to see the goodness in humanity and to be humble in her powers. Now it was up to New Salem, for the rest of eternity, to enforce those values in order to keep the world safe. The future relied on their success, or their contingency plans in case they failed.

"What do you say, Mom?" Isis asked with excitement. "Can we try?"

Selena's face perked up, maybe for the first time since her sister's death. After all they'd been through, and considering Sacha's sacrifice, Tia really didn't want to deny their request. But she had her apprehensions toward yet another such display in the middle of their village. Her vice-president did as well. Tia didn't need Wiccan powers to know when Paul's brain was filled with concerns. It practically radiated off his body. But he was also a man with a lot of heart who genuinely cared about the residents of this village. Even the new ones.

"Paul." Tia sat back in her chair. She threw her vice-president a huge smile. "You are the head of law enforcement in New Salem. I would like to defer this decision to your judgment."

All four members of The Witches of Vegas looked to Paul. Isis and Zack flashed hopeful, yet innocent eyes. Tia had to remind herself that, despite the innocence across their young faces, they were now immortal vampires. Then again, so was Simon and he had become a prominent and beloved member of New Salem. Well, maybe beloved was stretching it. But his contributions to their society and enthusiasm were second to none.

Paul took a wobbly step closer to the desk. He finally answered. "More than anyone, I understand the importance of a mentor and the need to get closure when he passes. That is why I feel we should approve this request but with a few conditions."

"Which are?" Sebastian asked.

"I want a wide perimeter from other residents. That's on us," Paul explained. "But we agree that this is the last time. It can never happen again. That's on you." Paul focused his attention on Selena. "Plus, you cannot share the knowledge of how to open a dimensional rift with anyone. That includes your family. The last thing we need around here is our witches experimenting with opening portals to other worlds."

"I will take that knowledge to my grave," Selena answered. "I give you my word."

"Then you have our approval," Tia said with a smile. "We will even return your empowered crystals in order to increase your chances of success."

"I thought our crystals burned out," Zack said.

"The witches combined an illusion spell to make you believe that," Tia responded.

Sebastian's eyebrows rose. "It was part of the illusion?"

"That wasn't the intention, but I'm sure you know how unpredictable Wiccan magic at times can be." Tia grinned. "Doctor Mac will need those crystals to replace the ones that were lost. However, he can wait on obtaining them until after your journey. You let us know when you are ready."

"Immediately," Selena said. "We'd like to get started immediately."

"Okay, then." She did appreciate their enthusiasm. It was almost intoxicating. "We'll make room in the quad and you can reopen your portal."

Selena and Sebastian jumped out of their chairs. The four turned around and walked out of the office. Tia had a hunch this new family would make life in New Salem just a bit more interesting. And maybe that was exactly what this village needed. She also sensed that, once fully acclimated, they were the types who would put their best efforts into helping New Salem thrive.

Chapter Thirty-five

Zack couldn't believe he and Sebastian were about to go back to the Other World. At least this time he wouldn't need to sneak in behind Sebastian. They would walk through the portal together. Even more surprising was that he couldn't remember the last time he slept, yet he didn't feel the slightest bit of fatigue. He certainly didn't expect that to be the end result when they first teleported to the village. Or that it would become home.

Just as Paul promised, their end of the quad was empty of people. Most of the residents were either back to work or in their cottages recouping from the day's adventures. Many of them claimed they needed time to digest it all even though none were ever directly involved in the battle with Valeria. A few groups of villagers lingered around to watch from a distance. Apparently, word that they were reopening the portal spread quickly.

"Okay, are we just about ready?" Sebastian asked Selena who placed the last of the crystals in position.

"We need Isis," she said.

"I'll get her," Zack replied.

Isis stood across the quad watching from a distance a woman sitting on the grass, cross-legged, with an acoustic guitar in her lap. A group of children sat across from the lady singing along with her. The group consisted of three boys, two girls, and a German shepherd. None of the children could have been older than six. The youngest, a girl, had to be around three years old. The dog sat next to her.

Zack jogged the length of the quad. Once next to Isis, he was able to hear the song the woman sang with the children. Perhaps they would have been in a classroom...if the building's top floor wasn't destroyed by Valeria.

Isis' eyes were almost trance-like watching the group. Her head turned to Zack. "Hey," she said to him. She refocused on the singalong.

Zack draped his arm around her shoulders. "Are you enjoying this rendition of the alphabet song?" he asked jokingly.

"It's better than Club 90's," Isis answered with a smirk.

While most of the children were focused on the adult with the guitar and her song, one little boy with jet-black hair, a dirty white T-shirt, and jean shorts peeked over his shoulder at Isis and Zack. He stood up from the grass and ran over to them. Isis stepped forward. Now, inches away, the boy stopped in his tracks. His eyes were wide and maybe a little bit fearful as he looked up at Isis.

"Hi," Isis said to him. "What's your name?"

"Brandon."

From the dirt on his hands, Zack had a hunch he was one of the farmer's kids.

"I'm Isis," she replied. "I'm new here."

"I know. My mom says you're a witch and you're a vampire, too."

"I am." Isis' voice was barely above a whisper. She

dropped to her knees. It made the boy slightly taller.

He stepped forward with a hesitation in his step. "Are you a bad witch?" Brandon asked.

"No, I'm a good witch."

"Does that mean you're gonna protect us?"

"As best as I can."

"Isis." Zack rested a hand on the back of her neck. "Your folks need us. They're ready."

"Right." Isis leaned in and smiled. "It was nice meeting you, Brandon. You should go back to your class now."

"My big sister is a witch like you." Brandon grinned. "When we do our chores, she makes the vacuum move all by itself."

"That's really cool," Isis replied.

"I hope I'm a witch when I get older." Brandon ran to his group.

"Either way, you're important," Isis shouted. "Always remember that!"

Her focus stayed on the boy who sat on the grass with the other kids. He waved to Isis with a big grin before rejoining the others in singing their next song, "Itsy Bitsy Spider."

Zack knew that frozen stare well. It was the look Isis had whenever she was troubled or just lost in her own head. "What is it?" he asked. "What's wrong?"

"That little boy, Brandon," Isis replied, her gaze never wavering. "We're going to see him die. We're going to see all those kids die. Then we'll see their kids die, and then the kids after them die. All that time, we're still going to be this age."

Wow, that was an aspect of their immortality that Zack hadn't yet pondered, but it clearly had occurred to

Isis. That lives of people they would come to know and care about would pass by quickly. Generations would live their lives from birth to death, but for Zack and Isis, each life would fly by in what would feel like the span of a heartbeat. With that in mind, they'd need to make sure they never took any of their friends or loved ones for granted. If that happened, their humanity would truly be gone.

"They're ready to open the portal," Zack said to get Isis refocused and out of her own head. "How about you? Are *you* ready?"

Zack offered his hand. Isis took it and pulled herself to her feet. She straightened her shoulders and turned from the children. "Yes, I'm ready," she responded. "Let's do this."

Zack and Isis power-walked across the quad. It quickly turned into a mad dash, then an impromptu race. Zack won by a foot. Isis let out the first laugh he had heard from her since their turn. It almost felt normal except for the fact that neither of them were out of breath. Isis walked to Sebastian who cupped his hand against her cheek. His gaze spoke volumes. It said even though she was technically dead and a vampire, he still worried about her. Isis wrapped her hand around his wrist. "I'm okay," she said with a wide-eyed smile. Sebastian nodded.

Isis ran to Selena who stood several feet away. "Let's do this, sweetie," Selena said.

"I'm ready, Mom," Isis replied.

Selena dropped to her knees. Isis stood behind her. She placed her fingers along Selena's shoulders. Across from them, Zack joined Sebastian at his side.

Selena jumped into her fast-talking chant while

holding out her palms. Isis, meanwhile, closed her eyes with two fists at her sides. Her head pointed downward at Selena. It was several minutes before electrical sparks filled the air in front of them. The sparks increased in number and formed a circle between the pentagonal shape of crystals. Soon, the circle filled with static. Once the static stopped, Isis and Selena blurred as if Zack were seeing them through a huge soap bubble.

"I'll be damned, she really can share her connection," Sebastian mumbled to himself.

"You never taught her that," Zack said as more of a statement than a question.

"No, she picked it up all by herself." There was a glimmer of pride in Sebastian's voice. "Let's head in."

Zack and Sebastian marched forward and through the portal. The moment they crossed over, the bright blue sky and green grass around them turned gray. "Wow, I didn't think we'd ever be back here," Zack said.

"Let alone in the same day," Sebastian replied.

From the moment they walked through the portal, the heavy aroma from the long grass burned Zack's nose hairs. It had a rotten egg mixed with bad body odor smell to it, and it was a lot stronger than the last time they were here. Then again, it may have been that his senses were a lot more sensitive in this reanimated state. Zack shut his eyes and rubbed his nose to relieve himself of the stench. It didn't help. Man, did all grass stink this bad, or was it just here in the Other World?

Zack popped his eyes open. That's when he saw it. By his feet lay the wood spear across the grass. The wood no longer shined like when Simon first showed it off. Brown soot covered it from top to bottom. Zack was sure the soot was Luther's five-hundred-year-old blood. This was the spot Valeria had impaled him. It was also the spot she killed that animal with the same spear. Both bodies were gone. But how could that be?

"Is it possible Luther survived?" Zack asked. "If he did, where is he?"

"Zack," Sebastian called out. "Look ahead."

"What the hell?" Zack muttered with widened eyes.

A dozen of the bull-like animals sat in a semi-circle a distance away. Luther's stiff body lay inside the semi-circle. One by one, the animals howled at the sky, then looked back down at Luther's corpse. To Zack, it came off random which animal howled, yet it seemed they all knew when it was their turn. None of them noticed Zack and Sebastian watching from afar, or the portal behind them, they all stayed focused on Luther.

"What are they doing?" Zack whispered even though they were far enough from the animals that they wouldn't have heard him even if he spoke in a normal tone.

Sebastian answered. "It looks to me like a ceremony for the dead."

"They're having a funeral?" Zack's mouth opened wide. "How would they even know from—"

Zack wheezed at the sight of two of the animals, one at each end of the semi-circle standing on their hind legs. They walked around the pack and Luther. Once the second animal finished the circle, the first one let out a loud high-pitched squeal. At no point did either of the two animals drop onto all fours.

As if in response to the squeal, four of the animals

walked up to Luther. They dropped their heads and used them to roll the expired vampire's body to the nearby cliff. At the edge, in unison, they pushed Luther one last time, sending him over the cliff. The animals all lined up along the edge and stared down. This included the two who had walked on their hind legs.

"How are we going to get his body from down there?" Zack asked.

"We won't," Sebastian answered. "The idea was to bring Luther home and have a proper funeral for him. This was the place Luther called home and the endemic species just held a funeral for him based on their customs. Luther has been sufficiently put to rest."

"By dumping his corpse over a cliff?"

"I'm sure if we looked down there, we'd see all of their dead at the bottom of that cliff. Luther's body is now among them."

"I don't understand," Zack said. "Luther was their enemy, their predator. These animals have spent the last four hundred years fighting for their lives against Valeria. Then Luther joined her in slaughtering them for the last year. Why would they hold a funeral for him?"

"It's respect for a worthy foe." Sebastian sported a slight grin as the animals trotted away from the cliff's edge one at a time, all in various directions. "These creatures are more evolved than we realized. Even more than Luther and Valeria realized. Now they can continue to progress over generations but without a direct threat dictating their evolution. Who knows where the next fifteen hundred years will take them? They may have a more humanistic society by then."

The last animal turned away from the cliff. It

looked over at Zack and Sebastian, let out a howl, and galloped away.

"Where do you think the future will take our coven?" Zack asked.

Sebastian glanced over at Zack. "You mean in New Salem?"

"Yeah."

"For Selena and myself, I believe it will take us far." Sebastian patted Zack on the back. "For you and Isis, a hell of a lot farther."

"Isis still needs you." Zack shrugged his shoulders. "I guess I need you, too."

"I know, and we're here for now," Sebastian replied. "Selena and I, we always do the best we can, but realize, now we will only be around for a small fraction of your lives."

"I'm sure you have another fifty or sixty years, maybe a bit longer."

"And the two of you have another thousand years, perhaps a lot longer." Sebastian's face rose up toward the gray sky, then his gaze fell to meet Zack's eyes. "I know my adopted daughter well. For Isis to survive, she will need more than just blood. She will need a familiar face that she trusts."

"My face."

"Exactly." Sebastian placed both hands on Zack's shoulders. "I know it's asking a lot, but I want you to promise me that no matter what happens for the rest of eternity, you will be there for her. You know she will always be there for you as well."

"I do know that." Zack didn't need to think on this request. He didn't need to hesitate on his answer. "Of course, I'll be there with Isis," he answered. "Forever."

"Then when my time comes, I'll rest easy knowing that you will have each other." Sebastian turned to the portal behind them. "Come, let's not dawdle," he said. "The ladies are waiting."

Epilogue

Isis stared down at the graves in front of her feet. The one in the middle had Selena's name engraved on the tombstone. The one to the immediate left said Sebastian. The grave on Selena's right, which was the oldest of the three, belonged to Sacha. All the tombstones shined from the light of the morning sunrise. Isis stood in silence holding Zack's hand. It was something she had done at least once every single day for as long as she could remember.

"It's weird," Isis said to Zack. "I miss them so much, yet I barely remember what they look like."

"I miss them too." Zack let go of Isis' hand and stroked her curled brown hair. "I also miss having color in my skin."

Isis smiled and gazed into his glowing green eyes. They were the one feature he still had even after two centuries. His complexion, on the other hand, was now one or two shades darker than those pure white sticks that her elementary school teachers wrote with on the blackboards. At least Isis still had brown in her skin even if it had become washed out and faded.

"I wonder what they would have thought of the world today," Isis speculated.

"From what I remember of your dad, he would not have enjoyed being a vampire," Zack answered. "I'm not entirely sure I like it. The generations jump by so quickly and every generation takes longer to train in their connections to the energy than the last. Of course, it could be I just have less patience than when I was younger."

Isis let her eyes roll. "Try not to sound too much like an old man, Zack. Technically, we're still sixteen."

"In reality, we're both around two hundred—"

Zack's attention turned to a short, rotund teenage girl standing several feet away who kept a careful eye on them. She was an actual sixteen-year-old. Unlike Isis, this girl had perfect olive skin that hadn't died then withered over the course of time. It helped that she wasn't a vampire.

"Mister President, Madam Vice-President, please forgive my intrusion on your private time."

"It's totally okay, Domina." Zack waved her over. "Please, join us."

Domina approached but with a hesitation in each step. She stopped in front of Zack. Domina was a sweet girl and a big help to the village. Isis really wanted to befriend her. The feeling was clearly not mutual, evidenced by the fact she had moved onto Zack's right side, keeping as much distance as she could from Isis.

"Yesterday, you requested Mister Simon to gather the witches in the quad at this time. You said you wished to address them." Domina straightened her back and stood at attention. "He has done so. You are still looking to meet, yes?"

"Yes," Zack said. "Thank you, Domina. Please tell them we'll be right there."

"Is everything else okay?" Isis asked.

"If I may," Domina replied. "Will you address them right away and you should be brief? This morning, I see an attack from several at the northern border. It will take place soon, within the hour."

"Did you see how the battle ends?" Zack asked.

"The witches, they will succeed. I see no casualties." Domina's eyes went wide. "Still, my dreams, they are not always accurate. We go prepared, yes?"

Isis reached over and put a hand on Domina's forearm. "We knew each of your ancestors, going all the way back to when we first came to New Salem," she said with a huge smile. "From Jasper and on, they used their connection to see the future. But none of their visions were as clear as yours. They would all be proud of you."

Domina took a not-so-subtle step back. "Th-thank you for the kind words, Madam Vice-President, it is an honor to serve you both."

"You don't serve us," Zack said. "We work together."

"Of course, Mister President." Domina cupped her hands together and gave them a slight bow. "I join the others now. I tell them we must await your arrival."

Isis' smile faded the moment Domina took off. "She's afraid of me, Zack. After all this time, they're all still afraid. I don't want it to be that way."

"It's not fear, it's respect for your power," Zack said in an obvious attempt to make her feel better.

"You see the way they flinch during our classes every time I walk up to one of them? I make them all anxious. Domina is outright scared of me."

"Domina has always been an emotional girl." Zack said. "Just like you when we were alive."

"She's also a powerful psychic, Zack," Isis

snapped at him. "She can see into our souls. What is it she sees in me? I'm not evil."

"I don't know what she sees." Zack draped his arm over her shoulders. "But I don't believe she—or any of them—see you as evil."

"They call me 'the immortal witch,' whenever they think we're not listening." Isis shook her head. "That's what we called Valeria back in the day. I'm not like Valeria! I'm not looking to hurt anyone!"

"The people of New Salem appreciate how you saved all of our lives." Zack waved a hand up at the school's rooftop. "It's just the level of power they witnessed stays in their minds even today. You stood up there for three straight days turning the Earth's energy into a shield that protected New Salem from nukes flying all over the world. Domina and her peers were young children at the time. Each one of them were in single digits. They saw the panic around this village, even in their own homes. To their young eyes, you were like a god holding back the falling sky."

"I'm not a god, Zack."

"I know you're not, Isis." Zack threw her a teasing grin. "A god doesn't belch whenever she drinks animal blood."

"I'm never going to live that down, am I?" Isis widened her eyes and shot her head up. "That only happened one time and it was like a hundred and fifty years ago!"

"Yeah, but it was a loud one," Zack replied. "As I remember, it was so loud it scared away some of the animals and even a few villagers. They ran for the swamp jungle, never to be seen again."

"All right, Mister Dramatic!" A chuckle shot out of

Isis' throat. Zack always had a knack for making her laugh even though his jokes were like classic reruns she'd heard thousands of times but still enjoyed over and over…well, most of the time. To think when they first met, she was considered the funny one in the relationship, not the scary one.

Isis wrapped her arms around his waist and squeezed. Their lips pressed together. Even after all this time, intimacy with Zack made her feel warm-blooded. It also helped her forget the way her fellow New Salem residents backpedaled from every disagreement. At least her reputation left Zack with little resistance in his thirty-year tenure as president. Not that she wanted to help him in that capacity nor would she ever use her power in such an abusive way, but it did help with those who didn't want to get to know her.

"Are you ready to address your team of witches, Mister President?" she whispered in his ear.

"I am." Zack took Isis' hand. "Let's speak with our team."

Zack led the way from the graves through the field of cottages. Many of them had become aged and worn, stemmed from decades of neglect. At one time, renovations and infrastructure were priorities for New Salem. Now, all efforts, Wiccan and otherwise, had to focus on farming and feeding everyone in the village. This had become a difficult endeavor now that the sun's rays were blocked by the gray covering of the sky. Many of the old witches in the village had learned to create their own sunlight to make crops grow. It was a full-time job with all hands on deck. It was also New Salem's top priority now that there were no longer neighboring countries to work out trade deals.

"You know it could have just as easily been Madam President," Zack said. "And I would have been Mister Vice-President. You know I would have been fine with it."

"Then I'd have to make speeches." Isis stepped in front of Zack, stopping their pace. She placed her hands on his cheeks. "Speeches have always been your thing, honey."

"Yeah, I guess they are." Zack grinned. "I was a magician once, you know."

"You never let anyone forget." Isis laughed. She poked a finger against his chest. "You heard what Domina said. Our new class of witches will have to defend the village tonight. This will be their first time, so you need to be real motivational."

"I have something in mind," Zack said. They entered the quad.

"I knew you would."

The two walked side by side past the school and into the open field where a group of seven teenage witches huddled with Simon. Domina stepped away from the cluster and called to the others while pointing toward Isis and Zack. The conversation halted and their focus turned to their teachers and village leaders.

The oldest of the witches were nineteen-year-old twins named Cameron and Cindi. Each had bright red hair and dimples. Their hair color reminded Isis of Selena and Sacha. It was the one thing she could still remember about their physical appearances. Cindi's long, flowing red hair particularly gave Isis a sense of déjà vu.

The youngest was a boy named Elian who just turned thirteen. He joined the class three weeks prior, after his connection first manifested during an argument with his parents over finishing his math homework. He ended up accidentally setting his notebook on fire. The revelation became more important than the assignment he didn't want to finish.

Accompanying them were two girls and a boy all around the ages of fifteen and sixteen. Like the others, they were young and not yet ready for what would prove to be their first true test. They were all about to be called upon to lead the battle to protect New Salem. This was a responsibility that should never have fallen on a group so young, even if they were witches. But with the manifestation of power passing over an entire generation, there were no other options available. The previous group of witches—their grandparents—were too old for battle.

Simon clapped his hands and waddled to Isis and Zack. He still sported that excited smile, which was almost always inappropriate whenever it crossed his lips. "Our new gaggle of witches is ready for you, my friends," he said.

"Thank you, Simon," Zack replied. "We'll take it from here."

Zack strolled three steps forward. Isis stayed in place. She wanted the attention on him. Realizing that all eyes were on her, she focused on Zack as a signal telling these young teen witches to do the same. Simon stood off to the side. He offered a nod of approval. Isis returned the nod.

"Good morning!" Zack threw a glance to Isis, then refocused on his small but important audience. "You, and the people of this land, may be all that is left of the human race." He held out his arms. "Our job, and I mean all of us, is to continue on. We need to keep living and rebuild humanity. But if continuing on is going to happen, then our small group here has a more specific job." Zack paused and made eye contact with each of the seven newly trained witches standing a few feet in front of him. "For the first time in almost two centuries, New Salem faces a major threat. The last time, it was the infamous Valeria who I know you all learned about in your history classes. This threat is just as big, not because of power, but due to sheer numbers.

"I know you remember our world fell to nuclear war almost a decade ago. As far as we know it wiped out nearly everything outside our borders. It could have destroyed New Salem as well, but we survived." Zack once again focused on Isis. "We were lucky to have you here to protect all of us."

"That's my only goal, to keep the people of New Salem safe," Isis responded. She knew exactly what message Zack was sending and she followed his lead.

Zack turned his attention back to the witches. "Unfortunately, while New Salem stayed safe, the radiation that killed so many out there also reanimated the dead. Or maybe it was other vampires who turned the dead. We really don't know how, we just know they're out there.

"But they are not like Simon, Isis, or myself. Their minds were destroyed to the point they can no longer think. As we've seen, they now have one single focus. They want to feast on blood wherever they can find it."

Elian raised a hand. Zack nodded her way. "You're saying that everyone out there is dead and we're the only source left for blood?"

"That's exactly what he's saying, Elian," Cindi

snapped at him. "Pay attention."

"That's right," Zack responded. "Fortunately, we are surrounded by miles of swamp forest. But, maybe due to luck, chance, or other means, sometimes packs of these…undead zombies manage to find us."

Zack pointed to each witch. "Mother Earth has chosen us for her special gifts that can be used to keep our home safe! It is what you have been training to do. Now, you will have the opportunity to put that training into use. Domina has seen a group of these zombies entering New Salem from the north. We will be there to meet them and turn them back by whatever means necessary!"

Nervousness and excitement resonated in each of their faces. None of them, especially the younger ones, could hide it. But Isis, Zack, and the witches' grandparents had trained them well. Zack just needed to motivate them past their nerves. If anyone could, it was him.

The slight grin on his face meant he was about to end strong. "For a long time, the brave soldiers assigned to New Salem's protection were referred to simply as the village's law enforcement team. But with countless threats to our people lurking all around us, that role has become even more important. That's why I have chosen a new name for us. It may not make sense to you, but it holds enormous historic significance to this community. It is a name…no, it is a *title* you can accept for yourselves with pride."

Zack's voice turned to a loud roar. "As of this moment, you are *THE NEW WITCHES OF VEGAS*!"

The witches cheered, as did Simon. Zack raised his arms in the air. In turn, the cheers became louder. Soon, even the residents watching from around the quad's buildings displayed their excitement. Isis stared at Zack as her lips stretched into a huge grin. After all this time, she still didn't know if they were considered human, vampire, dead, alive, or something else. But none of that mattered. One thing Isis knew was that she loved Zack more than she could ever say. Now and forever, he was truly her soulmate. She could never imagine eternal existence without him.

A word about the author...

By day, Mark Rosendorf is a mild mannered high school guidance counselor for special needs students. He has also moonlighted as a magician. Today, he teaches magic to his students. By night, Mark is the author of The Witches of Vegas series, a young adult fantasy series which shares the adventures of Isis, Zack, their families and the residents of New Salem with the entire world. He has also published such works as The Rasner Effect through The Wild Rose Press.

Mark wishes to thank all of you who have read The Witches of Vegas series. He hopes you enjoy reading their stories as much as he enjoys writing them.

Their adventures continue…